INDISCRETIONS ALONG VIRTUE AVENUE

WOMEN OF THE WEST

Indiscretions Along Virtue Avenue

CONFESSIONS OF SADIE ORCHARD

Harper Courtland

FIVE STAR
A part of Gale, a Cengage Company

A Cengage Company

Farmington Hills, Mich • San Francisco • New York • Waterville, Maine
Meriden, Conn • Mason, Ohio • Chicago

GALE
A Cengage Company

LIBRARY OF CONGRESS CATALOGING-IN-PUBLICATION DATA

Names: Courtland, Harper, author.
Title: Indiscretions along Virtue Avenue : confessions of Sadie
  Orchard / Harper Courtland.
Description: First edition. | Farmington Hills, Mich. : Five Star
  Publishing, 2019. | Series: Women of the West ; 1
Identifiers: LCCN 2019012402 (print) | ISBN 9781432859442
  (hardcover : alk. paper)
Subjects: LCSH: Orchard, Sadie, 1859–1943—Fiction. | Business-
  women—Fiction. | Brothels—Fiction. | Prostitutes—Fiction. |
  New Mexico—History—1848——Fiction. | GSAFD: Biographical
  fiction. | Historical fiction.
Classification: LCC PS3603.O8868 I53 2019 (print) | DDC 813/
  .6—dc23
LC record available at https://lccn.loc.gov/2019012402

First Edition. First Printing: December 2019
Find us on Facebook—https://www.facebook.com/FiveStarCengage
Visit our website—http://www.gale.cengage.com/fivestar
Contact Five Star Publishing at FiveStar@cengage.com

Printed in Mexico
1 2 3 4 5 6 7 23 22 21 20 19

To my father, Huey Watkins,
a cartoonist who loves to tell stories

ACKNOWLEDGMENTS

Western novelist W. Michael Farmer challenged me to tell Sadie's story and offered much help along the way, often sharing nuggets from his vast historical research. I wrote this novel while battling cancer. During this struggle, my husband, Brett, took care of me and encouraged me to continue the research and writing. My lifelong friend Becky Saunders Warf spent much time with me discussing everything from plotting points to book promotion. Whenever I became stymied, I'd call my friend Daria, a.k.a. middle school novelist D. V. Kelleher, who provided laughter and inspiration. Several other historical researchers have helped me, including Harley Shaw, retired research biologist and member of the Hillsboro Historical Society, Garland Bills, retired professor of linguistics and author of *Sadie Orchard: Madam of New Mexico's Black Range,* and Marilyn Pope, administrator of the Geronimo Springs Museum in Truth or Consequences, New Mexico. Much gratitude is due to my content editor, Erin Bealmear, who went more than the second mile with me in reviewing revisions, and to Gordon Aalborg, acquisitions editor, for having faith in this work. Special thanks to my father, Huey Watkins, and to other friends and family members who offered support and encouragement, most notably: Anna Komsa, David and Michaelle Starr, Kelly Ward, Doris Gwaltney, Trip and Boni Lea, Dawn Riddle, and Matt Thomas.

PREFACE

Sadie Orchard is a real historical character and an enigma of the Old West. Born Sarah Jane Creech in Mills County, Iowa, on March 16, 1859, Sadie moved into Kingston, New Mexico Territory, in 1886, speaking with a British accent and claiming to be from the Limehouse district of London. Within a year, she had her own brothel on Virtue Avenue.

In many ways, Sadie might argue that she stayed on Virtue Avenue all her life. She and her girls helped raise money to build a church. In a smallpox epidemic, Sadie nursed the sick. She counted attorney and politician Albert Fall and territorial governor William Thornton among her friends and is reported to have been a friend of the actress Lillian Russell. In 1895, she married J. W. Orchard, owner of a stage line, and became one of the few women to drive a stagecoach.

In writing this novel, I followed the known details of Sadie's life, added an element of the supernatural, and let Sadie fill in the rest. If you find things in this story that seem hard to believe, remember that, above all else, Sadie was a liar.

CHAPTER 1

March 16, 1876, Kansas City, Missouri
Before dawn on my seventeenth birthday, I wanted to stay in the warm spot I'd created, away from the cold, wet place in the middle of the bed, but then I heard banging on the wall of the second floor hallway. "Everyone in the parlor! Now!" Chantelle shouted.

I left my bed, threw a chemise over my body, and trudged downstairs.

Chantelle Blanchard was a big-boned, mean-eyed Cajun who enjoyed using her fists. She had moved to Kansas City five years earlier to open her brothel. Knowing better than to cross her, I hurried downstairs, as everyone did, some shivering in night-gowns, some in undergarments, others, bare chested with arms across their breasts. No one dared to sit on either of the floral print sofas or in the overstuffed chairs for this strange meeting.

Some of the girls got near the fireplace, but I knew they'd just have warm asses and cold tits because they'd never dare turn their backs on Chantelle to warm their fronts. There were six of us, but my only real friend in the house was a frail-looking Ukrainian immigrant named Oxana, who didn't speak much English. She was wearing a bandage across her left breast and had a frightened look about her. The first time Oxana came to my room, she was new to Madam Chantelle's. She stood in my doorway in a blue dress, one tiny hand over her breast.

I told her to come in, and she stepped forward, turned to

11

close the door, and broke into sobs. Soon, I was holding her like a child, stroking her back. I asked what was wrong. She said something in a language I didn't understand and opened the bodice of her dress. I saw that someone had bitten deeply into her breast just above the nipple, and the area around the bite was hot, red, and swollen.

I asked if Chantelle knew, and Oxana nodded. "She say I deserve, say serves me right." Fresh tears came to her eyes as she started talking in her native tongue again. When she repeated it in broken English, using hand gestures, I surmised that she was slow to do what a man wanted because she didn't understand English, so he bit her and then shoved her into kneeling position.

"You need a doctor," I said.

"No money," she whispered.

Having just made a payment to Madam Chantelle for clothing bought on her account, I only had a few dollars, but I walked with Oxana to the nearest doctor's office and held her hand as he cleaned the wound with carbonic acid and put in two lines of stitches, which hurt enough to make Oxana cry out.

"Make her shut up," he said. "Getting hurt is a risk in your profession. No need for her to screech about it."

I put a finger to my lips, rolled up a clean handkerchief, and gave it to her to bite down on. Finishing the stitches, the doctor applied ointment to the wound and bandaged it. Then the ruddy-faced bastard robbed me, charging three dollars for his services and the tin of ointment. He told us to change the bandage every day.

Now Oxana peered at me from across the room. I stood near one corner and watched a flickering gas lamp on the wall, the one next to a needlepoint piece that read "We Aim to Please."

Madam Chantelle paced back and forth, glaring at us. "My gold coin necklace was on my dresser last night. Now it's gone, and the *couillon* whore that stole it is gonna regret it."

The girls looked around at one another. Some of us might have been stupid, or *couillon* as Chantelle put it, but I didn't think any of us were dumb enough to steal from her.

Chantelle's favorite, Pretty Face, was the only one I hated. She was standing by the grandfather clock with a smirk on her face. Of a sudden, I remembered seeing her come out of the madam's room last night just before I went upstairs with a red-faced, gray-haired river man. I figured she was the thief.

I said nothing because I didn't care what had happened to Chantelle's necklace, but, even if I had cared, I knew the foul bitch would never believe Pretty Face had anything to do with it. What puzzled me was why Pretty Face was favored. She was anything but pretty. She was petite like me, but she had small, close-set, piggy eyes. Her brown hair was thin and stringy, and, to top that off, she always wore red lipstick and painted perfectly round circles of rouge on her cheeks.

Of course, I could get beyond a person's looks. I couldn't stand her because she was an asshole. Pretty Face liked to brag that, although the merchants charged other whores a lot more for things bought on the madam's credit lines, they offered her the same prices Chantelle got. I hoped she was lying. It galled me to think I'd have to pay more for things than that stinking bitch would pay. I thought I wouldn't have to worry about it long, though, because I was very close to paying off my debt to Chantelle. Soon I'd be free to leave this hellhole and work for a better house.

I made the mistake of taking another quick glance at Pretty Face, who was still in the shadows beside the clock. She looked back at me and scowled, and I felt sure she knew I'd seen her come out of Chantelle's room. Then Pretty Face said, "I saw Curly Kate come out of your room last night."

It took an instant to register that she was accusing me because

I still thought of myself as Sarah Jane Creech, or Sadie, my childhood nickname, not the name I'd picked to avoid shaming my family. I knew Pretty Face had never liked me, but I wasn't prepared for that level of treachery. I had a quick, gut-level reaction of fear, and, for a moment, time seemed to slow down as Chantelle moved toward me like a big barge.

She grabbed my arm and demanded, "What were you doing in my room?"

Stunned, I stammered, "I . . . I . . . wasn't—" Before I could finish the sentence, Chantelle punched my left jaw, knocking me on my back, and then she was on me, groping at my breasts and running her hands all over me to find the necklace I didn't have. I was appalled when her rough hands moved under my chemise. She probed my vagina and my anus, cutting into me with her fingernails. Finding nothing, she stood.

Imagining I'd been cleared, I got up, and then Chantelle backhanded my other cheek, causing my lip to bleed, and told Pretty Face to go check my room. I stood there with my insides stinging, and a bit of blood ran down my legs. Several minutes passed before Pretty Face appeared at the top of the stairs with Chantelle's necklace in her hand. "Found it!" she called.

It was clear to me that Pretty Face had stolen Chantelle's necklace, lost her nerve, and accused me. I could picture her pulling it out of her own pocket on her way upstairs and then claiming she'd found it in my room.

Chantelle retrieved her necklace, dragged me to the door, opened it, and slung me out into the cold. I landed hard on my right hip on the slate-covered porch. "You don't work here anymore," she snarled. "Now git!"

"But my things and my pay from last night," I said.

"Mine now. And you're damn lucky I'm not having you thrown in jail." She slammed the door and locked it.

It must have been near freezing at that predawn hour. God,

how I wished I had my coat and my shoes. As I slowly picked myself up, I felt like screaming and kicking the door, but I didn't want Chantelle to give me another beating. My teeth began to chatter.

I'd come here from Mills County, Iowa. For six months, I'd worked to pay Chantelle back for things I purchased on her credit account: five fancy dresses, three feathered hats, a woolen coat, seven sets of naughty underwear, five chemises, a razor to protect myself, cosmetics, and two bottles of perfume. I had been so close to paying my debt to her, but now everything I'd worked for was gone, except the chemise I was wearing.

Feeling dazed, I headed for my usual place of refuge, the livery stable. For as long as I could remember, I'd known horses, and they'd always known me. While trying to get ahead, the only indulgence I'd ever allowed myself was riding horses. If I didn't have money to rent one, I'd shovel stalls, curry horses, or do whatever in exchange for the privilege. Jake Wilson, the nearest liveryman, traded for stable work. He was the only man in town who treated me with respect. I appreciated that he never suggested a sexual arrangement. From what I'd heard, he was sweet on a cattleman's daughter. As I hurried along in the dark, a harsh wind stirred the dust in the road, stinging my ankles.

My vision blurred, and I realized my left eye was swelling. At first, I didn't cry. At least I had sense enough to know that wouldn't help. Few people would show compassion and help a whore. The tears came only when I remembered that Mama's locket was still in a wooden chest at Chantelle's house. That heart-shaped locket on a gold chain was all I had left from my girlhood. I had to get it back.

All was quiet as I slipped into a stall with a brown and white paint and petted his nose. The smells of horses and hay were comforting to me. My thoughts kept coming back to the fact that I was cold and had no clothes, no money, and no weapon. I was never a thief, but I searched for any saddlebags left lying around to see what I could steal. Finding nothing but an old saddle blanket, I decided to enjoy the warmth of the horse for a while and then go hide in the loft. I made the horse lie down, snuggled next to him, piled the blanket and some hay over me, and wrapped an arm across his neck.

Pretty Face will pay, I told myself. *I'll get even with her, and, someday, I'll own a necklace that's better than anything Chantelle will own in her whole, sorry life.*

CHAPTER 2

I woke to the metallic squawking of a rusty water pump, and it took me a minute to remember where I was. When I realized Jake was filling a trough for the horses, I jumped up quickly and hid in the loft because, although Jake was a friend, I thought it was probably best if no one knew where I was. He came in whistling and holding his pitchfork a few minutes later. He stopped when he got to the middle of the stable and said, "You might as well come out, Miss Kate."

Slowly, I came down from the loft with the saddle blanket wrapped around my shoulders. He took a long look at me and asked, "Rough night?"

I nodded. "Chantelle threw me out. How did you know I was here?"

"I came in earlier, heard you snoring, and found you sleeping in a stall."

I scowled at him and said, "I don't snore."

"You do when your face is all busted up. I heard about your run-in with Chantelle over breakfast at Sal's Restaurant. She's telling folks you stole her necklace and warning them not to hire you. You're finished here, Kate. No one will even hire you to wash clothes after they hear her story." Jake paused and flashed a crooked grin. I liked his smile because he had a space between his front teeth that gave him a boyish look, though he must have been about forty. "You shoulda hid it better. You coulda crammed it up your snatch."

17

"I didn't take it. Besides, she checked for that."

Wrapping the saddle blanket around me, I sat down on a rail and told Jake what happened. Then I started crying and became furious with myself for crying. I fiercely wiped the tears from my face and said, "I want my stuff back."

Jake laughed. "Go back in that house, and you'll get yourself killed if Chantelle catches you. You'd best just cut your losses. I can give you some old clothes if you'd like to work as my stable boy for a while. Lord knows you've proven yourself around here."

I smiled and said, "That sounds good."

"You can start by filling the feeding trough with hay." Before he left, he added, "I got one rule for you—no talking to customers unless it's about livery business. Things could get out of hand."

I'd thrown down bales from the loft and filled the feeding trough before he came back with his arms loaded. He handed me a pair of old boots, newspaper to stuff in them to make them fit better, wool socks, black pants, a blue shirt, an old black coat, a belt, and a porkpie hat.

"Soon as you get dressed, you can clean the stalls," he said. When he left the stable, I put on the clothes, which were far too big for me, rolled up the cuffs and sleeves, and stuffed my hair under the hat. I was small in the bust, so the big shirt hid my breasts. I had to find a punch and a hammer and make a new hole in the belt to hold the pants up. Getting around in Jake's big boots wasn't easy, but I managed.

An hour or so later, a tall man with a gray mustache came and asked for Jake, so I ran to fetch him. When Jake came back with me, the man shoved his chin toward me and asked Jake, "Who's that? Got quite a shiner."

"Him? That's Tom Jenkins, my new stable boy. He's a good worker but not much of a fighter. Got his ass kicked in an alley

18

last night by a feller half his size."

"Must have been a dwarf!" the man shouted. They laughed, and then the man paid Jake, took the paint I'd snuggled near earlier, and rode out.

"Now you've got a name," Jake said.

"Nice having things handed to me on a silver platter," I muttered.

"No need to be grumpy." Jake walked over to me and took something from his pocket. "Here, I brung you a ham biscuit. There's coffee in my office."

I thanked him and ate it, even though it hurt my sore jaw to chew.

For part of that first day, I thought about hiring a man to slit Pretty Face's throat. I wanted him to tell her why she was dying before he did it. In my mind, I saw the fear in her eyes and felt her earnest wish that she'd never done anything to cross me. I knew she wanted to plead for her life, but she was gagged and couldn't say a word as the man tested his knife's sharpness against his thumb. As the afternoon wore on, the killer became my tall, dark-haired lover, who took care of Pretty Face and Chantelle to avenge my loss. Then I married him.

Just before suppertime, the man with the gray moustache came back. He called out, "Tom Jenkins, see to my horse, will you?"

"Yes, sir."

He handed me the reins. "What's the horse's name?" I asked.

"Johnson. Named him after an old friend." He paused and added, "I'm Norton Stallings, of Greenville, Mississippi."

"Nice to meet you, Mr. Stallings."

"Hand me my saddlebag, will you?" I did, and he dug through it for a few minutes before he tossed it back in the stall.

After he left, I saw that he'd dropped an old newspaper and left it, a copy of *The Greenville Times*, dated February 26, 1876.

19

I picked it up and started reading by lantern light. A story about a spiritualist called the Chicago Fire Queen who bathed herself in fire at a spiritualist meeting intrigued me. After she did her trick, two men in the audience said they could do the same thing without help from the spirits, and they did it right there before her audience. Then a doctor and several other skeptics offered the woman ten dollars to hold her thumb over a lamp's flame for forty seconds, but the fire queen refused. I tore the story out of the paper and kept it for reasons I could not explain.

I wondered how those people had made it look like they were bathing themselves in fire. I looked back at the story, and Jake came in and said, "I didn't know you could read."

"Of course, I can read. I went to school until I was fourteen. Could have gone longer if my mother hadn't died. My teacher thought I should become a teacher."

Jake didn't seem impressed. "Can you cook?" he asked. "I'd like some help in my kitchen."

Three days later, my arrangement with Jake was still working out fine. He let me sleep in the loft with a couple of his old blankets and the hay to keep me warm, and he shared his food with me and paid me a little each day.

Within a week, my bruises, including the one on my hip, had faded from nearly black to pale purples and yellows. I remembered a little twist on the Golden Rule: do unto others *before* they can do unto you. It was a little late for that now, but I vowed never to let my guard down or let anyone run roughshod over me again like Chantelle and Pretty Face had.

It bothered me that Chantelle had beaten the hell out of me, but I hadn't put a single scratch on her. *Next time someone hits me,* I told myself, *I'll fight back. Next time, I'll inflict some damage.*

Then it hit me that there was no reason Tom Jenkins couldn't go into Chantelle's house. I considered paying for some time with Oxana, letting her see who I was, and snooping around to try to find my things. Nevertheless, I quickly saw the idea would put Oxana in danger. Besides, I didn't really have the guts to try it.

Fear helped me reconcile to the idea of cutting my losses and starting over. Even so, I still agonized over losing my mother's locket, which my father had given me a few days after her death. My mother's initials were on the front. It opened to reveal daguerreotypes of my mother and father, taken when they were about twenty years old.

My plan was to save up enough money to take a stagecoach, plus a little extra for food and other expenses, and work my way toward Dodge City. Then I'd find a better house and buy even nicer things on the owner's account, but I'd be able to pay it back quicker because I'd make more money in a better house. Then I would save a big enough pile of money to go wherever I wanted and live just like I'd never been a whore. I'd never wanted to be a whore in the first place. I just wanted to be rich, and working the brothels seemed like the easiest path to that end. Since my family hadn't been particularly religious, I'd never felt the guilt some girls feel over entering the business.

On Monday, March 29, Jake left me in charge while he rode out to the Calloway ranch to look at some horses. Like my father, Jake sometimes bought horses to resell. Business was slow, but in the early afternoon, a gentleman came in to board his horse overnight and asked me to curry the brown gelding. After he left, I was brushing that horse when Pretty Face came in calling for Jake. I had my back to her, but I recognized her voice and felt my heart thump faster.

"He ain't here," I said, making my voice sound deeper.

"Well, go find him, boy."

I felt my anger rise as I put down the brush and turned toward her. I saw a shovel leaning against the stall beside her. The light was dim because she'd pulled the door partly closed when she came in, probably because of the cold wind. "I'm in charge while he's gone. What do you need?"

She laughed. "You're in charge of horse shit, boy, and that's exactly what you smell like. Chantelle and I want to rent a carriage, but we only do business with Jake."

"Then I reckon you'll have to wait a few hours," I said, though I figured Jake could come back at any time. I was trying to think what to do. I still didn't have a weapon, but I was sure Pretty Face did. At that point, I'd moved almost close enough to touch her, and I could smell her cloying perfume. Then a gust of wind pushed the stable door wide open. As more light came in, I caught a glint of sun on gold. My mother's locket was hanging around her neck.

My hands found the shovel, and I swung its butt end against the side of her head with all my might. She dropped like a dead weight, bleeding from her head, and through the blood, I saw a small dent on the side of her head.

Her eyes rolled back in her head, and her body twitched. She opened her eyes, blinked twice, and said the strangest thing: "Our paths will cross again." Then she lay silent.

I shivered as an ugly, black knowledge came upon me, the sort that comes the first time a person kills someone. It was a separation, a darker stain on my soul, a knowing in my heart that things would never be the same. There was little time to dwell on it, though.

I quickly took back my mother's locket and heaved Pretty Face into the nearest stall. Next, I searched her for money and found thirty dollars. She also had a Colt derringer in her pocket, so I took it. I didn't see this as stealing, just recovering some of what she'd taken from me through her lies. I was about to leave when I saw her feet sticking out of the stall, so I took time to bend her legs to get them in. My breath was coming hard and fast, and I wanted to get out quickly, as someone could walk in at any minute.

When I left through the side door, hidden from the street, I bumped into Jake and tried to get by him, but he caught me by the arm. "Where are the horses?" I asked, wondering if I could barter with him for a horse.

"What horses?"

"The ones you went to buy."

"I ain't bought any yet. You never get a good deal when you're in too big a hurry to buy or sell anything. I'll let Old Man Calloway stew for a day or two and see if his prices come down." He held out a brush and said, "Here take this and—"

I stopped him mid-sentence. "Sell me a horse."

"What?" He stood there looking at me for a moment. "Why, you're trembling all over. What the hell's the matter with you?" He had me sit on the corral fence.

When I told him what had happened, he let out a low whistle.

"I didn't mean to kill her."

He frowned and said, "Let me take a look, and we'll decide how to handle this." I sat there, still shaking, as he walked away. Soon, he came out and announced, "You ain't killed nobody. She's still breathing." He sat on the fence beside me and sighed. After a few minutes, he said, "You go get the doctor. We'll tell him you rode out to pick up a load of hay this afternoon, and I'll say I rode up on you and the wagon on my way back to town and that we found her when we came in, so it must have happened while you was gone."

"What if she wakes up and tells the doc I did it? What if he sends for the sheriff?"

Jake ran his fingers through his dark, curly hair. "Way she

looks, I don't believe she'll be saying anything anytime soon. By then, you'll be long gone, stable boy."

I was slow to move, so he reminded me, "No offense to you, Kate, but ain't no sheriff gives a damn what happens to a whore. They ain't got time for that. Nobody's gonna come looking for you or your alias, Tom Jenkins, once you leave here. It ain't like you bashed in the head of a respectable woman."

CHAPTER 3

After Chantelle learned that Pretty Face was hurt, she sent for her. The next morning Jake said Chantelle was caring for her as though she were her long lost daughter, although the doctor offered no prognosis for her recovery other than, "Time will tell." The irony of the situation was not lost on me, but I knew it was time to move on. I gave Jake some of the money I'd taken off Pretty Face and asked him to buy me some clothes and a pair of shoes. He returned with black shoes, two white shirtwaists, a dark-blue skirt, and a brown skirt, the sort of things any respectable woman might wear. "You could have at least gotten me a pair of bloomers," I said.

"You'll have to buy those for yourself."

I laughed when his face and ears turned pink. I bathed in Jake's quarters, put on a shirtwaist and the blue skirt, and went to pay my fare for the next stagecoach headed west. There was enough time to buy a few more things, including some makeup to cover what was left of my bruises, a cotton nightgown, some undergarments, a valise, and a box of .41 rimfire cartridges for the derringer I'd taken off Pretty Face.

The stage driver loaded a padlocked strongbox into a compartment under his seat while a guard with a shotgun stood alongside. Soon, I was traveling the Santa Fe Trail, along with two men and a heavyset woman with light-brown hair that had a touch of gray at the temples. I had the single-shot derringer and some extra cartridges in my skirt pocket.

The men sat across from me, and the woman to my right. I enjoyed the feel and smell of the cushioned leather seats while eying the men, who appeared wealthy and were reading newspapers. Their hair tonic smelled of spearmint and lime. They were either unaware that I was studying them or didn't care. Neither seemed familiar, so I was sure they weren't former customers. I sensed a hint of danger in these men—not danger to myself particularly, just a sense that most men wouldn't want to tangle with these two.

Soon after the stage started moving, the woman, who had an English accent, introduced herself as Mrs. Evonia Spangler in a voice louder than necessary. Feeling her eyes on me, I smiled and said, "I'm Katherine Jones. Pleased to meet you."

"And you are?" she demanded of the older man, whose hair was dark brown mixed with silver.

"G. J. Stanard," he replied. Looking to his right, he added, "And my son, Joshua." Immediately, his eyes went back to his paper. The younger man, who had lighter hair and looked nothing like the older man, looked up and asked, "Are you from London, ma'am?"

"Yes," she said, "from the Limehouse District."

"Pleased to meet you," he said and went right back to his paper.

She turned to me and said, "Men! They've simply forgotten the art of pleasant conversation." I offered a consoling smile while she looked me over.

At last, she asked, "Why are you traveling alone, dear?" I hesitated and was about to turn as cold as the men sitting across from us and tell her it wasn't any of her business, but she held up a finger and said, "Wait . . . let me guess. I fancy I'm good at reading people." Mrs. Spangler frowned, as if in deep thought, and then her face brightened. "You've just set out hoping to find work as a school teacher or a nanny."

I relaxed and smiled. "Why, that's right! How did you guess?"

Mrs. Spangler smoothed the skirt of her blue, velvet dress. "It's simple, my dear. You dress modestly and carry yourself well. You're obviously intelligent because you sit up straight and appear very alert. Also, you have a slight flush in your cheeks as if you're excited to go out, see the world, and conquer it. So what else could you be?"

I smiled even more broadly, suddenly liking this naïve, older woman. "Are you traveling to meet your husband somewhere in the West, Mrs. Spangler?" I asked.

"In a manner of speaking, yes. My husband died two years ago, but I'm not averse to finding another." She squealed with laughter as if she'd told a hilarious joke, and I laughed, too, as I watched the Stanard men cringe at her high-pitched shrieks. When she settled down, just for fun, I sent her into another fit of laughter by whispering, "If those two sourpusses across from us were the only men in the world, which would you choose?"

When she recovered, she fanned herself, and said, "Oh, my. You're so much fun to travel with."

"Thank you, Mrs. Spangler. Where are you headed?"

"Oh, I'm just going from place to place. I want to see this country. I'm on no schedule, but, eventually, I plan to make my way out to San Francisco."

I noticed that she pronounced *schedule* as if the *c* wasn't there. I said, "Tell me more about yourself."

Instead, she told me about Mr. Spangler and how he made his fortune selling pickles. "Sweet pickles, dill pickles, any kind of pickles you can think of, he sold them. Surely you've heard of Spangler pickles, haven't you?"

"Of course," I said, though I hadn't. "Do you still sell them?"

"No, dear. They're still sold under the Spangler name, but I sold the company last year."

"What happened to Mr. Spangler?"

27

"A worker found him drowned in a barrel of kosher dills."

I bit my lip to keep from laughing while she removed a handkerchief from her pocket and dabbed at her eyes. I glanced over at the Stanard men and found them stone-faced. "That's dreadful, darling," I murmured, patting her shoulder. "Here, let's talk about something more pleasant. You haven't told me about yourself yet."

She sniffed and brightened a bit. "I'm a poetess." She sniffed again and added, "A published poetess."

"Do you have a book of poems?" I asked.

"Not yet, but I'll have one as soon as this journey ends. I'm traveling throughout the West to capture its essence for my readers."

"That sounds very exciting," I said.

She suddenly clasped my arm. "You don't have a job yet, do you?"

"No, ma'am."

"Then why don't you work for me until you find one? You could be my secretary and traveling companion. I'll vocalize my poems as they come to me, and you can write them down, and you can also help me with other things as needed. I can offer you ten dollars a week. What do you say?"

The idea of traveling for a while, sightseeing, and helping Mrs. Spangler was appealing, regardless of whether her poems turned out to be any good. I knew that, with ten dollars a week, I could save money and buy some beautiful clothes and lingerie. Then I could start working in a fine house without becoming indebted to another madam. However, on thinking through it, I remembered I'd likely have to spend much of my earnings on hotels, food, and stagecoach travel. "But I can't afford the fine hotels you'd want to stay in," I said.

"Oh, fiddlesticks. Then your room and board will be included. If the stage fares become a problem, I'll help with that, too."

I could see no real harm in the plan, as it could lead to my meeting a wealthy man, getting married, and settling into a life of luxury, which was my ultimate goal. I thought that, at worst, she could discover my past and fire me, but how hard could it be to keep my secret?

"Then it's settled, Mrs. Spangler. I'm going to write my family and tell them about this new venture." At the time, my sisters thought I was a nanny for a well-to-do family in Kansas City. At least I wouldn't have to keep fabricating stories about the antics of imaginary children.

At the first stage station, the Stanard men got off, and I thought they were going to walk away without offering to help us down, but the older man turned and offered, first me, and then Evonia, his hand. After we freshened up, our driver, a short man with a potbelly and yellow teeth, announced there was going to be a delay to repair a damaged stage wheel.

To make the best of it, Evonia decided we should work on her poetry book. She gave me some paper and a pencil, and we sat on a wooden bench under an apple tree about fifty yards from the stage station. "You must transcribe this in ink later," she said. "I'll speak each line and each punctuation mark for you, and I'll pause after each line."

Then she sniffed and sat still until I asked, "Is anything wrong?"

"Oh no, dear, I'm just waiting for my poetic trance to come upon me . . . oh, oh, yes, I believe it's coming now." She sniffed again and motioned for me to begin. "Behold exclamation point . . . Mountain grandeur period." Considering the landscape around us, I was surprised by her subject matter.

She continued, "I comma the reviewer . . . Stand muted by the beauty . . ." Then she paused and asked, "Do you think I should use that exclamation point after the opening word?"

"Oh, yes," I said, though I didn't care one way or the other.

"You don't find it overly dramatic?"

"No, not at all."

She pressed her lips together and said, "Good. That makes me feel better."

Our work was interrupted briefly when we saw two men ride into an area at some distance from the stage station and dismount. The Stanards walked over to them, but they were so far away I was unable to eavesdrop on their conversation. Even so, I noticed the beauty of the riders' horses, so I pointed and said, "Look, a palomino and a dapple gray."

"Yes, lovely." The riders then set out across country, not following the road, and we watched them for a few moments.

Turning her attention back to her work, Evonia said, "Let me see what you've written thus far." I showed her the page, and she repeated, "Stand muted by the beauty . . . comma . . . For a moment neglecting my duty . . . To share a sight so grand . . . Shaped by the creator's hand . . . period . . . The wild untamed vista . . . The snowcapped . . . Hmm. Dear, can you think of a word that rhymes with vista?"

I set the pencil down and asked, "What about sister?"

She frowned. "No, no, no. I want an exact rhyme. Precision, dear. Think precision."

"What about bravista?" I asked.

"Is that a word? I've never heard it."

"It's French for brave explorer. I learned it in finishing school," I said, smiling to myself.

Mrs. Spangler clapped her hands. "Marvelous! Now where was I?"

"The wild untamed vista."

"Ah yes." She cleared her throat. "The wild untamed vista . . . Awaiting the bold bravista . . . Snowcapped in summer . . . Hmm. Oh, dear, I think the trance has left me." She pushed a sweaty strand of hair from her forehead, slumped, and appeared defeated.

I didn't want my job as a secretary to come to a hasty end, so I said, "Oh, don't give up, Mrs. Spangler. You're doing so well. How about: Snow-capped in summer . . . I stand here dumber . . . than Zacharias before the birth of his son . . . Will that work?"

"What?" Mrs. Spangler asked. "Who is Zacharias?"

"You know. He's the father of John the Baptist, in the Bible, the one who was struck dumb by the angel."

"Indeed!" she exclaimed. "It's always good to include a literary allusion in poetry. You know, it just may be that you also hold promise as a poetess. Now where was I?"

I glanced down at the page and was very glad to hear our driver call for us to board the stage for the next leg of our journey. I was also happy with my arrangement with Mrs. Spangler. As a whore, I understood the value of pretending to be interested in every customer's conversation. I felt sure I could humor this ridiculous woman.

31

CHAPTER 4

After we'd ridden for about an hour, I heard the crack of a whip and felt the stage lurch forward at a much higher speed. "Is the driver trying to break our necks?" Evonia asked no one in particular.

"No, ma'am," the older Mr. Stanard replied. "We must have a problem. Josh, why don't you stick your head out and see what's up?" The younger man opened the stage door, thrust his upper body outside, and yelled, "Two men are chasing the stage! Must have been hiding in that copse of trees we just passed!"

Evonia cried, "Oh, God, we're going to be killed!"

Mr. Stanard said, "Not if my boy and I can help it."

I touched the derringer inside my pocket, but I didn't bring it out.

We heard gunfire, and Mr. Stanard turned to Josh and said, "Go out there and help the driver while I cover you." Josh climbed out of the passenger compartment on one side while the older man opened the window on the other side. He said, "You ladies stay down."

Evonia moved to the empty seat behind us and settled her body over the length of it. Her eyes were tightly closed, and her lips moved as if in prayer. I got on the floor near Mr. Stanard to watch the action.

There was more gunfire, and Mr. Stanard fired off a couple of shots, but I noticed his arm was angled toward the ground, as if to purposely miss the riders. When they came alongside the stagecoach, I saw the masked riders. One was on a palomino, and the other rode a dapple gray. Mr. Stanard was still hanging out the window, firing his gun and making himself a very easy target, but they never shot him. No bullets came through the passenger compartment, either.

I realized the Stanards were in cahoots with those riders. Then I saw the rider on the palomino get shot and go down, but I was positive Mr. Stanard didn't shoot him.

I felt a rage growing inside me. I wasn't going to let these stinking scoundrels win. My father had taught me to shoot during my girlhood in Mills County, Iowa, so I knew how to use a gun.

I drew the derringer, and, when Mr. Stanard ducked inside to reload, I touched his arm. He ignored me until I said, "We have another problem, sir."

When he looked up and saw my gun, he pointed his gun at me, apparently forgetting it was empty or thinking I didn't know that, and said, "Give it to me."

"All right," I said as I gently squeezed the trigger and put a bullet through his left eye. In a sort of shock, I watched his blood splatter my white shirtwaist.

I needed to warn the driver, so I reloaded and pushed my upper body out the door on the other side of the stage just in time to see the younger Mr. Stanard take aim at the driver. I fired at him, and the bullet hit him between his shoulder blades. He turned, forgetting to bring his gun around, and, for an instant, a look of astonishment passed over his face before he fell off the stage.

As we went over a dip, I nearly fell out of the coach, but I managed to hold on and pull myself back inside. There was no need to warn the driver of anything at this point, so I decided to let him assume the remaining rider had shot the young Mr. Stanard.

The other rider was still shooting, and so was the driver. At last, the driver hit the rider, not killing him, but injuring him enough to make him give up and ride off. I knew I'd do the same if I'd seen my three partners get killed. When the driver stopped the stage, I went to him and saw a large, dark bloodstain growing on the front of his blue and black checkered shirt near his collarbone. The bloodstain at the entry hole on the back of his shirt was small. I didn't know what to do for him except to climb up, open his canteen, and give him some water. "Are you ladies hurt?" he asked, looking at my bloodstained shirtwaist.

"We're fine," I said. "This is Stanard's blood, but I doubt that's his real name."

"Oh, that's his name, all right," the driver said. "I heard he was fixing to run for Congress."

I told him how I'd observed the Stanards speaking with those riders and how Mr. Stanard wasn't trying to hit them with his shots. "They were in cahoots. He pointed his gun at me when he saw my derringer. I had to shoot him. Didn't you see those riders near the stage station?" I asked.

"Nope, too busy with wheel repairs." He picked up the canteen and winced before taking another drink. "I want to see Foster's wound," he said, pointing to the guard slumped beside him, so I pulled the man's hat off. "Damn," he said, "look at that powder burn. Stanard's son got him behind his left ear."

The guard looked only a few years older than I was. "What did he die for?" I asked. "What was he guarding?"

"A cash shipment." The driver, who was growing ashen, wiped his wind-chapped face with a handkerchief and asked, "Miss, do you think you can help me drive this team?" Then he passed out.

I'd never driven a stagecoach, but I'd always known horses, and I knew I'd have to drive the stage if we got to the next station because Evonia sure as hell wouldn't be able to do it. I heard her babbling inside the coach, so I took her some water. "Here, it's all right now," I said. "The bad men are gone." Then I saw her looking over at the body of G. J. Stanard on the stage floor.

"I'll take care of him." I got out, walked around, and dragged him out, and then I remembered to check his pockets. "You owe me a new shirtwaist, asshole," I explained, as I took his cash roll and his pocket watch. It seemed a very fitting thing to do.

I left him there face up, one blue eye staring skyward, the other, just a bloody, black hole. Naturally, I also troubled myself to walk back a ways and relieve his son of his money.

I didn't touch the downed rider, but I fired a shot into his head just to make sure he was dead. I hoped someone would find his palomino and take care of it properly. When I got back to the stagecoach, Evonia was keening softly. "It's over, Mrs. Spangler," I said. "We'll be at another stage station soon."

Next, I went and spoke softly to the horses, which were still very edgy. Once I'd petted all six and told each of them what a good horse he was and how brave he was, I addressed them as a group. "In a minute, I'm going to take the lines and prompt you very gently, and you're going to take us to the next station, and you're going to get us there safely without any foolishness on your part." I climbed into the driver's box, ascertained that the driver was still alive, pushed Foster's corpse over as far as possible, and clucked for the horses to move out.

Driving the team was no problem for me in that terrain, except that the unconscious driver kept slumping over on me as we rode along. Eventually, I stopped shoving him off my shoulder and let him lean on me.

When the next station came into sight, I poured some water onto a handkerchief and washed the driver's face to see if I could revive him. As he began to come around, I put the lines in his hand. "We're almost there," I said. "You got us this far. You can make it." I did this because I didn't want to draw unwanted attention to myself. It seemed better to let him be the hero. He sat there, glassy-eyed, holding the reins, apparently believing he'd driven us thus far.

The sun was sinking low when the station workers gathered around to hear our story. I kept my story simple, repeating it like a parrot. "Some men tried to rob us. All the men on the stage were killed, except for our driver." Every time I said it, I let my voice slip further toward seeming hysteria. Jim and Susanna Ormond, a middle-aged couple who ran the station, told Mrs. Spangler and me to help ourselves to a meal of baked ham, boiled cabbage, potatoes, and biscuits with tea, and, when we tried to pay, Susanna said, "Put your money away. I wouldn't think of taking payment after what you've been through." Short and thin with strawberry-blonde hair, she reminded me of my mother.

She and her husband tended the driver's wounds as best they could and put us up for the evening. Our driver, Tom Johnstone, was unable to eat much, so Susanna gave him some potato soup. While two of the station workers rode out to get the sheriff and take him to the site of the attempted robbery, I spoke quietly with Johnstone and asked him not to tell anyone I had shot Mr. Stanard, and he agreed. He said he could understand why a lady wouldn't want that sort of notoriety.

That evening, Susanna offered me a bottle of laudanum, and I gave two large spoonfuls of it to Mrs. Spangler after we settled into the bedroom we'd share that night. Once she was sleeping, I pulled the Stanards' money from the front of my dress and counted it by candlelight. Two hundred and eleven dollars. Smiling, I pushed it back into my bosom, took a bit of laudanum, and crawled into bed. I couldn't help but wonder how much cash was in that strongbox and whether I might have taken it and gotten away with it. I thought, *Surely not. Besides, I'm not a thief.*

Chapter 5

With the money I had taken, I could have walked away from Evonia Spangler at any moment, but I decided to stick with her for a little while to see how things would pan out since I was a respectable woman, as far as anyone knew, and I had her to prove it. Within a few days, I understood exactly what she expected from me as we moved from town to town.

First, she preferred that I call her Mrs. Spangler when other people were around. She needed help with her bathing, as she had trouble reaching her back, and she was able to get dressed much more easily if she had help with her shoes and stockings. That's all she required, aside from a bit of conversation from time to time and having me transcribe her poems, which she composed whenever her poetic trance came upon her, usually about twice a day at odd hours.

Fortunately, Evonia valued time to herself, so she was not overly demanding of me. She treated me much as my mother would have, had she lived. Of course, I often found myself mothering Evonia, calming her fears, as I had on the stagecoach. She had no idea I carried a gun because she'd been too busy cowering in the stage to notice.

If a place appealed to her, we stayed for a while. Sometimes we rode the stages at night and slept upright in our seats if local lodging wasn't available or didn't meet Evonia's approval. I soon found that Evonia had two personalities, the ladylike one she presented most of the time and a private one she let me see after we'd traveled together for a while. She had a salty tongue, and, while I was with her, I learned a string of British swear words that would be the pride of any sailor. I was also able to unravel the finer points of etiquette by watching Evonia and imitating her as we traveled about.

We arrived in Dodge City in the early afternoon of April 24, 1876, and Evonia promptly headed for the Bellmore, a three-story hotel with Persian rugs and heavy brocade draperies. I'd never seen a nicer place. I stood near the entry, taking in the rich, burnished wood paneling and its winding stairway, while I read a poster about a dance that evening and thought how this would be a fine place to meet a wealthy future husband.

The hotel clerk greeted Evonia with, "Good afternoon, ma'am." He then glanced over at me, gave me a little frown, and said, "Miss, you might find more suitable lodging at—"

Evonia cut him off. "Nonsense. This is my secretary, Katherine Jones. We need two rooms, close together, please."

"Absolutely. For how long, ma'am?"

"I haven't decided yet. Until further notice, I suppose."

"Of course." The man called for a boy to carry our luggage, took keys from a grid of pegs on the wall behind him, and escorted us to the second floor to rooms five and six. "Which do you prefer?" he asked Evonia. "The rooms are very much the same, except one faces the street."

"If you take the one with a view of the street, you won't miss anything," I said, "but the other one will probably be quieter, more restful." I was hoping she'd decide to let me have the view of the street, and she did.

Both rooms had a comfortable bed, a washstand, a wardrobe, and a small table with two chairs. I was about to take the pitcher on Evonia's washstand to fill with water when she asked the boy who brought our luggage upstairs to have someone bring water up for us. As he hurried downstairs, Evonia said, "Help me off with my shoes, Katherine, and then you can go get some rest. I'm just going to wash my face and take a little nap."

By the time I had her shoes unbuttoned, a colored maid in a gray skirt and white apron came upstairs with two heavy pitchers and filled our washbowls. I wet a washcloth, wrung it out, and handed it to Evonia. When she had washed her face, I helped her out of her skirt and arranged it across a chair while she got into bed, so it wouldn't get wrinkled.

Once she was settled, she said, "That clerk was a pretentious rotter, wasn't he, suggesting you find a room elsewhere. Why if he didn't work here, management would tell that little tosser to go elsewhere the minute he walked in this place."

"Tosser?"

She used a rude hand gesture at lap level to show me what it meant, and I laughed.

I started to go. "I'll let you rest now," I said, and then I turned and said, "I saw a sign downstairs that says they're having a dance here tonight at eight, and I'd like to go."

She lifted her head from the pillow. "Really? Then, yes, of course, we'll go. What will you wear?"

"You've seen my whole wardrobe now. The blue skirt and the brown one. Which do you like best?"

"That's all you have?" she asked.

"That's it."

"Then for God's sake, go out and buy something new. You have your pay for your first three weeks. Where's my purse?" I handed it to her, and she gave me another ten dollars. "Use some of this if you need to."

On that first night there, I felt a sense of the joy of life I hadn't felt since I was a young girl. I wore a green, satin dress with a low neckline, but I'd stitched in a bit of lace to cover part of my cleavage so Evonia wouldn't gripe about it.

40

To my delight, Evonia didn't cling to me, as I'd feared she might. She sat at a table, drinking and talking to a stout, sandy-haired man, who appeared to be enjoying her company.

A stringed ensemble on a small stage above the dance floor played classical numbers, mostly waltzes, not the music I'd expected to hear in Dodge City, but fitting for a snooty place like the Bellmore. Soon, a young man asked if I'd like to dance. When I said yes, he said, "Ma'am, I should tell you I'm not much of a dancer. Could we get something to drink instead?"

I might have been irritated if he hadn't been so handsome with his blue eyes and reddish-blond hair. I liked the sheer size of him, so tall and solid looking, so I said that would be fine. He offered his hand and said, "Garland Spade. And what's your name, pretty lady?"

"Katherine Jones," I said, enjoying the chance to pretend I was an ordinary girl with no mark of shame on her life, "but my friends call me Kat." I smiled, let him lead me over to the bar, and told him I'd like tea.

"But this is a special occasion."

Giggling, I asked, "What's the occasion?"

"Why, it's the night I met you." He ordered a bottle of champagne instead. The bartender popped the cork and poured two glasses. Garland raised one and said, "To the night we met."

Of course, I could see he was a smooth talker and surely full of cack, as Evonia would say, but I was having fun, so I took the other glass, clinked it against his, and took a demure sip. He downed his quickly and stood there looking at me.

Finally, I asked, "If you aren't good at dancing, then what are you good at?" I suppressed a smile, half-expecting some wild claim about his sexual prowess, and I was ready to pretend I was innocent in asking and feign offense.

"Gambling," he said, as he refilled his glass.

"Then you're the kind of man my mama told me to stay away from."

A tall man with a dark moustache stepped toward me and said, "Now that's the truth."

Garland smiled and said, "See, even our new sheriff affirms I'm good at gambling. Kat, this here is Mr. Wyatt Earp. Wyatt, Miss Katherine Jones."

Wyatt Earp tipped his hat. "I only affirm he's the kind of man your mama told you to stay away from," he said as he walked away.

"Don't listen to him," Garland said, guiding me to a table and pulling out a chair for me.

"I'd like to learn about poker," I said, and I meant it.

"I could teach you. Poker is really two games. You're playing the cards, and you're playing your opponents, but you have to learn to play the cards first." He pulled a deck of cards from his pocket and started showing me different hands and explaining which hands were higher. Then he told me stories about beating opponents that might have beaten him if they'd had more nerve. I was fascinated and had no idea how much time was passing.

Garland was about to deal us a couple of practice hands when I felt a small, soft hand on my shoulder, and Evonia said, "It's almost time for me to turn in, and you should consider doing the same, luv. Some people might think it scandalous if you remain here unchaperoned."

Garland turned and smiled broadly. "Is this lovely lady your sister?" he asked, drawing a bright smile from Evonia.

"No, but people tell me we favor one another," I said, helping him pile it on. "This is Mrs. Evonia Spangler, and I'm her secretary. Mrs. Spangler is a poetess."

"A poetess. Now that's something special. Pleased to meet you."

"Likewise. It's so refreshing to meet a man with refined manners."

Garland leaned toward Evonia and asked, "May I have a few more moments with Miss Katherine?"

"Of course."

Garland smiled at her, then pulled me a few steps away and asked, "Are you staying in the same room with her?"

"No."

"What's your room number?" he asked, and he winked at me.

"Are you crazy? You can't visit me in my room, and it's not just because of Mrs. Spangler. It's a matter of common decency."

"You could receive a music teacher in your room if you were taking music lessons," he said.

"Not at this hour."

Garland grinned. "Poker teachers keep different hours. What's your room number?"

"Five," I said, and I smiled despite myself. "Give me at least half an hour to get her settled."

"Will do." Leading me back over to Evonia, he said, "It was very nice to meet you, Katherine. I hope to see you and Mrs. Spangler again this week."

As Evonia and I headed upstairs, she said, "What a nice young man. What a splendidly fine young man."

As promised, Garland Spade arrived at my door about forty minutes later. He had two clean glasses and our bottle of champagne in an ice bucket. Seeing no one was in the hallway, I quickly let him in. I pointed toward the table and chairs. "Poker," I said. "You were about to deal us some practice hands."

Garland sighed, took a seat, and began dealing the cards. I won the first two hands, each time with two pairs. "Either you're no good at gambling or you aren't even trying."

He sighed. "The ambience isn't right. When I play poker, I'm usually drinking and smoking." He got up, poured two glasses of champagne, and lit a cigar before dealing the next hand. I took a small sip of champagne and won the next hand with three queens.

"I think I need a better teacher."

"No, the ambience still isn't right. When I play poker, I'm usually looking at the ugly mugs of other men. You're too pretty. You need a moustache." He dipped his finger into the ashtray on the table, reached over, and smudged my upper lip. He dealt again, and I won with a full house. "The ambience?" I asked, and he nodded.

"I hesitated to mention it, but when I play poker, I usually play for money or some other consideration. We could play for nickels or pennies, but that wouldn't seem realistic because I wouldn't take the smallest bit of your money." He sighed and glanced about the room. "Of course, we could play naughty poker, where the loser would have to remove an item of clothing."

I shook my head. "Wyatt Earp was absolutely right about you, but I'll try it. Deal the cards."

After that, Garland's luck took a turn for the better. I removed a shoe after the next hand, and then another shoe, but that's as far as I cared to go, being in the role of a proper lady. "From now on, the only person taking clothes off is you, win or lose," I said.

Soon Garland was sitting across from me bare chested in nothing but his underwear, and I was admiring his muscles while considering the possibility of letting this end the way he was hoping it would.

Then there was a knock at the door. Garland quickly grabbed his gun from the heap of things on the floor.

"Put that away, and hide yourself," I whispered, pointing to the wardrobe.

There was more knocking, louder this time.

"Who is it?" I asked, once Garland was out of sight.

"Hurry and open the door," Evonia said softly. "I'm not fully dressed."

When I let her in, she said, "I have news. Mr. Thurman Upton has asked me to marry him." She was literally trembling with excitement and wearing nothing but a blue, satin robe.

"Mr. Upton?" I asked, totally confused.

"Yes, the gentleman you saw me talking with earlier this evening."

"What did you say?"

"I said yes, of course."

"But you've only just met. How can—"

There was a clunking sound inside the wardrobe, and Evonia cried out, "What the bloody hell?" She opened it and found Garland in his underwear. He waved, but she ignored the gesture, turned back to me as if he weren't there, and said, "I'm certain marrying Thurman is the right thing to do."

"You're not upset with me?" I asked, as Garland pulled himself out of the wardrobe.

"Well, I guess I should be, but I have a rather delicate situation of my own to contend with."

She sniffed, ran her fingers through her hair, and said, "Mr. Spade, would you kindly put on some clothes and help me? I need to get Thurman back to his room, without being seen, if possible."

"Of course, Mrs. Spangler. Where is he?"

"Passed out on my bed in room six."

"What room is he staying in?"

"Twelve, and his key is in his coat."

As Garland pulled on his pants, he said, "You ladies stay

45

here, and I'll take care of it."

"How can you be sure Thurman is right for you?" I asked after Garland left.

"I could see right away we were compatible."

We sat for several minutes, and I heard no movement in the hallway. "What's taking so long?" I asked.

Evonia sniffed. "I suppose Mr. Spade's having trouble getting Thurman into his clothes."

I tried not to laugh, but I couldn't help it, and then Evonia laughed with me. When she could speak again, she said, "I wouldn't answer Thurman at first, but I invited him up for a nightcap of whiskey later, and then I tested to make sure I'd find no disappointments in—well you know what I'm talking about. Anyway, after a while, I said yes, and then the rat-arsed knob passed out in my bed. He'd best remember our engagement come morning!" She leaned closer to me and added, "Thurman owns a big ranch outside of town, and that's where we're having the wedding."

CHAPTER 6

True to his word, Thurman Upton married Evonia on Sunday, May 7, 1876, and they only waited that long to give some out of town guests time to arrive. Evonia bought me a beautiful peach-colored dress of satin and chiffon to wear as her maid of honor, and she chose a lace-covered ivory dress with seed pearls for herself, since this was her second wedding. Sheriff Wyatt Earp served as Thurman's best man.

Thurman's second cousin's daughter, fifteen-year-old Helen Louise "Nellie" Leonard, was there with her family, and, though they were technically third cousins, she referred to him as "Uncle Thurman." When he asked Nellie to sing Evonia's favorite hymn, "Blessed Assurance," for those gathered, I thought he'd singled her out for the honor simply because she was pretty, but I found her voice clear and strong. I didn't know it then, but she was destined to become a famous actress known as Lillian Russell, and the two of us would become friends.

Thurman and Evonia proposed that I stay in a guest room at the ranch for a while and continue as Evonia's secretary until I found other work, and I took them up on the offer. After begging her mother, Nellie was allowed to stay at the ranch for a few days after the wedding, though her family traveled back to Chicago the next morning, but this was only because Thurman knew the train conductor and had him promise to look after Nellie on her way home.

I was only two years older than Nellie, though I couldn't tell

47

her so while posing as Katherine Jones. To amuse ourselves, she and I spent the cooler morning hours riding horses while Evonia tended to all the details of decorating that ranch house to make it her own.

Evonia had purchased sidesaddles for all three of us to use, but she said she didn't care that much for riding, and she never went along. I knew how to ride sidesaddle because my family's English neighbors in Mills County, Iowa, had let me use one of theirs when I rode with their daughter as a child, but I had to teach Nellie.

On our first morning out, I asked Helen, "Want to go faster?"

"Can we? Mother said I should ride like a lady."

"I'm a lady. Watch how I ride." I prompted my quarter horse into a gallop, took him in a wide circle, and brought him to a halt within ten feet of her sorrel.

Nellie clicked her reins and said, "Go, horse," and soon she had her horse galloping across the open range. I took off after her, worried a bit too late that, if she fell off, I'd be blamed for it. I caught her at the top of a slight rise, and we stopped. Her cheeks were flushed, and she said, "Golly, Katherine, this is fun." I smiled, put my worries aside, and we took off again, the wind in our faces, our horses' hooves pounding the earth.

The time I spent with Helen was all I ever had of what anyone might think of as normal teenage life with a friend, and it was all compacted into a few days. My mother had died when I was fourteen, so I'd taken care of our house and my younger sisters for a couple of years until I'd set out on my own, leaving those worries to older siblings who'd married and lived close by. I dreaded to think of when Nellie would have to go home.

The morning before she left for Chicago, we took a picnic out to a meadow beside a stream. She told me about plays she had been in at school. "Why do you like theater so much?" I asked.

"Because my life is boring. Theater is my only source of adventure. I don't even have any secrets of merit." She sat with her arms behind her, leaning back on her palms. "Here, let me prove it. This is my best secret: I put a dead wasp in my voice teacher's desk once after he scolded me for not practicing enough." She took off her hat, leaned her head back, and let the sun shine on her face. "Make my skin black. Make it black as the night sky," she commanded. In that moment, I loved her so much. I wished we could be friends forever.

"Stop it," I said. "You'll regret it if you burn and blister." I watched her grudgingly cover her face with her hat and decided to take a great risk. "Would you like to know one big whale of a secret?" Before she could answer, I blurted out, "I'm only seventeen. My name is Sarah Jane Creech, and I was born in Iowa, just like you. Before I became Evonia's secretary, I worked in a whorehouse in Kansas City."

Nellie clapped her hands. "Bravo, Kat! You're so much fun."

That night, she gave me her address and made me promise to write to her, and I did. In time, she came to understand I'd told her the truth about my age and my past, but she didn't care.

The main topic of conversation everywhere I went in those days was the upcoming U.S. centennial celebration. From what I heard, this was to be the biggest and best Fourth of July in history. Parties, dances, picnics, fireworks displays, races, and games for people of all ages were on the horizon for people in every city and town across the United States. Over the next few weeks, I saw a lot of Garland Spade, and we made plans to attend a ball at the Grandview Hotel immediately after the town's fireworks display.

I learned that Garland worked for a builder named Oscar Basham, helping install roofs and flooring. "What I want to do,"

Garland said, "is build up enough money from gambling to start my own contracting company."

"Isn't that a risky plan?" I asked.

"Maybe," he said, "but you'd be surprised at how much I've managed to put in the bank so far."

Garland would often take me to supper or ride horses with me. Sometimes we'd walk along the Arkansas River. The sweetness of spending time with him made me realize what I'd missed by taking up whoring so young. It brought a poignant feeling to my heart that I couldn't name, similar to when I realized I'd missed the experience of normal teen years and had compressed it all into a few days with Nellie Leonard.

On June 5, Garland came out to the ranch around noon on his dinner break and invited me to accompany him to see *Our American Cousin* at the Dodge City Opera House on Saturday, June 10, 1876. I had never seen a professional production in an opera house, so I was thrilled with the invitation, and I was particularly eager to see the play when Garland told me it was the one Abraham Lincoln had been watching when he was shot.

Later that day, Evonia and I went into town together, and I bought a pale-yellow dress with Florentine neckline and a cinched waist for the occasion. I also bought a pair of white, lace-up shoes and a white, satin purse with seed pearls.

Garland rented a carriage to take me out that evening. We had supper at Frederick's, where the waiters all wore black coats, white shirts, and black bowties. Since Garland had made reservations for six o'clock, we were seated immediately at a table in a corner, giving us plenty of time to enjoy our meal and make it to the opera house before the play started at eight. I liked that the tables were spaced widely apart, giving us a sense of privacy. Again, Garland ordered champagne for a special occasion. "What's the special occasion?" I asked when the waiter was out of earshot.

"Don't you know?" he asked. "It's the forty-seventh day after the day we met."

Across the room, I saw a waiter seating Wyatt Earp and a woman with dark-brown hair, curled in the front and arranged in sausage curls down her back. She wore red lipstick and a sapphire-blue dress. Without being able to explain how, I immediately perceived that she'd spent some time as a prostitute. In my judgment, the woman had a very plain-looking face, but I thought any woman might envy her hair.

"That's Wyatt's wife, Mattie Blaylock Earp," Garland whispered.

After perusing a lengthy menu, we both decided on stuffed pheasant, sautéed vegetables, and rice pilaf with an apple torte for dessert. I thought the restaurant was very nice, but, later, I was overwhelmed by the lavish interior of the opera house.

The two-story brick building had a lobby with a white, marble floor, French mirrors in gold leaf frames, and crystal chandeliers. Above embossed, burgundy wallpaper, elaborately carved, gold leaf crown molding touched the ceiling. Garland took my arm and led me up a curving stairway to the right, and an usher seated us in a gilt box he'd rented, the second one back from the stage. I sat there speechless for a few minutes taking everything in. The stage area was encompassed by three huge arches, all with intricately carved palm leaves. Huge crystal chandeliers provided lighting as guests took their seats. "It's wonderful," I said, "like being in a palace or something."

Garland took my hand when the house lights went down, and the stringed ensemble began to play. I was near tears when the curtain rose, thinking, *This is the life I've always wanted.* I'd known it was available; I just hadn't known what it looked like until that night.

The play was a farce about an English family who learned an

uncouth American relative, Asa Trenchard, had inherited Trenchard Manor. The story was satisfying because it involved some treachery that was resolved and had several love stories intertwined, and, at the end, many couples got married.

Before he took me back to the ranch, Garland and I took a walk along a footpath by the Arkansas River. "Thank you for such a beautiful evening," I said. "I hope you enjoyed it as much as I did. You haven't said much this evening."

"That's because all my words and feelings are bound up in my heart like the rocks that are set so deeply into this riverbed. I enjoyed it more than you'll ever know." Then he bent down and gave me a kiss I felt all the way down to my toes.

Garland asked me to marry him, and I accepted, on Friday, June 16. "And where will we live?" I asked, in love and giddy with excitement.

"Name a place."

"San Francisco."

"Done." He promised he'd soon have enough money to build me a house in San Francisco. Then he'd start his own contracting company and give up gambling, except the small-time games for pleasure. I could tell he meant it. Looking back, I feel sure he would have done just that, given the chance. It never occurred to me to consider the dangers he faced at the gambling tables.

Evonia was delighted for me. She and Thurman said I might as well stay with them until the wedding, so Evonia and I started planning another wedding at the ranch. On June 20, we had just come in from town, where I'd been measured for a white wedding gown. I'd never mentioned my past to Garland, and he'd never asked, though I felt sure he had some idea I wasn't exactly a saint since I'd let him into my hotel room the night we'd met. I wondered how I'd explain using the name Katherine Jones to my family, but I figured that would be easier than telling Garland my real name was Sarah Jane Creech.

CHAPTER 7

For years now, I've wondered if Garland would have lived if I'd told him about my time in the brothels. As it worked out, my past was what killed him.

After we became engaged, I begged Garland to take me with him, to let me be his good luck charm at the gambling tables, even if I just sat at a table across the room. He flatly refused to let me go into the saloons with him. Then I learned Garland had been invited to play poker at the Red Dog Ranch on the outskirts of town on the evening of June 24, and I asked if I could go. He resisted at first, saying it would be a distraction.

Finally, I wore him down to the point where he said I could go if it was okay with Emmet Fowler, the ranch owner. Then he coached me on what to do and not to do if I were near the table. First, I was not to walk near and look at his cards because he worried that my face might reflect what he held. Second, I was not to touch or speak to him during any game.

I joined him, after Fowler said it would be okay, and I was careful to follow his instructions. Four men were sitting at a round table when we arrived, all known for their poker skills. Emmet Fowler's great room had log walls decorated with the mounted heads of buffalo and deer. On the hearth of a stone fireplace was a grouping of geese and ducks, flanked by coyotes. The curtains looked like brown sheets, hanging artlessly over the windows. Gas lamps on walls provided lighting. Rumor had it that Mr. Fowler divorced his wife while she was away on a trip to visit her family in the East and sent her a telegram telling her not to come back. I wondered if men could actually do that, but, whether it was true or not, it was obvious that Mr. Fowler didn't care that there wasn't a feminine touch about the place.

He was a gentleman, though, and he introduced me to the men as Garland's fiancée, Katherine Jones. "Miss Jones, that there's Sam Stulz," he said, pointing to a gruff-looking man with deep lines in his face." Moving clockwise around the table, he continued, "Paul Barrow, Grover Hutch, and Colton Lorne." The men ranged from their thirties to their sixties, and most looked friendly enough, except for Colton Lorne. I remembered hearing Lorne's name before. He was a bounty hunter. He appeared to be the youngest in the group, without a line of any sort in his face. Looking at him, I figured he never would have any lines in his face because it seemed his face never moved, only his eyes. He dipped his head as the others had and said, "Ma'am," but with only the slightest motion, as though his lips hadn't moved. I felt a chill when he glanced back up at me, as if he were skewering me to the wall with that look. I nodded and quickly backed away.

Just then, I felt keenly aware that I shouldn't have come. I was the only woman in attendance, for one thing, so Mr. Fowler had put a pitcher of cool lemonade, a clean glass, and a tray of cookies out for my refreshment on a table beside a large, brown sofa. He'd also brought some books out for my entertainment: a Bible, a book of Shakespeare's plays, and Thomas Hardy's *A Pair of Blue Eyes*. When he showed me these things and walked away, I understood I had been dismissed.

The men were playing five-card draw that evening. I understood how the game was played because, by this time, Garland had shown me how to play several types of poker. Before any dealing was done, each man paid an ante to get into the game.

They started with ten dollars, and the antes went up as the night progressed.

Emmet dealt every player five cards, starting with the man to his left, and then the first round of betting began. Next was the draw round, and each player that hadn't folded was able to discard up to five cards and draw that same number from the top of the deck. Then the second round of betting began. At last, it was time for the showdown, and the one with the best hand won. The dealer would then take all the cards and pass the deal to the player on his left.

This went on for nearly two hours, and I became engrossed with Elfride Swancourt's love triangle in the Hardy novel. I was aware of the men's banter from across the room, but only marginally. Then I came to the end of a chapter, and I heard Colton Lorne say in a soft tone, "Mr. Spade, your fiancée reminds me of a whore I knew in Kansas City." I closed the book and saw Garland giving him a deadpan stare, Lorne staring back, his face serene. I could only imagine the anger rising in Garland. I quickly glanced away.

Sam Stulz, who had his back to me, said, "Hush, Colt, the lady might hear you. You're just trying to get Garland riled up before he places his bet. Don't you know the man's already under pressure?"

There was a bit of laughter, and Lorne shrugged and murmured, "Can't blame a man for trying." My hands shook from anger as I held the book, and my interest in it was gone. Certain I'd never seen Colton Lorne until that evening, I wondered if someone else had recognized me and told him about my past or if his mention of Kansas City was just a co-incidence. No matter how much I'd have liked to strangle him, I couldn't make a scene because Garland had told me never to interrupt a game, no matter what happened. Garland had let it pass, and whether he'd take the matter up again later was yet to be seen.

Their games went on. I eventually settled back into reading to pass the time, as the stakes grew higher. Then the room became charged with energy I could feel even at a distance from that table. The last hand of the evening, a hundred dollar ante, and everyone was in. I was practically holding my breath as I waited to see if Garland would win. Then Grover Hutch dealt the cards. Sam folded. Colton bet a hundred, and Garland called. Paul folded, and Emmet called. When the draw began, I saw Garland take two cards. Just before the second betting round began, Colton Lorne said, "I'm puzzled."

"About what?" Emmet asked.

"About why Garland there would marry a whore. Last time I seen that girl, I poked her for five dollars."

I experienced what happened next as if it took several seconds instead of an instant, but I never heard another thing except for the gunshot. I saw Garland's hand reaching for his gun, bringing it out of the holster. Then I heard Colton's shot and saw Garland jerk back a bit on the impact, as if a big hand had pushed him. He had a stunned look on his face as the blood spread across his white shirt. Colton had shot him in the center of his chest.

Emmet Fowler said I was screaming that night, but I didn't hear any screaming. To this day, I have no memory of going to Garland and ruining my clothes with his blood, but it must have happened because Evonia took the clothes I'd worn that night and burned them. As I experienced it, it seemed I just watched Garland get shot, and then I was back with Thurman and Evonia, thinking I'd had a bad dream.

Evonia canceled the order for my wedding dress while I slept for days, doped up on laudanum. Later, they told me I attended Garland's funeral, but I had no memory of it. His funeral took place on June 26, 1876, the day after three hundred men of the U.S. 7th Cavalry Regiment and General George Armstrong Custer were killed in the Battle of the Little Bighorn. Of course, I was oblivious to it at the time, but, in the weeks to follow, I came to feel particularly empathetic toward the general's wife, Elizabeth Custer, in her loss.

CHAPTER 8

Five days later, Evonia started weaning me off the laudanum. By June 30, I started asking a few questions. I wanted to know if Colton Lorne was in jail for murdering Garland. Turned out, he was not in jail, as the shooting had been ruled self-defense. Worse than that, I heard that Colton Lorne had won that final hand and was living like a prince off the money, so, while the United States enjoyed its huge centennial celebration, I hunkered in my room at the ranch in a dark state of mind. Showing true friendship, Evonia stayed near me, avoiding the parties and fireworks displays she had been so eager to attend, though I urged her to go.

I knew I could reconcile myself to Garland being dead because I had no choice, but I couldn't abide Colton Lorne being alive. I didn't give a damn about anything else, but that one thing mattered to me.

Evonia and Thurman had been very kind to me, but, on July 7, I left their ranch and found myself a situation at the Wild Rose Saloon right there in Dodge City. I used much of the money I had made as Evonia's secretary to buy myself some dresses and undergarments fit for a whore, but not the fine things I'd once dreamed of owning. Evonia's jaw dropped when I told her what I'd decided to do for a living. The only thing I held back from her was the fact that it had been my profession before I'd met her.

"You gormless twit!" she yelled. "Do you want to become a

poxy minger?"

"I have no idea what you just said to me."

She sighed and said, "I called you a foolish idiot and asked if you wanted to become an ugly, disease-ridden woman."

"It doesn't really matter to me," I said.

She sighed and regarded me with sad eyes. "I suppose it doesn't," she said. "I wish I could kill the rotter that killed Garland Spade."

I was so numb at that point that I only felt the smallest pang of conscience for disappointing her. I figured everybody who'd heard what Colton Lorne had said about me believed I was a whore, so I might as well revert to being one. All I wanted to do was stay in Dodge City long enough to see Colton Lorne dead.

On July 18, I put the bulk of the money I'd taken off the Stanard men to good use when I hired a Mexican known as Tiny Ramirez to kill Colton Lorne. I'd heard Tiny was a former soldier in the Mexican army and had killed his share of men. Moreover, he had the reputation of being a man of his word. He stood six-four and weighed about three hundred pounds. At that time, he was doing odd jobs, carpentry work and such, for the brothels and other businesses.

Tiny didn't even blink when I approached him with my offer. "So how you want me to do it, lady?" he asked, while pocketing one hundred dollars as an advance.

"He killed my man, so I don't care. You can poison him, knife him, or shoot him in the back while he's dead drunk for all I care. Just watch him, bide your time, and don't get caught. If there's time and you're able to, tell him he's dying because he shot Garland Spade."

"You want I should bring you his head on a platter?" he asked, grinning.

"Just leave him where he falls."

August 2, 1876

I was at the Nuttal and Mann's Saloon in Deadwood, South Dakota Territory, drinking whiskey with a fellow named John Beeman, a bear of a man with gray hair just beginning to touch his temples and the sides of his beard. Wild Bill Hickok was playing five-card draw two tables over from where we were sitting, and I had a side view of Wild Bill, who had his back to the door. I could sense he was uneasy because he kept glancing around the room between hands, as if looking for trouble. He asked the fellow next to him to trade seats, but the man wouldn't do it.

John Beeman had paid good money to be with me. I liked John all right, but I was hoping to get to know Wild Bill, too, if you know what I mean, because I'd seen him win a pile of cash the night before. I also thought he was a handsome man with that red hair.

John was slowly running his hand up my skirt. I giggled and told him to stop because people could see. "No, they cain't," he said. "It's under the table." I was about to argue that there was no tablecloth when his hand stopped, and he clinched my thigh.

Jack McCall had come in with a strange look on his face. We both knew Jack had suffered heavy losses at poker the night before. Then, of a sudden, McCall got right behind Wild Bill, drew his .45, and shouted, "Damn you! Take that!" He fired into the back of Wild Bill's head, killing him instantly. Blood splattered the cards Wild Bill held—two pairs—black aces and black eights, cards forever after destined to be called the "dead man's hand." That was the first time I saw a man killed, and I was only seventeen years old.

Of course, I'd never set foot in Deadwood, but I loved to tell that story over the years, and people loved to hear me tell it. On

August 2, 1876, I was really still working at the Wild Rose Saloon in Dodge City, which was owned by Macon Tillman, an older man, still muscular, who'd once served as a second lieutenant in the U.S. Army long before the Civil War. The place had six rooms upstairs. Downstairs, it had pink rose wallpaper that looked like something any respectable woman in the city would want in her home, at least, of course, if she didn't know it was in that saloon.

We had a slow afternoon, so me and two other girls, Savannah and Blossom, started drinking a little. Macon didn't care if we drank, as long as we didn't get too drunk or become obnoxious. Savannah was a pretty, brown-haired girl with blue eyes, who spoke with a Southern accent that sounded overdone to me, but I'd never traveled to the South, so I really didn't know. Blossom was plain looking and chunky, but men liked her. She had black hair, and she was always smiling in a sly way. I had taken to calling myself Little Jill because I was petite, and I liked the fragile sound of that name.

I didn't like to take whiskey straight, so Savannah poured me another whiskey and water and asked what my real name was. "That's not your business," I said, but, for a moment, I was tempted to tell her I was Sarah Jane Creech, out of Mills County, Iowa.

"At least tell us how you got into this business."

"Yeah, tell us," Blossom said.

I took a swig of my drink and decided to entertain them with a story as an image formed in my mind. "I was at my mother's bedside, applying a cool, wet cloth to her forehead. She was so sick with a fever that she was barely able to get up to use the chamber pot. She needed medicine, but there wasn't any money in the house." I paused and watched little motes of dust floating on a shaft of sunlight by the window.

"So you sold your body to get medicine," Blossom said,

breaking into one of her biggest smiles.

"Shut up and let her tell it," Savannah said.

"Well, sort of, but I didn't want to. The people living near us were poor, but I'd heard that Mr. Seldom, a widower in our town, was wealthy. Not knowing what else to do, I walked more than a mile to his house to ask for help.

"His front porch was shaded by huge basswood trees. When I knocked on his door, he stuck his head out, standing behind it, and looked at me. The top of his head was bald, but he had gray hair on the sides of his head and a gray moustache. I said, 'Sir, my mother has a fever, and she needs medicine. Can you help us?'

"He eyed me for a moment, then smiled and said, 'Perhaps, but there's a price to be paid.' I told him I didn't have any money, but he opened his door and told me to come inside."

Blossom and Savannah were leaning toward me at this point, so I took another sip of my drink and made them wait. From behind the bar, I heard a glass break followed by Macon's cursing. I expected him to call one of us to clean it up, but he didn't, so I continued my story.

"I followed him into his kitchen where he pointed to a bottle of laudanum on a shelf and said, 'That there is new. Never been opened. Kind of like you.' I didn't understand why he was comparing that bottle to me, and I didn't know laudanum wouldn't do anything but make Mama sleep. I asked if it would make her well, and he said it would if anything would."

I paused again and downed the rest of my drink, spilling a bit of it on my dress, and Savannah handed me a handkerchief. "He told me he wanted to see me naked and put his hands on my body. I took a step back from him, wanting to run for the door, thinking he was going to grab at me, but he didn't, so I didn't run. Then he leaned down and said, 'It's a small thing, child, and no one will know. I certainly won't tell anyone.' "

Savannah had a stricken look on her face that made me wonder if I was telling a story similar to her own. I continued, "I thought of my mother and decided that having one evil secret would be worth it if she got well, so I let him lead me into his bedroom, where he had me take off my clothes, and I endured his hands on me for what seemed like a very long time. At last, he said, 'You like this, don't you?' When I shook my head no, he said, 'Say yes.' I said nothing, so he clamped his hands on my shoulders and shook me. 'Say it,' he said. 'Say you like it.' With tears streaming down my cheeks, I whispered, 'I like it.' 'You're a naughty girl,' he said, as he undid his belt and dragged me over to the bed.

"When he finished, he told me to get dressed and get out of his house. I pulled my underclothes on, soiling them with a mixture of my blood and his seed, and got into my dress, but I didn't leave. 'The medicine,' I said, and he said, 'Oh, yes, I'd forgotten. The whore must have her price.' He brought it to me, and I ran for the door. I felt filthy, and I knew I was ruined."

I paused and looked at my hands for a moment, then added, "By the time I got home, Mama was talking out of her head. I gave her two spoonfuls of laudanum, and she finally settled down, moaning in her sleep. Two days later, Mama was dead, and I found myself alone on the streets."

When I looked up, Blossom smiled and said, "Ah, go screw yourself," and we all broke into such laughter that Macon came over to find out what was so funny. "Little Jill just told us about . . . about," Blossom said, but she was laughing too hard to say the rest. At last, she took a deep breath and choked out, "About how she was raped and orphaned all in the same week."

"And then Blossom told her to screw herself," Savannah added.

He stood with one hand on his hip, shook his head, and muttered, "I find no humor in that," and the self-righteous air with which he said it sent us into new peals of laughter. He took the whiskey bottle off our table and declared, "You girls have been drinking too much."

Around ten o'clock in the morning on August 3, 1876, Tiny Ramirez came into the Wild Rose Saloon to let me know he had taken care of Colton Lorne. I took him upstairs to my room where we could talk. He said he'd waited for Lorne outside of town and shot him as he came in from another night of gambling at the Red Dog Ranch.

He said, "I know to shoot this gunslinger may be hard, so I sing when I hear him come and speak to him as he passes. Then I start singing again so he no hear me cock pistola before I shoot him in back."

"You're sure he's dead?" I asked.

"Oh, *si*. I no do work halfway. He reach for his pistola, and I shoot it right out of his hand. Then, I help him die before I take his money. This job work out well for me."

I felt something tight uncoil within my chest, and, for a moment, I could hardly breathe. The feelings that followed were relief and sheer satisfaction. I asked, "Did you tell him why he died?"

"*Si*. I tell him he die because Garland Spade's woman says it should be so. Then I slit his throat."

I took out another hundred dollars to finish paying him, feeling it was the best money I'd ever spent. Since we had to stay in my room a while to make the transaction look right, I decided to demonstrate my appreciation to Tiny Ramirez.

The next day, I watched Colton Lorne's funeral procession from the window of my room upstairs. I had intended to move on to another town after seeing him dead, but I had no energy or ambition left. I stayed put, as if the entire reason for my existence had been accomplished and I had nothing left to do.

By the end of September in 1876, it seemed no one could talk about anything except the upcoming presidential election. Voter mistrust of both parties was commonplace. From time to time, I'd find little cards left on tables in the saloon that read, "Of the two evils, choose the least." They puzzled me because I was never sure if the person who left them was rooting for Hayes or Tilden. My boss, Macon, supported Tilden, but he tried to tolerate the opinions of all his customers, no matter what.

The Republicans were fond of the saying, "Not every Democrat was a rebel, but every rebel was a Democrat." A popular Democratic slogan was "Throw the rascals out," and that's exactly what Macon did one night.

Around seven o'clock, I came downstairs wearing a low-cut, black, satin dress that turned every man's head my way. Scandalously short, it fell just below my knee. Martin Stone was playing "I'll Take You Home Again, Kathleen" on the piano along the back wall, and the place was nearly full. I walked through the smoky air over to Brayden Benton, one of my regulars, who waited by the bar. Brayden was a tall, stout man with reddish-brown hair and was clean-shaven except for his moustache. "Well hello, Little Jill," he said. "It's always a pleasure to see you."

I smiled, touched the base of his throat, and slipped my fingers ever so lightly up his neck, across his jaw, and around the curve of his left ear. "Same here." I was about to say more when some fool started making a commotion. I turned and saw a short, thin man with graying hair tapping on a glass with a spoon. The man was wearing a black coat with tails and a top hat.

"Could I have your attention for a moment, gentlemen?" he

yelled. The piano stopped, and all conversations ended. When the man had everyone's full attention, he said, "I am Mr. Chester Stewart, and I hail from Pennsylvania. I have a brief selection I'd like to read to everyone tonight, regarding Mr. Rutherford B. Hayes's opponent, Samuel J. Tilden. This observation was written by no less than the great newspaperman John D. Defrees."

He unfolded a paper, cleared his throat, and read, "Mr. Defrees describes Samuel J. Tilden as, and I quote, 'a very nice, prim, little, withered-up, fidgety old bachelor, about one-hundred and twenty-pounds avoirdupois, who never had a genuine impulse for many nor any affection for woman.' " A general murmur spread as he hastily added, "That's all I have to say, gentlemen. Ponder that when you cast your vote."

I was thinking the description he read of Tilden fit Mr. Chester Stewart quite well when I heard Macon ask Brayden, "Will you get that little prick out of here 'fore I kill him?" Without saying a word, Brayden walked over and lifted Mr. Chester Stewart, turned him sideways, and carried him to the door, as if he were a rolled up carpet, and slung him into the street.

He came back to the bar, blue eyes sparkling, and asked, "Well, Little Jill, where were we?"

"Right about here," I said, brushing his neck lightly with my fingertips. "I'm trying to incite a riot inside your trousers. Is it working?" He didn't have to answer. I saw it was, so we headed upstairs.

As it turned out, the presidential election ended indecisively that year. Tilden won the popular vote and 184 electoral votes; Hayes won 165 electoral votes with twenty in dispute. I was still young, and I didn't give a kitty one way or the other, though, in later years, I came to care much about political matters.

In the upheaval that followed, things didn't go well for Tilden. The Compromise of 1877 ended reconstruction in the South and secured Democratic support for Hayes, who became president on March 4, 1877.

Things didn't go well for Jack McCall that year, either. After shooting Wild Bill Hickok in the back, he went to Wyoming and started bragging about how he'd killed Wild Bill in a fair fight. Though he had been acquitted by an impromptu court in Deadwood, he was arrested in Wyoming and tried for murder after authorities in Wyoming said the court in Deadwood had no legal jurisdiction. He was hanged on March 1, 1877. I was very pleased to hear it.

CHAPTER 9

My sorrow over Garland Spade never completely left me. Eventually, I started moving again and working different towns, so many that most of their names all run together in my mind. All whores did this, as the men in certain areas grew weary of them and wanted new flesh. I made it a practice to shave a few years off my age when I moved because the men wanted younger women. This was how I managed to stay seventeen for so long.

Some people claimed I had a boy and a girl in my early twenties and that I lived with their father for a while, though he refused to marry me, but I won't speak of it. Some things should remain bound up in one's heart. Even so, it happened I was present when a whore tried to get a church-going woman to adopt her son. She walked up to the woman's porch and pulled back the baby's blanket to show how perfect and beautiful the boy was, and then she offered to give him away. The woman frowned and said, "I'd never take him. That child's a bastard and won't amount to anything."

That same whore then took her boy to the foul-mouthed, barren wife of a blacksmith, who made a great fuss over that baby and promised to love him as her own. Some claimed that boy was blinded in an accident some years later and that I lost track of a girl I'd given up during those years, but people say all kinds of things.

It happened I was there when a certain whore received word that her child had fallen off a wagon, hit his head, and lost his sight. I know she sent a lot of money to pay for his care in the years that followed.

In those early years after Garland's death, I became aware I'd lost my way, but I didn't know how to recover it. I worked in the lower brothels and took my share of beatings off drunken men, and sometimes I didn't care if I lived or died.

Even so, I kept in touch with my family, fabricating stories about my life. They'd write back with news from home and express envy over my ability to support myself and see so much of this great country. I also wrote to Nellie and Evonia at least once or twice a year, making my life sound better than it was. I was happy to hear about Nellie's debut as Lillian Russell at Tony Pastor's Theatre in New York City on November 22, 1880, but I couldn't help reflecting on the contrast between her thrilling rise into show business and my perilous existence.

Evonia basked in her success as a poet. She sent me a copy of her book, *Westward Ho! Poems,* along with a note explaining that she often traveled with Thurman after arranging to read her poetry at various ladies' meetings and sell books afterwards. I mentioned this to Nellie in one of my letters, and she wrote back, "Hahaha. Good for her. She sent me a book, too. Sometimes I read Aunt Evonia's work from the stage—but only when I want to produce a comic effect!"

Somewhere in those years, I tried laudanum again, thinking it would make life better, but instead of bringing restful sleep as it had after Garland's death, it brought nightmares, so I stopped taking it.

In the spring of 1882, I moved to Tin Cup, Colorado, and it was there that I read a newspaper account of how the outlaw Jesse James had been shot by fellow outlaw Robert Ford on April 3. Jesse had made the mistake of trusting Ford and allowing him into his home. I was taken with the newsprint picture of Jesse, and I thought about the frailty of life and how the choices we make take us in such strange, unexpected, and, sometimes, tragic directions. My own life made me feel like I was on a runaway stage with no way of controlling the outcome of the ride.

When summer came to Tin Cup, I heard news of a whore named Oxana who had hung herself from the post of a canopy bed. I heard she had a terrible scar on one breast and that she'd drunk half a bottle of whiskey to build up her courage. I'd had no idea my old friend was in the same town until I heard the gossip. It made me wonder how I'd ever manage to finish life better than she had.

The year after Oxana's death, I moved to Sneffels, Colorado. I was leaving a party at the Lucky Nickel Saloon near midnight on Saturday, June 9, 1883. My customer, who was renting a room upstairs, didn't bother to walk me home when he was finished with me. I was standing outside by a hitching post, just looking up at the stars, when I heard a man's boots approaching on the wooden sidewalk. Feeling tired, I touched the derringer in my pocket and moved back near the saloon door, planning to slip inside to avoid an unwanted encounter. Just as I reached for the door, it became apparent the man was paying no attention to me. He passed, never slowing his pace.

When he reached the place where the sidewalk ended, I heard a voice call out to him, "Hello, dearie. Can I offer you some small comfort this evening?" A woman emerged from the alley, keeping to the shadows.

Shoving her aside, the man said, "Sorry, I'm not in the market for old, dried-up, female flesh."

"You could just say no, you friggin' asshole," she said.

When he was gone, she was still muttering curses, so I ventured near the alley and called out, "Ma'am, I need someone to walk me home. I'm willing to pay."

She came out of the alley where I could see her weathered face by moonlight. Her hair was partly gray, and she was almost skeletal in her tattered, cotton dress. She moved as quietly as the mist after a rain. "Reckon I can protect you?" she asked, and I saw she had some teeth missing.

I didn't say it, but I reckoned she might scare off anyone that would harm me. I asked, "Do you work in the cribs?" The cribs were on the outskirts of town, just tiny spaces with beds, where the cheapest whores stayed, those who were older and unable to command higher fees. I figured she was in the alley because she'd been having a slow night there.

"Used to," she said, "but they done throwed me out and give my spot to a younger woman. Now I work the alleys."

"Where do you sleep?"

"Got me a little place to camp at night," she said, running her hands across her skirt to smooth it.

"But what will you do in the winter?"

She shrugged. "Don't know."

She was peering at me expectantly, and I remembered I'd just offered her employment. "I live about five blocks from here. I'll pay you a dollar to walk with me." I took the money out of my pocket and handed it to her. She thanked me, and, as we walked, I asked her name.

"Dovie," she said. "My parents named me Little Dove. I'm half Apache." For a moment, I wondered if she was lying about her past as all whores do, but then I realized no white whore would claim to be half-Indian because Indians weren't paid as well.

"So are you saying you don't mind living outdoors?"

"I'm saying I should have had a better life. My father married my mother and lived among the Apaches for several years. When she died in childbirth, he had to bury her and my baby brother. He took me with him to live with his parents when I was six years old. Five years later, when he died of consumption, my grandmother wouldn't keep me anymore because I was a half-breed. She sold me to a brothel owner, and I did housework for the madam until she decided to start selling my body when I was thirteen."

I suspected the woman was trying to get me to give her more money out of sympathy, and I decided I wouldn't do it. Any whore can tell a sad story to a bleeding heart. Then she added, "Three years later, I slit her throat, took her money, and left that place."

I took a sidewise glance at Dovie and saw a single teardrop roll down her cheek. That told me she'd never slit anyone's throat but wished she had. She sniffed and said, "Sorry, Miss. I'm chattering like a white woman. Apaches are strong. This winter, I'll be more Apache."

We walked on in silence. When we got to my place, on impulse, I gave her five more dollars. Back in my room, I started thinking of my future and wondering if I'd end up like Dovie. I didn't want to think about it, but I couldn't help it. At last, I slept and woke to the morning sun. Days and weeks passed. Eventually, I put her out of my mind.

The night after the first snow flew in that town, which was sometime in mid-October, I got up early in the morning, put on my coat and boots, went to the nearest livery stable, and rented a horse. I wanted to see the world while it was fresh and clean and while every branch and twig was coated in white. The sun was out, so I knew this beauty wouldn't last long. I headed out of town and rode uphill toward a wooden church with a cross on the top of its bell tower. Just beyond it, I took a trail along a ridge. At a place where there was an outcropping of rock overlooking a valley, I saw a figure leaning against a stray boulder. A chill passed over me, and I wanted to ride on but felt compelled to take a closer look. Then I saw it was Dovie, the half-breed whore from the alley. She was wearing her thin dress and had an old, snow-covered horse blanket wrapped around her shoulders.

When I dismounted to help her, I saw that she was already dead, though her eyes were still open, as if she were enjoying the scene before her. Snowflakes had gathered on her eyelashes. I thought of how cold the wind must have been on that ridge as it snowed during the night. I remembered her telling me she was going to be more Apache in the winter. Tears came to my eyes, probably the only tears that anyone would shed for Dovie.

I'd heard that elderly Indians of many tribes wandered off to die in the wilderness when they became a burden to others, and I supposed this was what Dovie had done, except she'd never had the option of becoming a burden to others.

I didn't touch her. I simply mounted the horse and headed back to town to report her death. On the way back, I saw a child making snow angels in a front yard. I knew the Methodists said it was too late to pray for someone after they were dead, but I said a prayer for Dovie and asked that she find peace.

Back in town, the snow was tracked up and dirty. Soon, I reached the sheriff's office to report what I'd found. "An alley prostitute," the sheriff said.

"Her name was Dovie."

He scratched his large belly and asked, "You mean that tall, skinny, half-breed woman?"

I nodded and glanced over at an empty jail cell.

"Yeah, I'm familiar with her, and thanks for letting me know." He sat down and picked up the newspaper on his desk.

"Aren't you going to retrieve her body and see to her burial?"

He laughed. "The coyotes and buzzards will see to that."

I leveled my stare at him and didn't move. "She's a human being."

"She's a half-breed whore, and nature will take care of her."

Inside, I was seething, but I tried not to let it show. "I know there's a potter's field outside of town where poor people are buried."

"It ain't for Indians," he replied, "so it wouldn't matter if you'd hauled her down the mountain on your own shoulders."

I took the horse back to the livery stable, no longer in a mood to ride in the snow. Then I returned to my room, feeling frantic about my future. I was very aware that my season of youth and good looks wouldn't last forever. Though I had once aspired to work the finest brothels and command the highest pay, I'd stopped caring about that when I came back to the profession after Garland's death. In my heart, I knew I didn't have the right connections or the confidence to reach that goal. I wondered if Dovie and I would share the same fate.

At last, I saw that the main reason I didn't have the right connections, aside from not caring, was that I didn't know enough about the people I'd met. I thought of the seemingly endless sea of men I'd been with and could have kicked myself for not trying to learn more about them. As soon as I realized this, I bought a black book with blank pages and started writing down the names of customers and things they told me about themselves and other people they knew. I made it a point to remember people's names and what I'd heard about them, studying my notes frequently.

This helped me greatly, and not just with making conversation. It wasn't long before I could talk about strangers as if I actually knew them and make people believe I did. This earned me respect and became my key to the better brothels. This personal conversion took place between November of 1883, when the U.S. and Canadian railroads instituted five continental time zones, which helped end the confusion of having a myriad of local time zones, and November of 1884, when Grover Cleveland was elected president of the United States.

Feeling more confident, I moved to nearby Telluride, Colorado, in April of 1885 and started earning top rates under the name Blushing Betty. The name worked like a charm for me, and I felt the heat rise in my cheeks at the smallest off-color joke. I kept my language clean, too, playing the part of a cultured woman as best I could.

Doc Holliday passed through Telluride in June that year and stopped at the Big Dipper Saloon where I was entertaining a wealthy young miner by name of Everett Tucker. We were drinking whiskey at a table when Everett pointed him out to me. I'd been enchanted with Everett's good looks until he told me Doc Holliday was in the room. Doc stood by the bar across the smoky room with a pistol on his hip. He appeared relaxed, but I could tell he was sizing up the men around him. I would have gladly traded Everett and his easy smile for a chance to spend a night with the renowned Doc Holliday, whose hair was turning prematurely gray. "Invite him to play poker with you," I urged. "I'd like to meet him. I'll be your good luck charm."

Everett shook his head. "I don't want to embarrass him. He's a broken man in poor health. He can't gamble worth a shit any more, and he probably doesn't have any money."

"What are you talking about? That's Doc Holliday," I said. "Haven't you ever heard of the shootout at the O.K. Corral?"

Everett gave me the sort of smile a man would give an ignorant child. "I don't suppose you heard about what happened at Leadville earlier this year when he ran out of money and borrowed five dollars off a bartender named Billy Allen. When it was time to repay the loan, Doc was broke. Allen reached for his gun, and Doc shot him in the arm. He was acquitted on self-defense."

I could hardly believe it. I'd been working so hard to know everything about famous people, but I hadn't heard that story about Doc Holliday. Everett ordered us another round of whiskey. "At least invite him to have a drink with us," I said, so Everett got up and invited Doc to our table. Then, in the presence of that great man, I felt awkward. All I could think to say was, "I met your friend, Wyatt Earp, in Dodge City about ten years ago." Of course, Doc soon set me at ease, and he stayed with us and talked for a while, mostly asking us about our families and things we'd done, which showed me he wasn't in a mood to talk about his past.

When he was about to take his leave, I said, "Please show me how you can shoot. I'd like to witness it once in my lifetime."

Doc gave me a sad smile and said, "All right, ma'am. Let's step outside, and you can pick a small target for me." Everett and I followed him into the street in the bright sunshine, and I started looking for something Doc could shoot. People walked the dusty boardwalks by the saloons and other businesses outside, so I looked up and saw a weathervane on a building in the next block. "That rooster needs an eyeball," I said, pointing to it. Before I could hardly think of bringing my hand back to my side, Doc fired. The weathervane spun around, and we all walked down the street to see where his shot had hit. Sure enough, there was a circle of blue sky showing right where that rooster's eye should have been.

In September 1885, I read a news story about the massacre of Chinese mine workers in Rock Springs, Wyoming. Twenty-eight Chinamen were killed, fifteen injured, and seventy-eight Chinese homes were burned. White men were angry because the Chinese were being hired before them since the Chinese miners were paid much lower wages. At the time, the story seemed far removed from me. Two weeks later, upon reading that P. T. Barnum's elephant, Jumbo, had been hit and killed by a locomotive in Ontario, Canada, I cried.

In those days, it seemed the world revolved around me. I figured I'd work until I saved up a big pile of money, move far away, pass myself off as a respectable woman, and marry well. That way, I wouldn't have to worry about being ragged, hungry, or cold in my later years. Soon I had a large, beautiful wardrobe to help me play the part. And save money I did. By the early spring of 1886, I'd set my heart on moving to the wealthy mining town of Kingston, New Mexico Territory, as a proper lady.

CHAPTER 10

As I traveled and watched the mountain passes give way to desert and back to mountain passes, I adopted Evonia Spangler's British accent, and I started telling people I was from the Limehouse district of London. When I was angry, I'd use the peculiar curse words I'd heard from her lips. I decided to call myself Sadie, a nickname for Sarah that my sisters had bestowed upon me. Even bolder, I took the risk of using my real last name because this time I thought I was going to make it and become a gentlewoman.

The railway ended at Lake Valley, where I had time to look around a bit and eat before taking a stagecoach into Kingston. The date was Friday, May 7, 1886. I headed toward a group of mostly weathered, wooden buildings to browse the storefronts and find a restaurant. There was a post office, so I stopped in one of the buildings of Keller, Miller, & Co. to purchase postcards to send to my sisters. The cards showed the buildings and mine-shaft tailings of Lake Valley.

As a group of miners went into Cotton's Saloon, I passed an assay office and came to the Meredith Building. From inside, I heard two Chinamen apparently arguing and banging pots and pans. The smell coming from their restaurant was divine. When I went in, one of the cooks approached me and motioned me toward a table. I smoothed my skirt and glanced around. The other customers, all men, varied from well-groomed businessmen to scruffy-looking miners. The Chinaman wore black pants, a white shirt, and a black skullcap. A pigtail of plaited, black hair trailed nearly to his waist. "What fine lady may I boast eats here?" he asked, bowing his head slightly, as he pulled a chair out for me.

A little thrill rushed over me. Without thinking, I gave my full, real name, not my nickname. "My name is Sarah Jane Creech."

"Thank you for coming, Miss Creech. I'm Tom Ying, own restaurant almost one year. Serve steak and stir-fry vegetables today. Is okay?"

"Yes, it's perfect."

"You like tea to drink?"

"That would be splendid." At that moment, I had no idea that one day Tom Ying and I would become close friends. It was unthinkable to me as a white woman.

I took the stage into Kingston that afternoon. Kingston was set in a canyon entrance, and I was taken by the beauty of the Black Range Mountains surrounding it. Upon arrival, my tiredness melted away. I felt I'd surely made a wise choice because Kingston had everything: drug stores, mercantile stores, restaurants, smelters, saw mills, a brick factory, an ice plant, livery stables, assay offices, saloons, and brothels. I took particular note of Pretty Sam's Casino, the Percha Bank, and a store that sold furniture and rugs. Finely dressed women shopped the stores. Piano music flowed out of the saloons, where cowboys and miners sat drinking and gambling. Businessmen moved with determination down the wooden boardwalks.

After looking around a bit, I settled into the three-story Victorio Hotel, the finest in town. The next morning, the first thing I did was buy a horse, a brown thoroughbred with a white face. I named him Long Shot and arranged to board him at Pete Judson's livery. I also bought a sidesaddle to help support my claim of being British. I wanted to create a spectacle, riding sidesaddle across the countryside in my fancy hats.

At this time, Kingston was practically swimming in money. I planned to join with the best of society, regale the population with clever conversation, and dazzle everyone with my regal bearing. I wanted to nab the richest bachelor I met, marry him, and enjoy an easy life. Of course, by this point, I should have known that things don't always go as planned.

Late that summer, I read in the newspaper that, on September 4, 1886, Apache Chief Geronimo and his band of warriors had surrendered to General Nelson Miles at Skeleton Canyon, Arizona. I actually shed a few tears when I read it, thinking of how the renowned warrior had fallen from glory. Looking back, I see most of my sorrow was really for me. I knew I was still without prospects and quickly running out of money, so I'd soon have to surrender to fate.

My ingenious plan had taken longer than expected, so I'd have to turn to prostitution again. To this end, on Monday, November 29, 1886, I went to see Joyous Lee at the Mother Lode, the finest brothel in Kingston.

A little brass bell tingled as I entered the saloon, and I half-expected someone to call out, "Company, ladies!" But no one did. Over a piano in one corner, I saw a framed needlepoint piece that read ALL THE COMFORTS OF HOME. The bartender glanced over at me and continued wiping down the bar, where several men were gathered, though it was only ten o'clock in the morning. I was about to approach the bartender, but a maid came in from another room and asked, "Can I help you, Miss?"

Before I could answer, the portly, middle-aged Joyous Lee entered the room and exclaimed, "Sadie Creech—what a delight! Will you have tea with me?" I was surprised she remembered me. That summer, someone had briefly introduced me to Joyous at a party at Pretty Sam's Casino, but we'd barely said more than hello.

I smiled and said, "Yes, that would be lovely."

She turned to the maid and said, "Emily, serve us in the parlor, and bring chocolates."

Joyous was known for her raucous laughter and her ability to set people at ease, but I'd heard rumors that she also had a foul temper. I followed her through a doorway into a parlor with red, velvet draperies and sofas and chairs covered in red and gold brocade. Gas lamps dispelled the shadows. A marble-topped coffee table stood between two of the sofas, and Joyous directed me to one of them and took a seat across from me. Her dark, auburn hair was plaited in a bun on top of her head, and she wore several rings on each hand, the largest of which appeared to be a ruby of the finest pigeon's blood color. I wondered if it was real.

She must have seen me staring at it because she suddenly shouted, "Of course, it's real!" She wiggled her fingers and added, "Every friggin' one of them is real!" I was appalled, thinking I'd already offended her somehow, but then she broke into laughter, and I joined her and laughed so hard I almost peed.

"Every single one?" I asked when I could catch my breath. "Are you a bloody mind reader?"

"That, I am," Joyous said, and I was tempted to believe her after the strange interview that followed. Emily came in, put a tea service platter on the table between us, and poured Earl Grey into silver-rimmed china cups with a delicate cherry blossom pattern. She handed me a matching dessert plate laden with pound cake, a fork, and half a dozen exquisitely molded chocolate candies. Then she gave me a linen napkin embroidered with a cherry blossom motif.

When Emily left, I ate one of the chocolates and took a sip of tea. Joyous took a bite of cake and said, "So you're starting to feel a bit constricted? Money's getting tight?"

I didn't know how she knew this, but I said, "Exactly."

She looked me up and down for a moment. "Tell me about yourself. Where are you from?"

"London, the Limehouse district." I kept my consonants crisp as I named the only district of London I knew.

Joyous snorted. "Horseshit."

"Pardon?" I asked, pretending I hadn't heard her.

She narrowed her eyes and said, "You look like a Midwest farmer's daughter to me, one that's getting a little long in the tooth, if you know what I mean."

I carefully put my plate back on the tray and said, "You can go straight to hell, Joyous Lee."

I stood to leave, but she snorted laughter again and said, "Enjoy your chocolates, darling. You're doing fine. I hate a girl who won't stick to her story. How old are you?"

"Nineteen," I said, taking my seat again, still angry, but less so.

"Nearing thirty."

"Nineteen," I insisted, remembering what she'd said about sticking to a story.

"Nineteen, and a bloody virgin, too, I'll bet," she said, breaking into laughter again.

"Nineteen and the best blooming poke in this city," I declared, taking another chocolate from my plate.

"Suppose I told you someone had told me they knew for a fact that you aren't English?"

"Then I'd say they're telling porkies."

Joyous nodded, eyed me for a moment, and said, "Your breasts are small."

I'd had about enough of Joyous Lee. I thought about saying,

Yes, and you're a chuffer with a huge ass, but I held my temper, shrugged my shoulders, and said, "Well, as they say, more than a mouthful's wasteful."

Joyous shifted her weight, and I steeled myself to absorb more abuse. At last, she sighed and said, "I have an opening here because one of my girls decided to move on after spending three years with me, but I don't just hire anyone with a sweet thing between her legs. First, you'll need a clean bill of health. I require my girls to be checked out by Doc Guthrie every two months. Our clients expect only the best."

I smiled and said, "That's exactly what they'll get if you hire me."

Joyous nodded and said, "You'll do. If you're happy with my terms and the doc says you're healthy, you can move in today and work tonight. My girls pay me fifty dollars a month for room and board, and I take half their regular fees. Emily collects the fees in advance from our clients, so you'll never have to talk money with men. Your fee will start at fifty dollars, two hundred if the man stays all night. You can keep any tips or gifts you receive. If you become extremely popular, your fees will go up accordingly. Don't get greedy and make our clients feel rushed in any way; do, and you'll be out of here as soon as I hear of it. Any questions?"

"Do you usually have—?"

"We have so many that we often have to turn men away."

"Could I see—"

"Upstairs on the right, room six." She took a key out of her pocket and handed it to me.

When I opened that room, I was astounded. It was about twelve by fourteen feet and had blue wallpaper with a gold floral design, a large oak bed with a carved headboard, and a marble-topped washstand. Pulling back the covers, I found crisp, white sheets of excellent quality. There were gas lamps on the walls, and a small, crystal chandelier hung from the ceiling. A huge mirror in a gilded frame hung on one wall. On the other side of the bed, there was a chair covered in pink and gold brocade. Across from the foot of the bed, there was a tremendous oak wardrobe with double doors, and, in the far corner, a commode with a chamber pot fitted in it. The window had metal bars, which had been painted white, to keep out thieves and unwanted visitors. Beside the window was a framed embroidered piece that read, "Forget Me Not." I liked that because I did not intend to be forgettable. I sighed and sunk onto that luxurious bed for a few minutes before I went downstairs to tell Joyous I was pleased with her terms.

"Good," she said. "Go see Doctor Guthrie. Get that note of health. Then go buy yourself some new dresses and lingerie on my account. Get some perfume and makeup, too, if you need it. You can pay me back when your money starts coming in."

I shook my head and said, "I'm a business woman, too. I don't want to start out owing you a fortune. I have plenty of lingerie and stylish dresses that will please your clients."

She laughed and said, "You think like I do." I left the Mother Lode thinking, *No, I think better than you do.* Even my thoughts had a British accent.

By this point, I was already planning to save up another large store of cash, but this time I wouldn't take a gamble and spend it all on what I hoped might happen when I moved to a new town. I'd learned my lesson. Before long, I was going to have a brothel of my own.

CHAPTER 11

I went straight to Doc Guthrie's office. I was curious to meet this man because I'd heard he had managed to survive being scalped and wore a wig. A little bell rung as I entered his small waiting room, and, from behind a curtained-off area, he called out, "Be with you in a minute." Then I heard him ask someone, "Now, what's your problem?"

"My baby no shit," said a woman with a Mexican accent. Then the baby started wailing, probably because the doctor was prodding its abdomen.

After a moment, he said, "Give her a quarter teaspoon of cod liver oil. That should take care of it. You have some cod liver oil?"

The woman repeated, "Cod lee-ver oil."

They came out into the lobby, and I asked the woman with the squirming child, "Do you know what a quarter teaspoon is?"

"Speak English not good."

Dr. Guthrie sighed, produced a spoon from a drawer, took a bottle from a shelf, and poured a quarter teaspoon of oil into it. He pinched the baby's nostrils shut, shoved the spoon into her mouth, and tipped her head back. Amazingly, the child swallowed instead of spitting it out. Then she started bawling again. The woman smiled and asked, "Baby fixed?"

He smiled and said, "Baby fixed." The woman left, and he

never said a word about a fee, so I thought he must have a kind heart.

He turned and thanked me for helping him see that she didn't understand him. I had to force myself not to stare at his wig, which called to mind a portrait of Thomas Jefferson that appeared in one of the schoolbooks from my youth. When he asked what I needed, I told him my name and explained that Joyous Lee had sent me. He told me to go back to his exam room and get undressed. "There's a sheet you can use to cover yourself," he said. "I'll be with you in a few minutes."

Doctor Guthrie made his examination mercifully quick, unlike some doctors in other towns who had ogled me and prodded my private parts much longer than necessary. While he was scrawling a note for Joyous Lee, he said, "It's not my business, but I'm curious why you'd go this route."

"It's either that or sell Long Shot," I said, and when he gave me a curious look, I explained, "That's my horse, and, even if I sold him, I'd soon be in the same financial shape. I've nearly run out of money."

He smiled and said, "Best reason I've ever heard from a working girl. I've seen you galloping about on that fine thoroughbred." He handed me his note and added, "Not many people ride sidesaddle around here. Where'd you learn that?"

"On my grandfather's estate outside of London." I reached for my purse and asked, "How much do I owe you?"

He winked. "Nothing, dear. Joyous Lee always covers my fee for her girls." Something about the way he said it made me wonder if he was sleeping with Joyous. I left the office smiling and liking Doc Guthrie.

My next stop was the livery. I told Pete Judson my plans of moving to the Mother Lode, rented a carriage, and had him harness Long Shot to it. Then I headed to the Victorio to get my things. I knew I'd lose more than a day's rent that month, but I hoped that would be small compared to what I'd gain that same evening.

Just as I turned the corner, I heard a woman shouting, "Git! Git on away from here! We don't need nigger boys loiterin' around here begging from our guests!" I recognized the voice of one of the waitresses from the hotel's restaurant. The boy cringed before her and started walking my way with his head hung low. He appeared clean, but his waist overalls were ragged, and he was very thin. He looked to be about eleven years old. The sleeves of his long underwear reached down to his hands, but the sleeves of his blue shirt did not. I wondered if he owned a coat.

When he got next to me, he asked, "Pardon, ma'am, but what does *loiterin'* mean?"

"It means hanging around, doing nothing."

He frowned and said, "I wasn't loiterin'. I was lookin' fo' work, and I wasn't beggin' neither." He stood there a moment, seeming to stew over that, and then he brightened and said, "Ma'am, there ain't no call for you to be driving yo'self when you can hire a fine driver like me to do it for you."

"What's your name?" I asked.

"Silas, like in the Bible."

I got down and said, "Well, Silas like in the Bible, why don't you drive me the rest of the way to that hotel and wait there with this carriage? I'm going to go inside and pack my things up. I could use someone to bring my bags down and load them." He started to climb up, but then I paused, as if reconsidering, and asked, "Are you strong enough to do that?"

"Yes'm, I'm strong all right. Want to feel my arm muscle?" He clenched his right fist and pulled it up toward his shoulder.

"That's okay. I can see it bulging up under your shirt."

Silas smiled and said, "I knowed it was gettin' bigger."

"When I'm ready, I'll call for you, and you can bring my bags downstairs for me."

"I'll be right here, ma'am."

On my way inside, I wondered if Silas had eaten that day, so I went into the hotel restaurant, ordered a sliced beef sandwich wrapped in butcher's paper, and took it out to him. "You can eat this while you're waiting," I said.

His eyes opened wide, and he thanked me. When I got upstairs, I looked down and saw him devouring it. After I finished packing, I opened the window to tell Silas to come up, and I saw the same waitress approaching him, hands on her hips. "Silas," I called, "pay her no mind. Come up here and get my things." To the woman, I said, "Leave my hired man alone." She scowled up at me as he ran past her and into the lobby.

True to his word, Silas managed to take a heavy trunk packed with my clothing and two valises downstairs and load them without any trouble. When it was time to go, I started to climb into the carriage, but Silas asked, "Can I drive you, ma'am?"

I was torn to the heart. I realized this child thought I was a respectable lady, and I couldn't bear to let him see where I was going.

"Not today," I said, "but you've been a big help. How much do I owe you for carrying my luggage?"

"You don't owe me nothin', ma'am. You done bought me a sammich."

His words nearly sent my emotions over the edge, and that didn't happen often, unless I was angry. I had to turn and look away from him for a moment. When I could speak, I asked, "How big is your family? Do you have a lot of brothers and sisters?"

"No, ma'am, just me, my mama, and my little sister."

"Is your mama nearby, where I could meet her?"

He shook his head and said, "She work at a laundry place, and they don't like for people to talk to her while she there, not unless they want wash done."

That answered my unspoken questions. His mother wasn't a drunk or a whore. She was just a woman trying to bring up two children on starvation wages. "Where's your sister?"

"They let Birdie play in the yard, and Mama keep an eye on her while she works."

I gave him two bits and said, "This is your pay. You've earned it. It's yours." Then I took my last four dollars from my purse and said, "Give these to your mama. Tell her I said to get some groceries or whatever she needs."

He stood there with the coins in his hand, while I looked around to see if anyone had seen the transaction. I didn't think anyone had, so I said, "Put that in your pocket, and keep this a secret until you give those dollars to your mother. I don't want anyone to steal that money from you."

He obeyed me and said, "Thanks, ma'am. Many thanks. God bless you, ma'am." I got into the carriage quickly and drove away, certain that he was staring after me.

CHAPTER 12

I brought the carriage around to the back of the Mother Lode just after four o'clock, and Joyous introduced me to a barrel-chested man named John Preston who kept order at her place. He stood at least six and a half feet tall. Apparently, John was a man of few words because he just tipped his head slightly in my direction and set about carrying my things upstairs.

When I started to follow him, Joyous touched my arm and said, "Our supper party starts with drinks at five, so the professor will be here soon. Then around eight, others start coming in for dancing and entertainment. Get settled, freshen up, and come downstairs as soon as you can, and I'll pair you with one of our guests. We serve an excellent supper at six o'clock sharp."

By "the professor," I knew she meant the man who would play the piano that evening. I hoped he was good because that always made for a nicer evening.

I hurried upstairs and began unpacking my things, while John took the carriage back to the livery for me. To my delight, when I opened the wardrobe, I found it was cedar lined and had a good supply of sturdy hangers for my dresses. I unpacked them all, smoothing them, before hanging them inside. I had six nice party dresses, two simpler ones, several simple skirts and shirtwaists, ten sets of naughty undergarments, and plenty of ordinary underwear. The wardrobe was big enough to hold more dresses. I put my lingerie in the lingerie chest near the window and settled onto the bed to rest. Half an hour later,

Emily brought me a towel and washcloth and some hot water for my washbasin. "Madam's already got you paired with a nice gentleman for the evening, Mr. Albert Fall, a young man who's studying the law. I think you'll like him because he's the decent sort, and he's not bad looking. Joyous says he just celebrated his twenty-fifth birthday three days ago."

I smiled. "Tell Joyous I don't care if she pairs me with a toothless old man, as long as he has lots of money."

"She'll appreciate hearing that, but tonight, I think you've got the pick of the litter."

I wondered briefly if Albert Fall would be the one to lift me from this lifestyle. I chided myself, but then I reminded myself that it wasn't unheard of for a man to fall in love with a whore and marry her. Emily started to go, but I pulled the wardrobe doors open and asked, "Which dress do you think Albert would like best?"

She pulled out a lavender, velvet dress with a high neck. "He seems a bit conservative. Try this one."

I walked over to the lingerie chest and pulled out a respectable corset and some white bloomers. Then I asked, "How many girls work here?"

"Sixteen, but some of them were hired to accompany men to a party at one of the casinos, so there won't be that many here tonight."

When Emily left, I wasn't feeling tired any more. I was looking forward to enjoying a fine meal and drinking wine with Albert Fall. I smiled and wondered if he was married.

Before I washed, I took out my black book and wrote *Monday, November 29, 1886,* at the top of the first blank page. Under that, I wrote *Albert Fall.* I still kept track of people I met. I kept notes on everything they told me: the names of their family members, their occupations, feuds, suspicions, and any secrets I could coax them to share with me. This information was very helpful, as I had developed an excellent memory and could usually extract it from my brain just from the exercise of having both heard it and written it down.

Doing this was invaluable to me for many reasons. For one thing, many of the men I dealt with were lonely, so it made them feel special when I remembered their names and asked questions about whatever was going on in their lives. They sought me out, bringing repeat business because of this. For another, I could use uncomfortable truths to convince men to do what I wanted them to do at times. I wondered what secrets I'd be able to extract from Albert Fall as I dressed and put a light touch of rouge to my cheeks.

Downstairs, I was pleased to see that, instead of pushing all the tables together as they do in some houses, Joyous had small tables for two set around the room. Each table had two candlesticks with lighted candles. The tablecloths were burgundy, as were the napkins, which someone had folded to resemble small boats. Little place card holders stood by each place setting, and someone had carefully written names in flowing script on embossed cards edged in gold. A number of men had already gathered in the saloon, which doubled as our dining room.

I was also pleased to note the professor was not only a good piano player, but a good singer as well, setting a light mood with "Buffalo Gals." Several of the girls and our guests were singing along with him. Joyous motioned me over, led me to the dapper, young Albert Fall, introduced me, and wandered off.

Albert had dark hair and deep-brown eyes that seemed to take in every detail. I sensed he was a very intelligent man. I smiled at him, and he offered me a little smile that quickly faded. *He feels guilty for being here,* I thought. Because of this, of course, I knew better than to ask him if he were married, though

I frequently asked men about their families. When I glanced down toward the floor, I found a way to begin our conversation. "Where did you find those wonderful riding boots?" I asked.

"I bought these in Silverton," he said, looking pleased. "How did you know they were riding boots? Do you ride horses?"

I told him about Long Shot and created stories about a grandfather's horse farm in England. When I spoke of my past, stories of a rosy childhood often rolled off my tongue, surprising me with their turnings. "When I was thirteen," I said, "I sneaked a ride on my father's black stallion. He named it Old Scratch—after the devil, you know. He'd warned me not to ride him because he was too spirited, but I rode him anyway."

"Did you get thrown?" he asked.

"Heavens no. Turned out Old Scratch wasn't a mean horse after all. I suppose he just tried to throw Father because he weighed over two hundred and fifty pounds. I mean, how would you like to carry a fat man about on your back?"

Albert chuckled and said, "I wouldn't like it at all." He leaned back against the bar and added, "I don't think I'd mind having you ride me, though."

I smiled, glanced about the room, and saw a couple of the other girls giving me cold looks. I didn't know any of them yet, so I figured they were just sour because they hadn't been paired with Albert.

Before long, Joyous came back and asked Albert, "Did I make a good match?"

"Fine," he said, nodding.

Joyous pointed to the table nearest the piano and dance floor area. "That one's yours," she said. "Supper will be served shortly, and, afterwards, a surprise for all our guests."

Albert held my chair for me and then took his seat. Before the kitchen maids brought out our supper, Joyous tapped a fork against a crystal goblet to get everyone's attention. "Best wishes to Mr. Albert Fall, who recently turned twenty-five. A belated Happy Birthday, sir!"

Albert stiffened slightly, and I realized she'd made him feel uncomfortable. From across the room, a red-faced man cried, "Hear, hear!" and everyone clapped and cheered.

"Who is that loud mouth?" I asked.

"That's Edward Doheny, one of my closest friends," Albert replied.

I touched his hand lightly and said, "It's not so bad. Every old geezer in this room would love to trade places with you. You know that, don't you?"

"If that's so, it's because of my companion. You're lovely with your blonde curls and bright-blue eyes."

Joyous continued, "I'd also like to introduce Mr. Fall's supper companion, the newest boarder at the Mother Lode, Miss Sadie Creech. She hails from the Limehouse district of London. Sadie, stand up so everyone can see you." Our guests applauded me, and then the professor started playing the piano again.

I glanced back across the room, and said, "Mr. Doheny seems very different from you. What does he do?"

"He's a miner. We both are."

"I heard you're going to be a lawyer."

Albert offered a sad little smile and said, "I hope to someday."

I could tell that whatever headway I'd made with Albert, Joyous had snatched away by drawing attention to the two of us. A kitchen maid in a black skirt and white shirtwaist came out and asked Albert about his wine choice for the evening. He was nice enough to ask what I preferred and ordered a bottle of rosé to please me. After we'd enjoyed a glass of wine, the server brought out exquisite china plates laden with duck à l'orange, sautéed green beans, rice pilaf, and pickled beets. I was hungry, but I ate with control, very slowly, as a lady should. The professor started playing soft music that floated on the evening, creating a dreamy effect. By the time we finished eating, several couples were on the dance floor, moving about to some nameless waltz, nameless to me anyway.

Another server brought drinks, whiskey for Albert and unsweetened tea brewed to the color of whiskey for me. This was every madam's way of helping her girls not get drunk. The maid took our plates while Albert slugged his drink in three gulps. "I'll bring another right away, sir," the server said.

"Bring another for the lady, too," he replied. I wondered if he was aware that mine wasn't whiskey, though it would cost him just as much as whiskey. I certainly wouldn't tell him if he didn't know.

By this time, the party was picking up. Edward Doheny was obviously drunk as he waddled over to the piano and announced that he'd like to sing a song. Without consulting with the piano player, he broke into "Blow the Man Down."

Before he'd finished the second line, the professor was accompanying him on the piano. Doheny danced a bit as he sang, and he gave a comic performance on the next line, first patting his backside and then holding his hands under his breasts, as if holding colossal melons, as he sang. Everyone laughed, and I found myself having quite a good time.

He sang many verses, and we all joined him on the repeated lines. Albert started laughing, singing, and apparently having a very good time. At last, Doheny ended his song, and Joyous Lee came to the center of the room, waited for the applause to die down, and said, "I have a very special surprise for our guests this evening. Many people are interested in spiritualism these days, and one of the finest mediums of this age has recently moved to Kingston. I'd like to introduce Lady Claire, who will demonstrate her powers for us this evening."

She gestured to her right, and a woman in a black, satin gown entered from the parlor. She wore a veil of black lace that covered her head and face. "Good evening," she murmured in an oily voice that seemed familiar. "I've been given a gift. The part of my past before I received this gift is blank to me, except for what my mother has told me. We traveled up and down the East Coast for years, helping people find peace and answers, and now my mother is gone.

"When I was a child, I took flowers to my grandmother's grave. Hours later, my mother found me fallen there, and I had hit my head against the gravestone. No one knows why I fell. I was severely injured and remained unconscious for days. When I woke up, I could see into the future, and I could call forth spirits of the dead. I've been told that my grandmother also had this power. I'll provide free demonstrations tonight. Afterwards, you may see me by appointment, for a fee, at my new residence on Grayson Street."

The woman paused and looked out across the room. "I can see a few of you are smiling, and I don't blame you for doubting my story, but I carry the mark of that injury, and I'd like to show it to you now to help you believe in my gift."

Slowly, she lifted the front of the veil, and I was staring at Pretty Face. Time had not been kind to her. She had deep crow's feet around her eyes, but she still carried a hint of a smirk about her mouth. She no longer wore round circles of rouge on her cheeks, but she was unmistakably the same girl I remembered from Madam Chantelle's brothel.

She removed the veil completely and turned in a circle so all could see the place where she'd shaved her head to reveal the indentation in her skull. The rest of her head was covered with stringy, brown hair touched with gray. Some people got up and moved closer to her for a better look.

She said, "What you see here tonight might disturb you, so I'll give you a chance to leave the room before I enter my trance if you don't wish to stay. I sense there are spirits in the room who wish to speak. Would someone please dim the lights?" Joyous nodded toward the bartender, who quickly extinguished all of the gas lamps, so there was no light in the room except for the candles on each table.

I touched Albert's hand. "Let's go," I said. "I can entertain you much better than she can." But he refused.

"I'm curious," he said. "I've always wanted to see something like this." No one made a move to leave the room as servers quietly brought out slices of chocolate cake.

A potbellied miner reached toward Lady Claire's head, then pulled his hand back, as if remembering his manners. "Go ahead. Touch it," she told him, and, when he did, her body began to twitch, and her eyes rolled back in her head. Joyous quickly brought a chair and pushed her into it, and soon the twitching subsided. Lady Claire's eyes came back into a normal position, but they seemed blank and unknowing. Then she called out in what seemed a little girl's voice, "Father! Father? It's Lois. Where are you, Father?"

The miner, who had taken his seat, stumbled forward again. "I'm right here, sweetheart," he said, kneeling before Lady Claire and taking her right hand into his own.

She stroked his cheek with her other hand and said, "Don't be sad, Father. I didn't really die. I live in a beautiful garden now, and someday you'll live here, too. I love you, Father, but I must go now." The man knelt there weeping until Lady Claire touched his shoulder and asked, "What happened to Lois?"

"She died in a house fire when she was ten years old," he said.

"And what is your name, sir?"

"Vestal Warren."

"Well, Mr. Warren, I want you to know that I feel completely flooded with her love for you. You can be at peace now, sir. You haven't really lost Lois at all. You'll join her in that garden someday, just as she promised." Mr. Warren thanked her repeatedly, still weeping, and made his way back to his seat.

I sat there not knowing what to think. Had someone told her that man had lost a daughter named Lois? If so, how had she simulated the child's voice to convince him? Was his desire to believe enough to make him believe?

"There are other spirits present," Lady Claire said, "and some bring gifts." Suddenly she was heading for our table. She stopped beside Albert and looked deeply into his eyes. "Would you care for me to look into your future?" she asked, and Albert nodded. She took in several deep breaths and let them out while looking toward the ceiling. "You will become a great man," she said, "but I see shame in your future. Prison doors and shame. A friend will be your downfall."

Albert laughed and said, "You're quite the entertainer, but I believe you're mistaking my future with that of some future client." She didn't dispute him but stood there staring at him for a few moments.

Then her eyes were on me. "And you?" she asked. "Would you have me speak of your future?"

"No, I don't believe in that sort of thing."

"Very well, then. Nevertheless, I bring a gift from Lewis Johnson," she said, holding her empty hand out, palm upward over the table. When she turned her hand over, a small, rounded, white stone fell onto the table. I couldn't help but gasp, recognizing what it was immediately.

"What does it mean?" she asked.

"I have no idea."

"The spirits are disappointed when we lie, but perhaps Lewis Johnson will understand, being a liar himself," she said, drawing a bit of nervous laughter from the crowd. Then she leaned toward me and whispered, "Evil follows you." I sat there trembling, not completely believing in her gifts, yet wondering if her words were a threat or a prediction. I never touched that stone.

Johnson was the man who'd killed my grandfather after an argument over a bet and been acquitted in a trial. Four years later, Johnson and two of his sons were found tied together, drowned in a river. Years ago, my sister Isabelle had written to tell me of their end, adding that some believed our family had killed them. I saw no way Pretty Face could have connected me to Lewis Johnson without supernatural help unless she'd done extensive research on my family.

I couldn't keep my eyes from moving back to that stone, which appeared to have been tumbled and smoothed by a river. If she really had some spiritual gift, I thought that stone was confirmation that my family indeed had killed Johnson and his sons. If not, it was just Pretty Face's way of telling me she knew who I was and planned to get even. Albert must have noticed I was shaken because he took both my hands in his and squeezed them gently. "She must have had training as a magician," he said.

Lady Claire continued to move about the room and gave several similar demonstrations, speaking in strange voices at times or dropping rosebuds, coins, or other objects onto tables, always drawing an emotional response from the recipients. Most of the people in the room seemed completely sold on her abilities.

I didn't want to believe Pretty Face had any supernatural powers, but I couldn't help thinking of how her body had twitched and her eyes had rolled back in her head years ago in that stable when she'd told me our paths would cross again. I wondered if she remembered me or knew what I had done to her, but, whenever she looked my way, I saw no hint of recognition in her eyes.

At last, she announced that all the spirits that wanted to

speak had spoken and left the room. She put on her veil and pulled the little black lace panel over her face. "It was a pleasure to be with you this evening. You may find me on Grayson Street if you need answers or consolation."

All was quiet in the room as she slowly took her exit through the parlor, and then the bartender turned up the gas lamps as people started talking again. Suddenly Albert stood up and shouted, "Sing 'Charlotte the Harlot,' Ed!"

"For that, you'll have to come and help me."

"I haven't hit the jug enough," Albert replied, drawing laughter from around the room. I was grateful to them for helping dispel the aura of the supernatural that remained.

Ed Doheny went to the bar with everyone watching him. Then he came over, handed Albert a glass of whiskey, and nodded. Albert slugged it down quickly and allowed his friend to lead him over to the piano, where the professor played a sprightly introduction.

Doheny sang the first verse. By this point, Albert had gotten into the spirit of the song. He sang the chorus with Doheny in drunken harmony.

People began clapping to the music, causing Doheny and Albert to sing even louder on the second verse. They continued, and we all joined in on the chorus after each verse.

For this, Albert and Ed earned a big round of applause. Albert came back to our table, flushed and smiling. Soon I felt his hand on my lap under the table. He gave my thigh a playful squeeze, leaned in, and asked, "Would you like to take a walk?" Of course, he meant a walk upstairs to my room. I smiled back at him and nodded, pretending to be eager, although I would have much rather stayed at the party for a while. He signaled Emily, who quickly collected my fee, along with payment for his bill for supper and from the bar.

Naturally, I hoped he'd stay the night, but I saw he only paid my regular fee. Later, Albert showed no interest in lingering with me. I was crestfallen when, after I undressed, he simply touched my breasts and had me kneel to do what no decent woman would do for him.

Within minutes, he'd left my room, and I took out my book and noted under Albert's name that he was a close friend of Edward Doheny. I didn't record the rest because I knew I'd remember what he'd required of me. I could tell it didn't matter if Albert Fall was married or not. He wasn't the sort of man who would take up with a good-time girl.

A little while later, I went back downstairs to see if new guests had wandered in. I went to the bar, took another glass of tea, and stood near the dance floor. I danced with several men that night, including Albert's friend, Edward Doheny, who had already spent time upstairs with a chubby brunette.

The men I danced with followed the house rule of buying a fresh drink for themselves and for me after each dance. I found the dancing pleasant except for a couple of times when drunken oafs stepped on my toes. Before an hour had passed, I felt I'd hit the jackpot when a gray-haired miner with a web of tiny purple veins on his nose motioned Emily over and paid two hundred dollars to spend the night with me.

CHAPTER 13

On November 30, 1886, I awakened with my head throbbing and became aware of a terrible stench emanating from the chamber pot. My whole room reeked of vomit and liquid shit, and the gray-haired miner who'd left it that way was gone. I got up, pulled on the lavender, velvet dress I'd worn the night before, splashed some water on my face, and poked my head into the hallway, where I saw a black woman with a pink cloth wrapped around her hair and a rug beater in her hand. She wore a simple white shirtwaist with a black skirt, and her brown skin shone as if she had oiled it. "You, there," I called. "Come empty this chamber pot and clean my room. You can beat the rugs later."

I kept my syllables crisp, as an English gentlewoman would. The command sounded so regal in my own ears, I wouldn't have been surprised if she'd curtsied to me. Instead, she snapped her head around and said, "Who you think you is ordering me around?"

"I'm one of your mistresses," I said impatiently. She came toward me as if to comply, but, before I knew it, she'd grabbed me by one arm and started flailing my bum with the rug beater. I shrieked, kicked at her, and tried to take it away from her.

Soon, Joyous Lee appeared in the hallway, obviously irritated by the commotion, and the woman stopping hitting me. I was amazed to see Joyous in a green, velvet dress and already fully made up, even down to red lipstick, so early in the morning. I said, "This impertinent bitch refused to clean my room, and then she attacked me."

Joyous took a step toward me and said, "This impertinent bitch is Vashti Jones, your next door neighbor and one of the best moneymakers in the house. You'd best learn to get along with her. The maids are downstairs, where I sent them. If you want your room cleaned quickly, do it yourself." She walked past us, her skirt and underskirts rustling, and went down the stairs at the other end of the hallway.

Vashti smirked and said, "I bet yo' ass be red as a monkey's ass. It stay that way, too, if you mess with me."

I scowled at her and vowed to myself I'd eventually get the best of her, but I was feeling too poorly to think about it. It wasn't until later that I thought to wonder why this uncultured woman could possibly work at the Mother Lode as anything other than a maid. Determined not to clean my own room, I went downstairs to get some coffee and found Emily sweeping the kitchen. "Joyous Lee said for you to go and clean my room at once," I told her. She nodded, put the broom aside, and headed toward the stairs. I figured Joyous would never know.

I poured coffee into a beautiful china cup from the cupboard and added cream and a spoonful of sugar. My hind end had stopped stinging, and my mood was lifting when I turned and found Joyous in the doorway. Being both tall and fat, she nearly filled it. "Where's Emily?" she demanded.

"I wouldn't know," I said, taking a sip of coffee.

"I think you would," she said, her eyes narrowing. I took a step back as she moved toward me, thinking she might strike me, but she broke into a laugh and clapped me on the back. "Sending her upstairs sounds like something I would have done. I like a resourceful girl. I know you'll do well in this business. Just don't expect to get anything over on me." Joyous then ordered me to fix her breakfast in Emily's place, eggs over easy, toast, and fried potatoes. "Make enough for yourself as well."

When we had nearly finished eating, we heard the little brass parlor bell jingle. "Company, Sadie," Joyous said, and we hurried to see what was needed.

A middle-aged man, who hadn't shaved in at least three days, stood inside the doorway, nervously turning his hat in his hands. "Hiram, what's wrong?" Joyous asked.

"Old Tom Beeson needs help. He's burning with fever up to his cabin. I came to find a nurse, but I need a woman that knows how to ride. Trail up there's hard, you know. She'd also have to look after Tom's horse and mule. Didn't know where to turn, so I asked Pete Judson at the livery stable, and he said one of your girls rides real well and boards a horse there."

"That's me," I said. "I've ridden horses all my life."

They both turned to me as if they'd forgotten I was in the room. I was holding myself as tall as I could, but Hiram frowned when he looked at me. "My father taught me in England," I said. "I used to go on fox hunts."

"Well, there's your answer," Joyous said. "Sadie's one of the top moneymakers in this house, so it's going to cost two hundred dollars a day, and we'll need Tom to pay for three days in advance. No refunds if he gets well quicker. He did send cash or gold, didn't he?"

Hiram nodded and started counting money into Joyous's hand. I remembered what she'd said to me regarding Vashti and noticed how whichever girl Joyous was discussing suddenly became a top moneymaker in the house. Joyous said, "Sadie, change into a plain skirt and shirtwaist. You don't want to mess up that lovely dress in the wild."

"Better pack some extra blankets and bedsheets, too," Hiram said. "You might have to sleep on the floor."

I turned to go, but Joyous called me back and said, "Before you leave here, get a bottle of whiskey from our saloon, and then have Emily wrap up two of those chickens she cut up for our supper. Take them and make soup for Tom. Tell Tom the chicken and whiskey are gifts from me." Then she asked Hiram, "Should we send medical supplies?"

"Naw, Doc Guthrie's done rode out ahead of us. I reckon he'll take care of that."

I didn't know it, but I was soon to have an encounter with the supernatural, one that seemed real to me. Within the hour, I was riding sidesaddle out of town, wearing a stylish black hat and one of Emily's old overcoats. Hiram muttered that he didn't know how I was going to stay on my horse all the way to the top of the canyon on that sidesaddle. "That canyon?" I asked, pointing into the distance. When he nodded, I spurred Long Shot and took off ahead of him.

He caught up with me about three quarters of a mile away, and we slowed down. "You ridden up here before?" Hiram asked.

"Sure, and, if I were a barbarian, I'd do it astraddle my horse like you do, but I always ride like a lady."

Hiram shook his head and smiled. "Hold up a minute. I ain't from that barbarian clan. Last name's Dawson." I could tell from the twinkle in his eye that he was warming to me.

"Glad to hear it, Mr. Dawson," I said and offered my hand. He shook it firmly, and I let him take the lead because I knew he'd eventually have to take it to show me how to get to the cabin.

We climbed up a narrow canyon in a cold wind to reach the halfway point, and I could see how that ride could become very challenging if there were ice or snow on the ground. Continuing, we rode narrow trails with steep drop-offs that would make my head spin if I looked down them too long.

I kept my eyes on the trail ahead and on Hiram's solid form, picking his way forward. After a long while, we came around a bend and met Doc Guthrie, who was on his way back to town. He nodded to us, in turn, saying, "Hiram, Miss Creech."

"How is he?" Hiram asked.

"Not the best. It could go either way. It's a good thing he's not sleeping in a tent out in the cold."

"Is it typhoid?" Hiram asked, and I noticed a touch of fear in his voice.

"No, I think it's just a damn good case of the grippe. It would lay a much younger man low. I gave him some laudanum to help him rest. Left two bottles on the table."

We rode on until nearly one o'clock in the afternoon, and then I saw smoke billowing from a chimney at the center of a one-room shack. An ample supply of firewood was stacked on the front porch. About fifty yards to the right was a small stable. Off to the left, I saw a cave-like structure, which I assumed was the mine entrance to Beeson's claim. There was no outhouse. I reckoned Old Tom saw no need for one in this rough terrain.

We stopped, looking over the scene for a moment, and then Hiram said, "I ought to prepare you for what you'll see inside. Tom only has one bed. He ain't much on furniture or finer things, if you catch my meaning. You can fix a pallet on the floor by the stove, or you can crawl into bed beside Tom, if you like."

"Thanks for having me pack extra blankets," I said, as we eased forward.

Hiram started bringing things in while I looked around. Although Hiram had warned me, I still felt dismayed when I saw the inside of that bleak cabin. There was no comfortable chair in sight. There were two straight-back chairs, a rough table, a galvanized bucket, and a tin dishpan that probably served for personal bathing as well as washing dishes. A few shirts and an extra pair of waist overalls hung from hooks on the wall, and an assortment of enameled dishes and utensils, both clean and dirty, were piled on the table. Under the bed, I spotted a chamber pot that looked like a soup tureen with a handle.

Tom Beeson's possessions were few, but his place was much better than many of the miners' camps. He even had a door in the floor in one corner that pulled up to reveal a stairway into a small root cellar. I knew many of the miners lived in tents, so I figured he was wealthy to have a place like this. An old axe handle stood by the door, its head on the floor beside it, and I figured it had been left there awaiting repair.

A wood-burning cook stove served as the heater, and I saw a trail in the dust on the floor from where the bed had recently been pushed near it. The sharp smell of sweat and wood smoke filled the place. Tom Beeson was shivering under two blankets, though the cabin was plenty warm. A thin layer of sweat covered his brow. I guessed Tom was in his mid-sixties. His white hair lay in waves, though he'd had it cut short. He was sleeping, so I didn't bother him.

After a long while, Hiram came in, took the large bucket outside, and filled it with water for me. He brought it in, took the dishpan out, and did the same. When I thanked Hiram, Tom woke up, so I walked over to him, took his hand, and said, "My name is Sadie. I'm here to take care of you."

He looked toward me, but I didn't get the sense that he really saw me, and then he muttered something about a black wolf, something that drove him to tears. "It's okay, luv," I said, gently squeezing his hand. I took a dipperful of water to him. He tried to receive it but squirmed so much when I lifted his head that part of it spilled down around his neck. I got another dipperful, and Hiram raised him into a half-sitting position and held him steady as he drank it.

"There's a spring out back of the stable, if you need more water," Hiram said. "I've rubbed your horse down and fed and watered it, along with Tom's horse and mule. That should hold them until tomorrow."

Again, I thanked him. Then he was ready to leave. I followed him outside and stood on the porch as he mounted his horse. "No matter what happens, don't leave this place before morning," he said. "I don't want you and your horse dropping hundreds of feet off a trail in the middle of the night."

That was when I realized I'd be sitting with a corpse if Tom Beeson died that day. I just couldn't let that happen, not out on that cold mountain in the dark.

CHAPTER 14

Clouds started gathering as soon as Hiram left, so I lit a lantern. Before long, it was pouring down rain. I took a pot off a hook by the stove and started boiling the chicken Joyous had sent. I felt sorry for Mr. Beeson, but he smelled like a polecat, and the stench was giving me a headache, so I decided to give him a bath.

I transferred some water from the dishpan into a large pot, heated it, and poured it back into the dishpan. From my own bags, I took out a bar of sweet-smelling soap. He tried to fight me when I pulled back his blankets and removed his union suit, but he was too weak. "It's okay," I said. "I'll cover you back up soon." I pulled the sweat-soaked clothes from him and marveled that he hadn't peed in the bed.

"After your bath," I said, "you'll get clean sheets. They should feel good to you." He was shivering, so I worked as quickly as I could, washing one arm, one armpit, then his chest, then his back and his rear end, then one leg and his groin. Then I washed his other side and asked, "Do you have to pee?" He didn't respond, so I rolled him onto his side and placed a Mason jar under his penis because the chamber pot was too bulky to use in the bed. I started rubbing his belly over his bladder, and he peed in the jar.

Once I'd dumped the piss into the chamber pot, I changed his sheets, as nurses do, with him in the bed, then covered him and got him settled again. He was shivering violently, but I just patted his hand and said, "There, now. That wasn't so bad, was it?"

I took the reeking sheets and underwear and stuffed them into an old burlap bag I'd found in a back corner and flung the bag out onto the porch. I also let the door hang open for a while to air the place out a bit. Before long, Tom eased into sleep, and he seemed to be breathing better. I went down to the root cellar and found some onions, carrots, and potatoes to add to his chicken.

As I worked, the wind kicked up on the mountain, whistling through the eaves of the cabin, as the rain continued. When I took the vegetables to the stove, I walked through a cold spot, and the hair on the back of my neck stood on end. *Drafty cabin,* I thought. I dumped the vegetables into the boiling chicken and salted the mixture. Then I dipped out a cup of broth and spoon-fed it to Tom, leaving the pot to simmer up a nice stew we could eat later. After that, I headed to the porch to bring in some more firewood.

Somehow, I managed to fall asleep in one of those uncomfortable chairs and began to have unpleasant dreams about something scratching at the door. For a while, half-awake, I wondered vaguely if there was a possum or a raccoon on the porch getting into that burlap bag to get at the salt from Tom's sweat. Then Tom startled me, crying out from his bed, and the lantern went out. I was unnerved, but I got up, lit the lantern, and stirred the chicken stew.

The smell of it reminded me that I hadn't eaten since breakfast, and I was ravenous. Ignoring Tom's whimpers, I took the pot off the burner, spooned a serving of soup into a bowl, and began to eat. Afterwards, I fed Tom another cup of broth I'd reserved for him and gave him more laudanum, which helped him settle back into sleep.

Rain continued to pound on the roof. I decided to sit up as long as I could because the idea of making a pallet on the floor was not appealing. Time slowly passed, and I found myself nodding off and jerking awake now and again. Eventually I did sleep at some length, and, the next time I awakened, Tom was making a high-pitched, keening sound, the exact sound a terrified child makes. I rushed to his side, took his hand, and asked, "What is it, Tom?"

"It's coming for me, Mama," he whispered. "It's—"

My heart started pounding. "What's coming?" I asked, trying to keep my voice level.

"The black wolf." Old Tom licked his dry lips, started keening again, and clamped down on my hand.

"Tom, nothing can get you when I'm here," I said. I stood by his bed until I finally had to pry his fingers loose when my hand went numb. I took a cool cloth, pressed it to his brow, and then bathed his face and neck. As soon as he slept again, I made my pallet on the floor and crawled into the blankets, but it took a while for me to sleep because a smell like that of a wet dog hovered just above floor level. I figured it had to be my imagination responding to the rain and all of Tom's crazy talk, along with my recent encounter with Lady Claire, formerly known as Pretty Face.

My hip was aching from the cold, hard floor when a loud noise awakened me. I couldn't tell what it was, but I supposed a tree limb had fallen. Apparently, it hadn't bothered Tom because I heard him crooning, "I knew you'd come back to me, Katy. Come and let me hold you again." I was glad his wild talk had taken a more pleasant turn, and he didn't have to say those words twice. I slipped out of my clothing and into his bed. I undressed because I didn't want his sweat on my clothes. I lay with my back to his chest, and he slipped an arm over me, his hand on my left breast.

In the wee hours, the sound of the door slamming shut awakened me, and Tom began to moan and toss about. I felt a rush of cold air, and the lantern went out again. I got up and lit it, and, of course, there was no one in sight, but I didn't understand how the wind could have opened that door, much less closed it again. I glanced into the shadowed corners of that cabin, but I saw nothing, so I gave Tom more laudanum and got back in the bed.

I lay awake while Tom whimpered and moaned until he finally fell asleep. Then a sound moved slowly across the room, not toward us, but toward the back corner. It was like a large dog's nails on the wooden floor. Heart pounding, my breathing shallow, I opened my eyes and saw the shadow of a wolf move across the circle of light from the lantern. There was no wolf, only a shadow. I wondered if I were losing my mind—if, somehow, I'd been drawn into Tom's delusions. Then I heard a low growl and sensed the presence of evil in that place.

I turned, grasped Tom's shoulders, and shook him. "What have you done to bring that thing in here?" I screamed. I knew I was acting like a crazy woman and didn't care.

Tom began his unnerving keening again and called for his mother. He appeared to be staring at something behind my back. I jerked around to see, but nothing was there. The wind whistled in the eaves as I struggled to get control of myself.

At last, I said, "Mama's sorry she talked mean to you, Tom. Did that black wolf scare you again?" He nodded, wide-eyed.

"Did you let the wolf in here?"

"No, Mama . . . I killed it. Killed its owner, too." His voice was soft and low. "Killed them outside Coloma." His voice trailed off, and he stopped, raised his head, and stared into the far corner, his face a terrified mask. Then his head fell back onto the bed, and he started mumbling incoherently.

It was of little comfort to be lying beside a man who had just confessed to murder. I wondered if he had really killed a man, or if he was just talking out of his head. I lay there beside Tom until he startled me again with his keening.

In the lantern's glow, I saw spittle dribbling down his chin as he curled himself into a ball. I tried to comfort him, but he looked at me, wild-eyed, and said, "It's coming!"

Then a low growling started in a back corner of the cabin, making my skin crawl. It came to me that, if I gave in to my fear and started screaming, the phantom wolf would kill us. I turned and saw two eyes reflecting the lantern's light, moving slowly toward us.

I might as well have had the same fever Tom had for what I did next. I sprang over to the door, still naked, and grabbed that old axe handle he'd left there. Then I charged the back corner and start bashing at the floor and the wall, following the glow of the shadow wolf's eyes and aiming at its head. All the while, it snarled and took leaps toward me. I kept beating at it until my arms ached. I fought like a woman out of her mind until the snarling stopped and my reasoning returned—until I realized the cold, gray dawn had arrived. There was nothing there. Then, exhausted, miserable, and feeling insane, I crawled back into bed with Tom.

CHAPTER 15

On December 1, I awakened to the smell of hot chicken stew around two in the afternoon. Tom told me his fever had broken earlier, so he'd gotten up to check on the animals and add wood to the stove. "Why didn't you wake me?" I asked. "That's my job."

"After the fight you put up this morning?" he asked. "I seen how you took on that black wolf with the axe handle. Seen it snarling and biting your arms and legs, and you bleeding all over the place, but you didn't let it get me. For that, I thank you."

I hadn't seen any biting or bleeding. That was his hallucination, not mine.

Tom brought me a bowl of stew and a spoon and slipped into bed beside me. Remembering my manners, I asked, "How do you feel?"

"Weak as a kitten."

"Aren't you going to eat?"

"Already did."

I ate, and then I got up, bathed, and put on my clothes. "Look, I'm glad your fever broke, and I'm sorry you're still weak," I said, "but I've got to get back now. I'm going to saddle Long Shot and ride out of here. I'll have Joyous send someone to come back and check on you." I wasn't planning to risk another night in his cabin.

Tom sighed and said, "You can't leave this late in the day.

You'd never make it back before dark, and it's too dangerous on that trail at night."

"I'll chance it."

He ran a hand through his hair and said, "Look, I lied when I implied I'd fed and watered the animals because I didn't want to scare you. The horses and mule are gone."

I pushed past him, ran outside to the stable, and found it empty. The stable door was lying flat on the ground, as if the horses had become spooked and knocked it down. I figured that was what had awakened me in the night. I whistled and called for Long Shot to no avail. Then I started looking around. In addition to Tom's boot prints, my footprints, and their hoofprints, I saw wolf prints inside the stable, but there was no blood. Walking back to the cabin, I saw more wolf prints, and I tried to stop the panic I felt rising inside me. Tom was watching me from the porch. "Where's the nearest miner's camp?" I asked.

"It's too far, and you'd never find it by yourself," he said. I sank down onto a porch step and started to cry. Tom waited until I'd finished and offered me a handkerchief. "I really think the battle's over," he said. "I been sensing that thing around this place for days, but now it's gone." He paused a moment and then pointed toward the sky. "See? The sun's trying to come out."

"But what about the horses?"

Tom took a pipe out of his pocket and started tamping tobacco into it. "I 'spect they'll turn up soon."

The rain had ended, so I decided to make the best of it. Fate had gotten me into a situation where I just had to hang on and do the best I could. I took time to do Tom's laundry that afternoon. He didn't have a scrubbing board, so I just heated water in the bucket and washed his dirty sheets and union suit as best I could, using a bar of lye soap I'd found on a shelf and adding some white vinegar to the water to help get the stink out. I dumped the water in the front yard and took the bucket to the spring to get rinse water. Then I hung his things on the bare branches of a young cottonwood tree to dry. I half-filled the bucket again and took it into the cabin, not wanting to lug a heavy, full bucket.

Tom was sleeping when I came in, and I noticed that he had more color in his face. As the day wore on, it grew dim in the cabin, so I lit the lantern again. Tom didn't wake up until I pulled a pan of fresh biscuits from the oven. I thought they would go well with our leftover chicken stew for supper. He got up and went outside for a few minutes while I set the table. When he came in, he brought the damp sheets and his union suit with him and hung them on pegs to finish drying, but the effort left him out of breath. He sat down heavily in one of the chairs and said, "Horses are back. Don't know where that dang mule is."

"Are they okay?"

"Look fine to me. By the way, that's a fine horse you have there."

I smiled and said, "His name is Long Shot. I go to the livery to pamper him and take him out for a ride nearly every day." I took the lantern outside to check on Long Shot, and he was fine. I found no cuts or other injuries. While I was outside, Tom's mule wandered back into the yard, so I fed and watered him before I went inside. Tom had already taken care of the horses. They stood in their stalls looking nervously toward the doorway and the stable door, which was still lying on the ground outside. Feeling a bit worried, I went back to the cabin and asked Tom if he thought the two of us might be able to pick it up and drag it over to barricade the stable. To his credit, he tried, and we did it, but then he had to lean heavily on me on the walk back to the cabin.

★　★　★　★　★

After our supper, Tom took out a pipe and smoked a bowl of cherry tobacco that left a wonderful fragrance in the cabin. "That was some dream you had about me fighting a wolf," I ventured, as I wiped the table off. I'd already washed the dishes.

He scowled and said, "That weren't no dream. Go see what you done to that corner of the cabin."

I'd already seen the many dents in the floor and gouges in the walls in the daylight. "But you said I was bleeding," I argued. "I don't have any wounds."

He shrugged and said, "I can't explain that. I'm just telling you what I seen."

I put away the dishcloth and said, "I heard that thing growling, saw its eyes, heard it walk across the floor." I picked up my coffee cup, but my hands were shaking, so I set it back on the table.

"Did you see old Burt Honen walk in here with that hole in the middle of his forehead and the back of his skull blown off?"

"The man you killed?" I asked.

Tom nodded and said, "He's the one what opened the door."

I started feeling light-headed and sat down. "Is your face on a wanted poster somewhere?"

"Only in hell." He started telling me about what he'd done back in 1852, during the California Gold Rush. "Honen had a claim on the American River outside Colomo. The talk was that his mother had assimilated into a tribe of Miwok Indians in the Sierra Nevadas long before she had him. That made him an Indian in my book, and I didn't give half a damn for an Indian. I figured I'd kill him and take over his claim. At that time, I was a very callous man."

"But you've changed since?"

"I had to when an Indian saved my life a few years later, but that's another story. That's when the weight of that sin began to feel heavy on my shoulders, and I changed my way of looking at things."

Tom dumped the ashes from his pipe and lit another bowl of tobacco. He then told about how he had watched Honen get drunk in a saloon and followed him back to his tent one night. He was about to shoot Honen when a huge, black wolf came at him. Of course, he shot the wolf instead. Honen was too drunk to react quickly, and Tom easily killed him. He loaded Honen's body on Honen's horse, led it to a distant canyon, found a good hiding place, and covered the body with stones. He then slapped Honen's horse on the rear to send it running.

"Weren't people suspicious about his disappearance?" I asked.

"Some men looked for Burt, but I didn't think they'd find him, and no one had any idea I had anything to do with his being gone."

"Didn't it bother you, killing a man?"

He shook his head. "Nope, and I certainly weren't bothered by the bullshit I heard in the bars the next week. Guess I shoulda been, but I weren't. People started wondering why Burt had stopped coming around. By that time, I'd already filed a claim on his place, saying it was unused. People said Burt Honen was a Miwok Indian of the bear clan. The Miwoks reverenced certain animals they called totem animals. Some claimed that Burt had raised that wolf from a pup after a bear killed its mother. They said no one could get near it besides Burt.

"One of the miners said if Burt had been killed, whoever killed him had better watch out because that wolf would come and get him. I snickered and said, 'What if the wolf's dead, too?' There was an Indian feller of a different tribe standing by the door. He looked at me and said, 'Wolf more powerful in death than in life.' "

Tom put his head in his hands and sighed. "I got the oddest

sense that Indian knew what I'd done and was about to accuse me, but he just stared at me for a moment and walked off. Since then, I've heard that some of those tribes believe we have two spirits, one that dies when we die, and another that wanders the earth. I reckon it was Burt's spirit that wanders the earth what came in with that wolf's spirit."

"Is that what Burt Honen believed?"

"It's a little late to ask him."

I remembered I had whiskey in my bags and went to get the bottle because it seemed like a good time to take a drink. Tom brightened when he saw it. "You know why I think the battle's over?" he asked.

"Why?" I asked, as I poured whiskey into our empty coffee cups.

"Because a thought came to me while you was fighting that wolf that I'm being given a chance to do something good to make up for what I've done. I'm thinking on what that might be," he said, after taking a long draught of whiskey.

I pushed the bottle toward him, and he refilled his cup while I took a single sip and enjoyed the warmth sliding down my throat. "Why do you think the wolf waited thirty years to come for you?"

Tom leaned his chair back on two legs and frowned. "I been studying on that. Only reason I can think of is maybe time is different on the other side."

"What happened after you killed Honen?"

"I kept working Honen's claim. Honen had done all right there when he was living, but he never saw the half of what was there. I got rich then, still am."

I swirled the whiskey in my cup and asked, "Why didn't you quit mining and settle down?"

"My Katy got the typhoid, stepped off into eternity, and left me." Tears welled up in his eyes, and I considered the irony of him taking one person's life with hardly a thought and weeping over the loss of another's life. He looked up at me suddenly and asked, "Could I persuade you to stay past the morning?"

"You've actually paid for me to stay through tomorrow night," I said. "I was going to give part of it back if I left."

"I have? How much have I paid?" Then he waved his hand and said, "Don't answer that. I don't want to know. Whatever it was, it was worth it, worth it and more. I'd give you a bonus right now if Hiram wasn't holding my money for me. I'll take care of that 'fore long."

I stayed with Tom three full nights and left on the morning of December 2. He simply clung to my body the second night, but the next morning, after I bathed, I put on my garter belt and hose, leaving my cunny bare. This made a huge impression on old Tom, and I could have sworn I was with a much younger man. After he'd ravished me, I took a book out of my bag and recorded the story he'd told me.

CHAPTER 16

When I returned to the Mother Lode, I told Joyous Lee Tom was on the mend, and she gave me three hundred dollars, which was my half of the fee she'd charged him. I lugged my things upstairs, where I met Vashti in the hallway. She nodded and said, "So you still alive." I wondered if she'd hoped I'd catch Tom's fever and die. I ignored her and went to my room to lie down. In a couple of hours, I'd have to dress for our nightly supper party.

After my supper companion left my room that evening, I freshened up and went back downstairs to join what was left of the ongoing party. It was nearly two in the morning, and most of the girls had retired to their rooms for the final time that evening. As I made my way to the bar, a drunken man with a walrus moustache warbled a song about his mistress's cunny.

I felt a hand on my arm and turned, only to find myself staring into Vashti's face. "Let me introduce you to some of the girls," she said. "You still don't know nobody that live here."

"I thought we weren't friends."

"Oh, we be friends jus' fine, long as you don't try to make me yo' servant."

"Fair enough," I said, letting her lead me to a table near the back of the room, where a plump brunette sat talking to a thin blonde.

"Sadie, this is Jiggly Jane," Vashti said, gesturing toward the brunette. "And this here is Bobtail Betty."

Jiggly Jane invited us to sit down. Then she said, "Just call me Jiggly for short. That's what everyone else does, and you can call her Bobtail." She paused and said, "You're the girl that got paired with Albert Fall the other night."

"Yes, and you got paired with Edward Doheny, the life of the party."

She brightened and said, "He requested me."

"Well, Albert requested me in a roundabout way. Joyous told me he wanted whichever girl a doctor had checked most recently."

At that, the girls burst into laughter. "Afraid his dick will turn blue!" Bobtail shouted, which made them laugh harder.

Vashti must have seen my perplexed look because she said, "There's a song about that."

"What was Albert like?" Bobtail asked.

"The quiet type."

"Was he any good?" Jiggly pressed. I shook my head.

"And I thought you were having more fun than I was that night," Bobtail said. "I was stuck with that sour-looking Elmer Finch who runs a general store. He always asks for me when he comes here, and he always tells his wife he was out gambling with his friends when he goes home."

"Most men lie," I said. I looked at her for a moment and said, "Bobtail is an unusual name."

"And it's her birthright," Jiggly said. "She's got the nub of a tail at the end of her spine, and she can even twitch it."

They giggled, and I said, "You're full of shit."

Jiggly looked at her friend and said, "Show her." No one else was paying any attention to us, so Bobtail stood up, turned her backside to us, and lifted her skirt. She had foregone underwear, as I often did, and, sure enough, she had a little two-inch nub that she moved back and forth. I could hardly believe it. Jiggly looked at me and burst out laughing again. "Ain't that the damnedest thing you ever seen?" she asked. I had to admit it was.

Bobtail settled back into her chair and asked, "What did you think of that creepy woman dropping a stone on your table?"

"I think she learned some cheap magic tricks somewhere down the line," I said, trying to appear completely unconcerned.

"What I wanna know," Jiggly said, "is why you let her get by with calling you a liar."

"She was just mad because I didn't give her anything to help further her reputation. I reckon she expected me to go into hysterics or beg her to tell me about the man that supposedly sent it, but I don't care for such shit."

"So you don't believe in the supernatural?"

"No, not at all."

Jiggly turned to Vashti and said, "I can't believe you're keeping your mouth shut."

Vashti shrugged and mumbled, "The woman got a right to her opinion." Then Vashti told us about the party she'd attended that same night, and I told them about the miner that left my room reeking of shit and vomit. We sat and talked until Jiggly and Bobtail went upstairs, and it was just me and Vashti in the empty saloon.

"I've been waitin' all night to tell you about a dream I had on that first night you was at Tom Beeson's place," Vashti said. "I saw you fightin' off a big, black wolf with a axe handle, and it was bitin' yo' arms and legs, takin' out chunks of meat. I kept thinkin' you was gonna slip and fall on your own blood."

I felt goosebumps rise on my arms. I hadn't told a soul about what went on at that cabin. She had no way of knowing that if she hadn't dreamed it. *Or did she?*

"That must have been quite a dream," I said in a level voice.

"Sho was. You had it backed in a corner, and it kept tryin' to get at yo' throat while you was swingin' that axe handle, but I could tell you was gettin' tired. When I woke up, I figgered you done dead. Then you come in this mornin' like nothin' happened."

Vashti told me she was from New Orleans and knew some things about magic and voodoo. She claimed she had a sixth sense into the spirit world, but I didn't believe all of that. As good-time girls, we all tried to build a special aura about ourselves. My gut said she was probably just a South Carolina field worker turned whore who had traveled west.

Still, her story about the dream troubled me. I wondered if it were possible that Tom had told someone about what had happened, creating a path for the story to travel to Vashti, but then I doubted that. For one thing, I didn't think he'd speak of it because he wouldn't want people to think he'd lost his mind. My heart started pounding when I realized Vashti must be telling the truth about her dream.

"One time I seen that wolf looking at you 'fore he leaped," she added. "Those teeth missed yo' throat by a inch."

I didn't want her to know she was frightening me, so I shrugged and said, "Take some laudanum before you go to bed. It'll help stop your nightmares."

At that, Vashti banged her fist on the table and said, "Stop talkin' to me like that! I tryin' to help you!"

Although I'm generally not very open or trusting, I finally told her what had happened at the cabin. I ended with, "I must have killed it. Tom even said he thought the battle was over."

Vashti shook her head and said, "Naw, it ain't over, and you didn't kill it. That thing done marked you. It gonna come back."

"If it's going to do that, why didn't it get us while it was there?"

"I don't know." She sighed heavily and looked toward the ceiling, and then she said, "Yes, I do. It left 'cause the sun come up. It coming back. It just bidin' its time." She folded her arms across her chest and said, "You betta be ready for it."

"And how do I get ready?"

Vashti frowned. "Don't know. I'll have to study on that a while."

The whole conversation seemed insane, and it suddenly became more than I could bear. I stood to go upstairs and asked, "Will you keep this to yourself?"

Vashti nodded. "I keep plenty things to myself. One day the weight of all them things gonna pull me down in the ground."

I left her there to mull on the heaviness of her secrets. Before going back to my room, I stopped at the bar and swigged a double shot of whiskey, knowing I'd be awake all night thinking about that black wolf if I didn't.

CHAPTER 17

Sunday, December 5, 1886

Every day, I went to the livery to visit Long Shot, and I always took him riding if the weather wasn't too bad. I had slept until around eleven after my late night talk with Vashti, so I bathed quickly and put on a black skirt, a white shirtwaist, my black coat, and a black hat with a large ostrich feather that stuck up a foot higher than my head. For protection, I tucked my pistol into my pocket.

Long Shot whinnied when he saw me, so I took a few sugar cubes from my pocket and offered them, one at a time, off the palm of my hand. "That stuff's pretty good, isn't it?" I asked, dropping the British accent. I never played a part when I was alone with Long Shot because he was my closest friend. Feeling a bit lazy, I had Pete saddle him for me while I went to get something to eat. Then I took Long Shot riding out toward Lake Valley, where we hadn't been in a while. We were well out of town when I came to a spot that overlooked the railroad depot, and I stopped to enjoy the view. A middle-aged man with brown hair and a cleft chin rode up. "Howdy, Miss," he said.

"Hallo."

"Hey, you're that English girl I've heard about that works at the Mother Lode, ain't you?"

"Yes, I am." It pleased me that word was getting around about me. "Do you work in the mining camps?" I asked.

"You might say that," he said. "I'm interested in a little

entertainment." He urged his horse over until he was right beside me, uncomfortably close. "How about it?"

"No, I'm not working right now, so—"

Before I could finish, he cold-cocked me with a jab of his fist to my right cheek, causing me to fall off my mount. I was stunned for a few moments, and my left hip was hurt by the fall. When he dismounted, I reached for the gun in my skirt pocket, but he said, "Take it out slow and easy and throw it to me." I saw he had his gun aimed at me, so I did as he said. Then he opened his fly with his left hand and said, "Time to get to work."

"My hip is hurt," I said.

"Not my problem. You wanna wait til I hurt the other one before you get movin'?"

Actually, I didn't. I crawled over to him, and he ripped the bodice of my dress open.

When I thought he'd finished with me, he stood and gave me three good kicks, sending the steel toe of his boot into my right hip, my ribcage, and my shoulder. Then he mounted his horse, a black and white roan, took a dollar from his pocket, and threw it on the ground. "Nice doing business with you," he said.

I lay in the dirt and cried. It was the first time I'd cried that hard in years, and a good cry is cleansing, so they say. Long Shot came over and nuzzled the unhurt side of my face, and that made me cry even more. It seemed he understood I needed to be loved, and he offered his love. I don't know how I'd have gotten back to town if he hadn't been such a good horse. I made him lie down, and I managed to get onto my sidesaddle and put my arms around his neck to hold on to him while he stood up. I tore part of the skirt off my dress to cover my breasts. Then Long Shot slowly took me back to the Mother Lode.

★ ★ ★ ★ ★

John Preston was outside when I rode into the yard, so I briefly told him about the incident, and he helped me dismount, picked me up, carried me up to my room, and settled me on my bed. Then he offered to take Long Shot back to the livery stable. Soon Joyous came up to see me and gasped.

Sticking her head into the hallway, Joyous called for Emily to bring raw steak to put over my bruises. Then she asked, "Had you ever seen the man who did this before?"

"No, I don't think so," I said, touching the wounded cheek lightly with my fingertips. Joyous sat by my bedside, frowning.

After Emily brought a cool slice of beef, I told Joyous what had happened in full detail. Then Joyous patted my hand and said, "You rest now, and don't fret. I told John to fetch Doc Guthrie so he can have a look at you. Whoever did this, we'll find him, and we'll get him. We'll hire someone to take care of Mr. I'm-Interested-in-a-Little-Entertainment."

I pushed myself up to a sitting position and said, "I'd rather take care of him myself."

"We'll see," she said.

Just as she was about to leave, Emily brought Doc Guthrie upstairs to see me. He winced when he saw my face, and said, "I hate a man who will hit a woman." He turned to Joyous and asked, "Do you have any ice in the house?" She said yes, so he turned to Emily and asked her to bring an ice pack for my face. After he examined me, he called for ice packs for my hips, side, and shoulder, which were also bruised. "You'll need to rest as much as possible for a few days. If you get up, use a cane or a walking stick. Use the ice packs several times a day. Take laudanum for the pain."

"I'll send John over to the ice plant for another block of ice," Joyous promised.

★ ★ ★ ★ ★

Later on the afternoon of the attack, Vashti, Jiggly, and Bobtail came to my room to chat. Our talk soon turned to how to settle the score with my assailant. "You could lure him out to the canyon and push him off a cliff," Bobtail said, giggling.

"She ain't gonna lure him nowhere," Vashti said. "If he got any sense, he gonna know she want to kill him."

"Then she could take him by surprise, maybe light a stick of dynamite and throw it in the outhouse while he's taking a shit," Jiggly offered. Bobtail laughed, and I wanted to, but I tried not to because it hurt.

Vashti just shook her head and said, "Mm, mm, you girls is pitiful."

"First, I have to find out who he is," I reminded them.

"What you need is a find-me spell," Vashti said. "I'll work one for you today."

It seemed Vashti always tried to make people think she had some kind of power the rest of us didn't have, and that irritated me. "I don't have a lot of faith in that," I said.

"You don't have a lot of faith in nothing 'cept the value of your cunny."

Over the next few days, I grew very fond of Vashti, Bobtail, and Jiggly, who took turns bringing meals to my room so I wouldn't have to walk downstairs. I appreciated their pampering. I found them kind and true, bawdy and fun.

One day, I awakened and found Vashti in my room sitting over a little bowl in which she'd set some sage grass afire. "What are you doing?" I asked.

"That's yo' find-me spell," she said. "Now be quiet." I watched as she uttered some nonsensical words and threw a pinch of something onto the flame, causing it to turn blue.

"Aren't you supposed to do that at midnight or something?"

"I supposed to do it when I say I supposed to do it," she snapped. "It done now. You can 'spect that man to show hisself real soon."

"And you can expect to fly to the moon any time now." I knew she was full of shit. I just wanted her to know I knew it.

"You lucky I done worked the spell befo' you open yo' mouth. I ain't doing nothin' else to help you."

My scorn toward her powers didn't keep her from bringing me breakfast the next day, and her bringing it didn't keep me from getting into a fight with her afterwards. She brought a tray of scrambled eggs, grits, and coffee. As she settled the tray over my lap, she asked, "How you feelin' today?"

"Lousy," I mumbled.

"You my little ray of sunshine."

She plopped down in my pink and gold chair and gave me a few minutes to eat before she asked, "How you get yo' name?"

I didn't want to admit it was my childhood nickname, so I said, "I just like it. It sounds friendly."

"It do sound friendly, but I think you ought to change it. I'm not sure it suit you."

"Who are you to talk about my name when you have a stupid name like Vashti?"

She scowled at me. "Vashti ain't no stupid name. It's a Bible name, the name my own mama picked out for me." Then she told me the story of Queen Vashti, who refused to disrobe in front of a room full of drunken men when the king wanted to display her beauty.

By the time she finished, I was laughing so hard I had tears in my eyes, laughing so hard it hurt my face. "You were named after a woman who was too modest to take her clothes off in front of drunken men? Oh, that's rich! Your mama wanted you to be the epitome of modesty."

"I *am* the epitome o' modesty. You ever seen my titties come out at a drunken party or seen me show off my ass like Bobtail did in the saloon?"

"No, but I haven't been here very long." She sat there frowning, and I remembered she'd been nice enough to bring my breakfast, so I tried to smooth things over. "Sorry I laughed. Vashti's a fine name."

She took a little Bible from her pocket and read a passage to me from Proverbs 31 on the virtuous woman, which included, "Her children arise up, and called her blessed; her husband, also, and he praiseth her."

She stopped and looked up at me. "That's gon' be mine," she said. "Someday I'm gonna have a husband, and my husband and chirren gonna rise up and call me blessed."

"When did you start reading the Bible? I didn't know you could read."

She gave me a sour look and sighed. "I was sent to a Catholic orphanage when I was eight years old. The nuns taught me to read."

I couldn't resist asking, "Why didn't the nuns clean up your grammar?"

"I know grammar as well as you do. I use my dialect because it makes me feel more connected to my family. When Joyous pairs me with a well-educated man, I make adjustments. Do you feel a need for me to make adjustments for you?"

"No," I said, feeling humbled and embarrassed.

"That's good, 'cause I shore ain't makin' no a'jusments on yo' account."

I smiled and said, "We're sort of alike, you know, both looking for that rosy future, both molded by the past."

Vashti shifted her weight. "Tell me about yo' past. I done tol' you a lot about mine."

I shook my head. "I don't feel like talking about it."

Vashti said, "Don't matta. You ain't gotta tell me nothin',

'cause all I has to do is look at you, and I can read yo' story. I been readin' people all my life, and I know a story when I sees it. I seen yours many times."

"You can't read shit."

"Yes, I can. I can read the way you hold yo' neck and walk like you got a corn cob up yo' ass. Somethin' made you feel lower'n a dog turd, and you tryin' to hide it. Ain't why every whore's in this business, but that's why you in it."

I felt the color rising in my face. "You bloody munter, you think you know everything, but you don't. I'm a business-woman. I saw a good opportunity, and I took it."

She stood, took my empty breakfast tray, and turned to leave. Looking back over her shoulder, she said, "Say what you will, but I knows a story when I reads one."

CHAPTER 18

True to his word, Tom Beeson brought me a bonus on Tuesday, December 7. When Emily told him I'd been hurt, he asked to see me, so she brought him upstairs. I saw fire in his eyes as he gave me another hundred dollars. "Thank you, Tom," I said.

"Who did this?" he demanded.

"I don't know," I said, and I told him about what had happened, describing the man with the cleft chin and his clothing carefully, hoping that Tom might know who it was.

"Was he riding a black and white roan?" he asked. I nodded. "Sounds like it could have been Bill Dunn, one of the foremen at the Lady Franklin mine. He's a mean son of a bitch, that's for sure. Why don't you get John to ride you out on that ridge above the mine? Take a spyglass along, and see if you find the man that did this. If you do, point him out, so John can get a good look at him. He knows Dunn. If you say he's the one, I'll take care of him for you."

"But I want to get the sorry blighter myself," I said.

Tom shook his head and said, "He's dangerous and unpredictable, especially when he's been drinking. Ain't no job for a woman."

On Friday, December 10, John and I rode out toward the Lady Franklin mine. We rode in a comfortable silence, except when John would murmur directions such as "Careful." Joyous had loaned me a brass telescope an army officer had given her a few years back. When we found a good spot above the mine, I hid myself behind a rock and started searching the faces of the men below. There were about fifteen of them outside at the time, so it took some time to catch them all in a position where I could see their faces, as they were moving around quite a bit. There was a horse-driven mine hoist out front. I saw many bearded men going in and out of the mine, and all of them were wearing hats that shaded their faces. I was about to lose hope when I spotted the man with the cleft chin and recognized my attacker. I stared at him for a moment, and then he turned and looked up at the ridge, as though he knew I was there. Then he smiled. I felt my skin crawl the way it had in Tom's cabin when I heard that phantom wolf walk across the floor, and I felt the same sense of evil. "I think he saw me," I said to John. "The rotter was looking right at me."

"That's impossible," he said. "The most he could see is a glint of sun off the lens, and even if he saw that, he wouldn't know who was watching him."

"The bloody bastard smiled at me," I said.

"Let me see," he said, reaching for the telescope. "Which one is he?"

"The one in a blue shirt, standing nearest the mine entrance."

John studied the man for a few minutes and said, "Yep, that's Bill Dunn." He stood and took my hand to help me stand, and I was trembling. "It's all right, Sadie. He's never going to hurt you again. He'll be in hell soon."

"Not soon enough," I said, as he helped me mount Long Shot for the ride back to town. I knew then that Tom was right. I no longer felt I had the nerve to deal with him myself. I thought he must be the devil.

By Saturday, my wounds were much better. That morning, I told Joyous I felt like working that night so that she could plan to pair me with one of her supper guests. I knew a little makeup would cover what was left of my bruises. Looking back, I now wish Vashti had worked a "find-him" spell instead of a "find-me" spell. Her wording was off. Of course, her spell may not have had anything to do with what happened, but who can say for sure?

I went to the livery to see Long Shot right after breakfast. The weather was so fine I decided to take him for another ride toward Lake Valley, but this time I was more prepared. I had brought along a pistol, as usual, but I also had a mean switchblade up my sleeve. This, I had borrowed from Vashti.

I rode out through the valley, and then I turned toward the hills. The cloudless sky made me feel glad to be alive. Even the raucous cawing of crows gave me joy. Around noon, I stopped along a ridgeline overlooking Lake Valley and spread a blanket to sit down on and bask in the view. Long Shot whinnied, and I said, "Beautiful isn't it?" I sat there talking to him as I usually did. "I'm going to buy some land and build a nice stable and a corral for you," I said. I kept chattering, explaining how big it would be, what fine oats and hay Long Shot would enjoy, and how I'd bring him apples and lumps of sugar every day.

When I got up, I turned and found Bill Dunn standing right behind me. "Nice day for a ride," he said. I started to reach for my pistol, but he said, "Keep your hands where I can see them. I'm a lot faster than you."

I stood there motionless, almost ready to faint. "I'll scream," I said, which caused him to laugh.

"Go right ahead. There's no one out here to hear you but me." He took a step toward me. "I've missed you," he said. "I figure you might be sore at me, but my mama always said, 'Let bygones be bygones.' No hard feelings, okay?" He gave me that same smile I'd seen through the telescope.

"None at all," I said, as I thought of how best to kill him. I became angry with myself when I heard my voice quaver. I knew if I couldn't conquer my own fear, I'd never win against this man. I thought of what he'd done to me, and then I felt the same rage come over me that I'd felt when I saw Pretty Face wearing my mother's locket.

"That's good," he said. "Now throw your pistol over to me nice and easy, and come here." I did as he asked with a smile because he didn't know I had that knife up my sleeve.

"You know, luv, we could handle this more friendly-like than the last time," I said as I moved toward him. "Why don't you kiss me?"

His lips never touched mine before I had the knife deep in his gut, and I held fast to it and jerked it from side to side to do as much damage as possible. In his eyes, I read surprise, then pain and rage, then total befuddlement, as he must have realized he would die from his wounds. He might have had time to draw his gun and shoot me, but he held tightly to my upper arms instead, as if that would stop the cutting. When I pulled Vashti's knife from his gut, he tried to stuff his intestines back into his belly, while I wiped the blade off on his shirt. I looked down, saw his blood all over me, and said, "You've made a mess of my clothes, but no hard feelings, okay?"

He finally fell, and I picked up my gun and put it in my skirt pocket as he writhed on the ground. My clothes were ruined, so, as if I had a chill, I wrapped a saddle blanket around me to hide them and mounted my horse.

Because my hips hadn't fully healed, it would hurt to ride fast, so I urged Long Shot into a gentle canter, rode to the backyard of the Mother Lode, and dismounted. Still wrapped in the blanket, I went inside and told Joyous Lee what I'd done, and, being the wise, motherly type that she was, she advised, "Don't tell anyone else. Not John Preston, not Tom Beeson, not Jiggly or any of the other girls—no one."

"Why?"

"Because Dunn has friends around here, and, if someone finds out and has you arrested, the law generally doesn't favor a whore. The way I see it, we can't prove he assaulted you, and no one can prove who killed him if you keep your mouth shut."

She had me wait in the kitchen while she heated water on the stove for me to bathe and went to get clean clothes for me to put on. When she came back, I undressed, washed myself, and slipped into the clothing she'd brought for me. Then we took all the clothes I'd worn that day, even down to the underwear, and burned it in the back yard. When there was nothing but ashes left, she said, "Now go get some rest, and then get ready for our supper party. You're going to like it."

I knew I would because our parties were becoming ever more elaborate as Christmas drew near. Joyous wanted our customers to feel as if they'd come home for a holiday supper. I later heard that Bill Dunn's horse came into town while we had our supper that evening. As Joyous had said, the man had friends, and several men went out to look for him. I understand they found some shreds of Dunn's clothing a few days later, but it was hard to tell what had happened to him because the coyotes and buzzards were such greedy bastards.

On my first Christmas Eve in Kingston, a fat, buck-toothed miner was in a drunken slumber beside me. I was hoping to sleep myself, but I heard Vashti yell from the room next door, "What you mean, you ain't bring me no Christmas present! Get yo' ol' wrinkled ass outta my bed, and don't come back. I means it!"

I sighed heavily and pulled the blankets over my ear, but I still heard her customer make the mistake of saying, "You think I'm Santie Claus?"

Something large and heavy broke in Vashti's room, and she

screamed, "I ain't thinkin' you nobody, you son-of-a-mongrel-dawg! You gonna wish you was Santie Claus when I gets through with you!"

The man sputtered, "Wait . . . wait a minute now . . . I was just joshing. I meant . . . I meant I didn't bring no *present* present 'cause I figgered you'd rather have a *cash* present."

"You bring me a money present?" Vashti crooned. "Let me see it." A moment passed, and I heard her squeal loud enough to rouse the town. Then she said, "Come 'ere, Sugah. I been feeling the heat fo' you all day long."

Vashti had no shame. I had no doubt she'd charge the man double for working on Christmas Eve, gift or no gift. That's how she worked those men. She became my role model. I went to sleep that night to the sound of her fake moans and the squeaking of bedsprings.

CHAPTER 19

Tom Beeson rode into town on Tuesday, January 4, 1887, and called for me around nine o'clock in the morning. I happened to be downstairs in the saloon when he came in. "Would you like to take a walk?" he asked.

"Sure," I said, offering my brightest smile. Emily, who was dusting the gas lamps on the walls, apparently heard him because she started moving toward us to collect my fee.

Tom waved her off, saying, "Not that kind of walk—a real one."

I shrugged and said, "All right. Let me get my coat." Halfway up the stairs, I turned and asked, "Where are we going?"

"It's a surprise," he said.

We walked the wooden sidewalks and turned onto Virtue Avenue, continuing until Tom stopped in front of a large, two-story house. This was in the brothel district off Maiden Alley. "Like it?" he asked.

The house was freshly painted in white with red shutters and a red door, and it had barred windows, as most brothels did. A row of rocking chairs stretched across the front porch, and an assortment of cactus plants grew on the front lawn. Purple and yellow pansies were in bloom up near the house. I noticed the sign out front was painted over in white, awaiting a new name. "It's nice," I said.

Tom squinted at me and scratched his head. "Do you know how to do figures?" he asked.

"Of course, I do. I went to school in England where they have better schools and stricter schoolmasters." I was telling the truth about understanding how to do figures. I had gone to school until my mother died, and I'd always been good at mathematics. In my opinion, no one was better at accounting than I was, and no one could pull anything over on me, either.

"Reckon you could run a brothel?"

"Are you offering me a job?"

"Better than that—a partnership. I've decided to branch out, not keep all my eggs in one basket. You could run this place, and we could share the profits, sixty–forty, you taking the 60 percent because you'd have to stay here and run it while I mine my claim. What do you think?"

"Sounds good."

"Want to see the inside?" We walked onto the porch, and Tom took a long key out of his pocket and opened the door. "Bought the house and furniture together the day after Christmas," he said. "Had it cleaned and painted inside and out." We walked into a room that had a mahogany bar and barstools and matching tables and chairs. As at the Mother Lode, an area near the piano stood open for use as a dance floor. Double doors led into the light-blue parlor, which held sofas and chairs upholstered with navy-blue and gold brocade. Matching draperies hung on the windows. I smiled when I saw a needlepoint saying over a sideboard by the window: "If at first you don't succeed, try, try again."

There was a kitchen with a pantry, of course, and one large, nicely furnished bedroom downstairs, which would be mine. We walked through all of this and went upstairs to look at the girls' rooms, of which there were eight, half as many as at the Mother Lode, but still enough for a very profitable business.

When we left, he locked the door and stood staring at the blank sign out front. "What you reckon we should call the place?" he asked.

In my dreams, I'd already picked out a name for my first brothel. "How about the Horny Toad?" I asked.

He clapped a hand across my shoulder blades and said, "Now that will do just fine." I started to step off the porch, but he said, "You remember I said I'd give you a bonus, don't you?"

"You've already given me a hundred dollars."

Tom appeared flustered and said, "That was the smaller part of your bonus." He pulled a folded paper from a pocket inside his coat. "This is the bigger part. I bought the house in both our names, so it's half yours. When I'm gone, it'll be all yours." I shrieked and hugged him. I could hardly believe my good fortune.

Tom took me to Percha Bank that day, introduced me to the manager as his new partner, and had an account set up for our business. Then we went to several stores, where he did the same. Regarding Joyous Lee, we agreed it would be best to give her some notice until she found a replacement for me. We certainly didn't want her badmouthing us. Regarding where I'd live after I left the Mother Lode, he offered to put me up in the Victorio Hotel until our grand opening. He said he didn't want me staying in that big, old empty house by myself.

We got back to the Mother Lode around two that afternoon, and Tom stood there in the parlor while I told Joyous Lee the news in the saloon. Joyous let out a stream of profanity that I took to indicate anger, but then she hugged me and said, "I always thought you'd do well in this business, but what in the hell did you do for old Tom to make him do such a thing?"

Tom said, "Now, that's a secret." Then he winked at me.

While Joyous pondered that, I said, "I can stay here for a while until you find someone to take my place."

"Just stay here until Sunday morning. I've just heard that Jiggly Jane's sister would like to start boarding here. I'll wire her some money to travel in from Texas."

Of course, there are folks in town who claim it didn't happen that way at all. Some said Tom was getting soft in the head and I talked him into an unwise arrangement that day, leading him to the Percha Bank after I'd seen a house for sale.

I was like a woman in a dream during my last days at the Mother Lode. I was so busy thinking about my new business that I hardly heard what anyone said to me. I must have responded to whatever it was, but I just made the motions of moving through life while so deliriously happy that life was about to improve. Already, I was commanding a new level of respect from the other girls, except for Vashti, of course.

Over the next few days, as the news of my partnership spread, I could see that townspeople were looking at me differently. Madams were respectable members of society, although whores were not. Tom left most of the planning of the Horny Toad's grand opening up to me, but he spent several evenings with me at the hotel discussing matters, and I invited him to stay the night each time, as I was becoming quite fond of him.

One night while we were lying in bed together, I said, "When we were up at your cabin, you said an Indian once saved your life. Tell me about that."

"It happened one evening in a Telluride saloon. I was drunk, and an angry whore was attacking me. My buddies were laughing because a woman was about to kick my ass. They knew I wouldn't hit a woman. Then she brought out a switchblade."

"Why did she want to kill you?"

He turned on his side to face me and said, "You won't like it."

"Okay, but why?"

"Because I called her a dog-faced, gold-digging slut. She sailed into me like a storm. She woulda killed me if an Indian named Red Hawk hadn't grabbed her wrist and disarmed her."

I laughed and asked, "Was she dog faced?"

"Naw, she was purdy."

"Then it sounds like you deserved it. Why did Red Hawk help you?"

"I don't know. Maybe just to show how quick he was."

I ran my fingers across his chest and asked, "Was she a gold-digging slut?"

"She was the mother of them all."

Over supper one evening, Tom said, "Sadie, if you want, we could have more than a business partnership. I know I'm old, but I'm still strong, and I'll marry you if you'll have me. You think on that. If you show me a sign, I'll ask you proper."

I did think on that. I thought on it until I was quite giddy. I could love Tom Beeson. I knew it because I was already starting to, and all I had to do was say the word, and I'd have a rich husband and be able to enjoy the life of a gentlewoman. Smiling to myself, I decided to wait until a few days after our grand opening to give him a sign by bringing up the idea of building us a big house to live in on the outskirts of Kingston.

The next day, I went to the Horny Toad to do some decorating, hanging pictures and embroidered pieces and setting out a few new lamps and doilies I'd purchased. Suddenly, a feeling of heaviness came over me, and the room darkened as though a cloud had blocked the sun. I looked through the parlor window and saw Pretty Face standing outside saying something from across the street. Irritated, I opened the front door and found that her mouth was moving, but no sound was coming from her mouth. I figured she was trying to curse our new business with her mumbo jumbo. "Need a job, Lady Claire?" I asked.

She took time to finish her soundless speech before she answered, "I just wondered if I could have a few of those pansies from your front yard."

"Help yourself."

She made no move toward the flowers, and I gave her an icy stare, but she stood there staring back at me for the longest time before she finally walked off. I went back inside to finish my work, which must have taken about an hour. When I came outside, all the pansies in the front yard had wilted and turned brown. I wondered if that sorry slag had come back and put salt on them or something. I pulled the ruined flowers out of the ground and threw them into a barrel used for burning trash, wondering how I could make her leave me alone, short of killing her. I told no one of the incident because I wasn't about to help build her reputation as a powerful hoodoo woman. When Tom asked what happened to the flowers, I said, "I don't know. They died."

That week, I had several cases of canned, smoked oysters shipped in from the California coast because I planned to put them on our bar menu. As I ordered food and drink for our party, I had a bit of trouble with Elmer Finch, who wanted to charge me two dollars a bottle for a California wine I knew Joyous purchased for a dollar a bottle. "That's ridiculous," I said. "It's too much."

"Well, I'm sorry, but I can't do any better than that," he said, eying me. He had a wrinkle that ran between his eyebrows that gave him a perpetually angry look.

I narrowed my eyes and gazed at him. "I think you can do a lot better."

"Then you're thinking wrong."

I walked around the store for a few minutes, trying to place where I'd seen that rotter before, and it came to me that he'd been at the Mother Lode the first night I was there. I'd seen him with Bobtail, and I remembered the secret she'd shared with me about the lie he always told his wife. By this time, he had started stocking shelves with canned vegetables. I walked over to him and asked, "Mr. Finch, do you enjoy being married?"

"Huh?" he asked.

"There are so many single men around here . . . I was just wondering if you like being married. Do you have a happy home?"

He scowled at me and said, "Of course, I like being married. Nothing better."

"That's wonderful," I said. "Do you think your home would be as happy if your wife knew you were out screwing Bobtail Betty when you claimed to be playing cards with your friends? I reckon you tell her you've lost at poker when you go home with your pockets so much lighter. I happen to know that Joyous Lee gets that wine for a dollar a bottle, and I think I should, too, you miserable wanker. Hmm, I wonder what your wife would think?"

Needless to say, I got my wine for a dollar a bottle.

My first hire was a lovely mulatto girl, who called herself Tigress and had the whitest teeth I'd ever seen. I knew she'd appeal to Buffalo soldiers and white men alike. I also hired seven white girls: Tilly, Sweet Thing, Clementine, Jade, Crystal, Ruby, and Nectarine.

I decided on the Saturday before Valentine's Day as the perfect evening for the grand opening. Our invitations were engraved on ivory paper with a gold border. We sent them to the most prominent men in and around Kingston. They read:

Tom Beeson, Sadie Creech, & Eight
Beautiful Young Ladies
request the pleasure of your company
at the grand opening of The Horny Toad
616 Virtue Avenue
Kingston, New Mexico Territory
on Saturday, February 12, 1887
from six o'clock in the evening until the wee hours

Selling oysters, which some believed were an aphrodisiac, seemed like a stroke of genius to me. I planned to sell smoked oysters for two bits apiece. I'd have the bartender offer them with a choice of hot sauce or lemon butter.

The wine I bought for a dollar a bottle, I would sell for five dollars a bottle. I'd instruct my girls always to ask men to buy a bottle of wine to take upstairs, and I'd give them a portion of the profit. If they distracted the men, kept it unopened, and turned the bottle in, we could sell it again, and I'd give them an extra dollar. I could just see the money rolling in. I then turned my attention to hiring a professor.

Of course, I realized I'd need someone to do housekeeping, and I thought about Silas, the boy I'd met outside the Victorio Hotel, who'd said his mother worked at a laundry. I considered finding his mum and offering her a better-paying job, so I went looking for Silas on a Sunday afternoon and found him on a street near the Victorio.

"Hallo, Silas," I said as I approached him. "Will you take me to your mother? I'd really like to talk to her."

He led me to a little two-room shack on the outskirts of town. I waited outside as he ran inside, yelling, "Mama, the lady that sent you a big pile o' money want to see you!" He'd left the door wide open, so I peeked inside and saw his mother set aside some sewing. She came to the door with a little girl, about three years old, following her and peeking out from behind the skirt of her tattered calico dress. The woman was tall and thin. I guessed she was around thirty years old.

"Hallo, I'm Sadie Creech," I said offering my hand. "I really admire your son for his efforts to find work and help you."

She shook hands with me, smiling, and said, "Thank you, ma'am. Silas is a hard worker. I'm Alma Simmons. Thank you for sending that money. It put new shoes on our feet and bought some groceries."

Her little girl peeked out and slowly stepped forward, smiling and pointing at the black leather shoes on her feet. "You can tell Birdie love them shoes," she said. "She been prancing around like a princess in 'em." Then Alma ran her hands through her hair and asked, "What can I help you with, ma'am?"

"I'm now part owner of a new brothel on Virtue Street. I was wondering if you might be interested in coming to work for me as a housekeeper. I can offer you more than you're making now."

"Would I have to be there when the girls is doing their shenanigans?"

"Well, that could happen at any time, but, for the most part, no; you'd only be there in the daylight hours, when business is very slow."

"Can Birdie play in a backroom somewhere out of sight when it's cold or raining? I don't like her being out in that laundry yard all day."

"She can play in the front parlor if she wants and go to a back room if a gentleman comes in."

Alma frowned while rubbing her forehead. "I just don't want no man doing nothing to hurt Birdie."

"I don't think it would happen, but, if anyone tries to touch her, I'll shoot him. I mean that."

Still frowning, Alma said, "I might do it if you promise me

one more thing. You can talk to Birdie all you want, but I want you to tell yo' girls not to pay no mind to her. I know she a cute little girl, but I don't want them trying to make friends with her or giving her little toys and such. However nice they might be, I don't want Birdie to get no idea that they nice or that they on the right path. I don't want her dreaming about being like them fancy women."

I told her I understood and agreed that would be part of the house rules. We talked a bit more, and I told her I had a fenced-in backyard the children could play in when it was warm outside, and that they'd be welcome inside, regardless of the weather. I was very impressed that she didn't make her decision solely on money, so I offered her a little more than I'd planned and brought her on at four times what she was making at the laundry. Although I didn't really need her yet, I offered to let her start the next day. I knew I'd made a wise choice when Alma insisted on finishing another week at the laundry to give the owners time to find and hire her replacement.

The next day, Tom Beeson said he was very pleased with all I had done, and he even bought a new suit of clothes, including new underwear and shoes, for our grand opening. "Why, Tom, you could get married in that," I exclaimed, and he winked. Regardless of whether he'd taken that as his "sign," I still planned to bring up the idea of building a big house for us.

My plans were finalized by February 5, so I had time to focus on getting myself ready. I bought several new party dresses, including one in red velvet with a sweetheart neckline to wear on opening night. As I reflected on how my dreams were coming true, I remembered that night I'd spent in the livery stable after being thrown out of Madam Chantelle's house. In particular, I remembered a promise I'd made to myself that I'd own a necklace better than anything Chantelle would ever own, so I went to a jeweler and bought a diamond lavaliere on a gold chain. On a whim, I also commissioned a necklace to be made with three twenty-dollar gold pieces set into a double serpentine, gold chain.

CHAPTER 20

The grand opening of the Horny Toad went unbelievably well, but, to my sorrow, I lost Tom the following day. Around one o'clock in the morning, Tom and I retired to my bedroom, and he held me in his arms as we drifted into sleep. Two hours later, I awakened and found him fully dressed. "I'm heading back to my cabin," he said. "I have a feeling someone's messing around up there."

"Come back to bed, you berk. It's nighttime, and you and Hiram Dawson both told me that trail is too dangerous in the dark."

"It is . . . for a woman. But I've ridden that trail hundreds of times, and I know it well."

"But it rained last night. The trail's wet." No amount of pleading would dissuade him. Tom took his shotgun and headed out. When I finally got back to sleep, I dreamed of the black wolf and woke up a little before dawn in a cold sweat. Not being able to shake the feeling that something bad had happened, I went to the livery stable, saddled Long Shot, and headed up the long trail to Tom's cabin in the gray light of dawn.

After more than an hour of riding up the canyons, I came across what appeared to be tracks from where a wolf had chased a horse. With my heart in my throat, I followed the tracks to a place where the trail ran along the edge of a ravine. I could see where the horse had lost its footing and fallen off the edge, but I couldn't see the horse or a rider. The wolf's tracks ended there, too. I rode up the trail a bit to make sure, but I saw no more wolf prints.

Weeping, I returned to town, and the first person I came upon was Doc Guthrie. "I think something terrible has happened to Tom Beeson," I said, telling him what I'd found.

Doc gathered several other men, and they rode with me to the site and examined the tracks. Two of the younger men in the group made their way to a place where they could get down into that ravine, and they found Tom's body and that of his horse, but they found no sign of a wolf's body. It chilled me to think of how terrified Tom must have been when he encountered that thing in the darkness. Of course, his death shook me for more reasons than one. I hadn't forgotten Vashti's prediction that the wolf would eventually come for me as well.

Vashti was beside herself when she heard the news. She came to visit me at the Horny Toad, sat down in one of the plush blue chairs in my parlor, and said, "I tol' you that wolf dog would come back. You seen it yet?" she asked. When I said no, she asked, "You *sensed* it?"

"No!" I shouted. I refused to tell her I'd dreamed about it.

The look she gave me said she didn't believe me. She folded her hands and said, "You will, so you betta be prepared."

"How do I get prepared?"

Vashti sighed and slumped back in the chair. "I'll have to study on that a while."

Then my sorrow over Tom flooded my heart, and, in spite of myself, I started crying in front of her. She misunderstood my tears and said, "It'll be okay. There's ways to protect against spirits."

We laid Tom out in the parlor of the Horny Toad for his wake and held the funeral there the next day. During the wake and for two days afterward, we were closed for business and kept black bunting on the front of the house. Tigress refused to stay in the house on the night of his wake and took a hotel room instead. The rest of us greeted visitors and sat up all night with his corpse. I paid a traveling circuit preacher to say a few kind words and read some scripture at a graveside service, and it wasn't long before a man named Grover Miles filed papers and took over Tom's claim. The Horny Toad brothel belonged entirely to me, but Tom was gone, and Tom had left all of his money to a nephew in California. Any happy years we could have enjoyed together were gone.

I couldn't help but think of Pretty Face's words from my first night at the Mother Lode: "Evil follows you." I also remembered how she'd stood outside the Horny Toad mouthing soundless words before we'd opened. *Did she somehow call forth this evil? Could she put curses on people?* I knew that, if she could, I was the one responsible. I'd inadvertently awakened her so-called gift with that shovel years ago.

Mostly I thought about Tom and what we could have had if had he lived. I tried to keep my sorrow to myself, but, from time to time, I'd be with Ruby, Tilly, or one of the other girls and my tears would flow. Or I'd go to the bank, become overwhelmed with emotion, and have to step outside for a few minutes.

Only Long Shot seemed to understand my sorrow in those days. "He was going to marry me," I whispered while he took lumps of sugar from my palm. "That would have made him your daddy. And we would have built a fine house for us to live in and a big stable for you."

CHAPTER 21

On a bright, early morning in the spring of 1887, I heard the little bell ring as someone entered the Horny Toad, so I went into the parlor, ready to call one of my girls down, and was surprised to find a well-dressed, middle-aged woman there. "I'm looking for Sadie Creech," she said.

"That's me, luv. If you're coming to find out if your husband's been here, I'm afraid I wouldn't know," I said, steeling myself for whatever came next—a show of wrath on her part, a venomous, self-righteous assessment of my way of making a living, or even a tear-filled diatribe against whomever she'd married. I was also fully prepared to lay a good cursing on her and run her off, if need be.

She laughed and said, "Do you really get that sort of call? I can imagine it would be awkward." Then she sobered and said, "Actually, I wanted to speak with you for a few moments about a deep need in this community. I hope to enlist your help."

All it took for me to respect someone was for them to show me some respect, and once she had done that, I warmed to her considerably. "Would you care to have coffee with me? I just made a fresh pot."

She nodded, so I motioned toward a sofa and told her to make herself comfortable. She laughed again and pointed to an embroidered piece on the wall, *We Aim to Please.* "That seems to be a brothel favorite. I wish I could hang one that says *I Aim to Please* over our bed," she said, breaking into laughter again.

"Well, you could—it wouldn't take long to make one."

"No, I couldn't. You see, my husband is a minister. With the visitors that tromp through our house, he couldn't allow it."

"Then tell him your thought. I'm sure he'd appreciate that."

At that, she laughed even harder. "You misunderstand. I was hoping to inspire him into finer action." Then we both had a good laugh.

"Oh, my, I like you already, and I don't even know your name," I said. "Wait just a moment, and I'll be back with our coffee."

When I came back, she ignored the cream and sugar, took a small sip of steaming black coffee, and introduced herself as Mrs. F. E. Farrow. After a few minutes of small talk, she said, "My husband and I would like to settle here permanently, but it gets tiresome to search out places to hold meetings. We've tried renting saloons, but the owners usually insist on staying open for business during the meeting, and it's distracting to have liquor being served in one corner while trying to share the gospel in another. This community needs a church, a sanctuary where people can turn their thoughts to God without distraction. We'd like to build one, but we haven't the money. I wanted to know if you might consider helping us."

"So you're seeking a donation?" I asked. Instantly, I decided I'd give her a hundred dollars, just because I liked her.

"No, ma'am," she said. "I was hoping you'd become an advocate and help us find ways to raise the money. We'd like to build a very solid structure that will serve the community for many years." She opened her purse, took out a piece of folded paper, and handed it to me. On it, she had sketched a simple church building with a steeple. "I'd like to make it big enough to seat at least a hundred people," she said.

"You're asking a lot of a woman whose employees wouldn't even be welcome inside the building," I said.

A distraught look came over her face. "But of course they'd be welcome," she said. "The purpose of the church is to reach out to all people and introduce them to God. It can't do that if it tells certain people to keep out."

I sighed. "You don't know what it's like to be a whore and be shunned by a bunch of self-righteous bitches, either."

Mrs. Farrow looked me in the eye and said, "With all due respect, you don't know what I know or don't know. If we say the whores will be welcome there, and they will be, can you suffer a few of those 'bitches,' as you call them, to attend as well? They need to learn about God, too."

With that, she won me over, while sending my thoughts off in other directions. *Is she telling me she's a former whore? If not, she doesn't seem to care how I take her words.* "Mrs. Farrow, I'll do anything I can to help you. In fact, I already have one idea—my girls and I could visit the saloons on Fridays as the miners start pouring into town but before they've gotten very drunk and rowdy. We could then pass a hat to collect money for the cause. You might be surprised at how quickly you could start construction if we did that. I don't think the girls would mind helping if they understood they'd be welcome to attend the church." Suddenly, my head was full of ideas. I asked, "Have you gotten an estimate on what the church would cost?"

"With a building lot and everything, it will probably be a little over two thousand dollars," she said, "at least according to Howard Everett at the lumberyard."

The estimate sounded too high to me, but that didn't bother me because I knew some dirt on Howard. I smiled and said, "I know quite a few businessmen in this town. If I have a chat with them, I think I can convince them to offer good prices on your building materials and the labor, too. We should go to the bank and set up an account just for the building fund. We need to do that so folks won't be worried about anyone holding the cash and leaving town with it."

In the weeks that followed, I decided to give my diamond lavaliere to the cause, so I sold it back to the jeweler I'd purchased it from for just a little less than I'd paid for it and put the money into the building fund. The jeweler was generous with his repurchase offer because he knew it was for a good cause and because he expected to do business with me again. Tigress and my other girls were proud to help raise money for the church, and the whole community pulled together in the effort.

The church was nearly finished when I read that Doc Holliday had died at the Hotel Glenwood in Glenwood, Colorado, on November 8, 1887, and I was sorry to hear of his passing. The story of his death was in newspapers all over the county. I remember thinking he would be pleased if he knew whores had helped build a church because a whore known as Big Nose Kate had been his common-law wife for a number of years.

Pastor and Mrs. Farrow had their church in time for Christmas that year, and it cost only fifteen hundred dollars for everything, even down to the altar cloth. When it was all finished, I asked Mrs. Farrow if she thought I'd done enough to earn a place in heaven. She smiled and said, "It doesn't work that way, Sadie. Eternal life is a gift."

CHAPTER 22

During the winter after the church was completed, my girls and I attended the church services each week, sitting on the back row. Though I didn't understand it, I lost Tigress to Jesus, and she left the Horny Toad, but I didn't mind that much. I just thought she was crazy for leaving a good income to work for pennies as a maid or laundress. I was pondering that in the kitchen one morning while I made a second pot of coffee and Alma cleaned the upstairs bedrooms. Breaking my thoughts, Silas came in and said, "Miz Creech, Birdie's sick." I followed him to the parlor and found Birdie on the floor, leaning against a blue sofa.

"What's wrong, Birdie?" I asked, touching the child's forehead. She was burning hot. Just as I reached down to pick her up, she leaned to one side and vomited on the rug.

"Silas, go get your mother, and then go and ask Doc Guthrie to come over here." I got a rag and started wiping up the vomit while he ran up the stairs.

Alma came down, saw what I was doing, and said, "Miz Creech, I'll clean that up. That's my job," as she hurried to check on Birdie. I had her put Birdie on the sofa and got a blanket and a pillow for her, along with a small bucket in case Birdie threw up again. Alma got a cool, wet cloth to put on Birdie's forehead.

"How in the world she get so sick so fast?" Alma asked. "She seem fine at six o'clock this morning. Is any of them whores sick?"

"Not that I know of."

When Doc Guthrie arrived, he examined Birdie with a somber look on his face. "I've seen a couple of others with this," he said, "and I wasn't sure what it was until this morning when one of my patients broke out in rash. It's smallpox, and it's dangerous, especially for a child this age. I want you to take her home and keep her as comfortable as you can. Keep using wet cloths to cool the fever, and use them on her back and chest."

"What else can I expect from this smallpox?" Alma asked.

Doc Guthrie drew a deep breath and let it out. "Well, she'll have the fever, vomiting, and severe pain in the back and maybe the abdomen for two to three days, and then she'll start to feel better. Next, she'll develop places that will fill with fluid, break open, scab over, and leave pitted scars. I'm very sorry to tell you this."

Birdie whimpered, "Mama, my back hurts."

Doc nodded. "That makes me even surer that I'm right," he said. "Take her home and get her to drink some chicken broth and water, maybe a little apple juice. You can give her a bit of laudanum if the pain gets real bad." He produced a bottle from his doctor's bag and handed it to her.

"I cain't take her home," Alma said. "I ain't finished my shift."

I assured her it was all right. "Birdie's the most important concern right now."

"Thank you, Miz Creech. That's what I was thinking, but I didn't wanna leave you with no problem." When she left, I got out my purse to pay for the house call, but Doc Guthrie wouldn't take anything.

"I've got a feeling a lot of people are going to be doing a lot of work for free over the next couple of weeks," he said. "I expect to see a lot more cases."

"Will Birdie recover?" I ask.

"I hope so," Doc Guthrie said, "but I don't know."

I went to Alma's shack the next day around noon and found her haggard. Silas had gotten sick sometime during the night, and she'd cared for both children without getting any rest since the night before last. I told her to go to sleep, that I'd take care of Birdie and Silas for a few hours. She made herself a pallet, stretched out on the floor, and fell asleep quickly. I soon found how hard it was to keep both children sponged off and to get them to drink water or apple juice. I couldn't imagine how exhausted Alma must be. After a couple of hours, Silas started moaning so much that I was afraid he'd wake his mother. "My stomach hurts," he said and then spewed vomit into the bucket beside the bed.

"Did throwing up help it?" I asked.

"No, it still hurts real bad."

Remembering Doc Guthrie's instructions, I gave him less than a teaspoon of laudanum, being uncertain of the correct dosage for a child his size. Soon, he slept for a while, and Birdie slept, so I sat in Alma's straight-back chair and rested a bit. When the sun was starting to set, Silas said, "Miz Creech, am I gonna die?"

"No, of course not. What gave you that idea?"

"I think Birdie done died."

I jumped up, went to the child, and found her very still. I didn't think she was breathing, but I couldn't bring myself to touch her to confirm it. Keeping my voice level, I said, "Silas, she's very sick. I'm going just a little ways to find someone to go get Doc Guthrie. Can you be very quiet and not wake your mama while I'm gone?"

"Yes, ma'am."

I went out in the street and gave a boy a dime to run for Doc Guthrie, promising him another dime when he returned. Before I could get back inside, I heard Alma scream.

She was keening and holding Birdie, rocking her in her arms, when I went in. "I didn't wake her up," Silas said. "She wake up on her own."

When Doc Guthrie arrived, I gave the boy who'd summoned him another dime. Alma refused to let go of Birdie while Doc confirmed that she was dead. I admired him for not trying to take the child from her. He said, "Now, Alma, you haven't had much rest, and you need rest. Little Birdie is at peace now. She feels no pain. I'd like to put Silas on a stretcher in the back of my carriage and take him to Sadie's house, where she can look after him. I want you to stay here with Birdie and sleep with her while she's at rest. Would you be willing to take a dose of laudanum and do this?" She nodded, and he gave her a very large dose. Alma took Birdie and crawled into bed with her, and Doc and I stepped outside.

"You can't leave her there to wake with a cold, stiff child in her arms!" I hissed.

"I don't intend to. When that laudanum takes effect, I'll be able to take the child from her, and she'll sleep until morning. Can you send someone back to sit with her and be here when she awakens?"

"Yes, one of the girls can come, but there'll be hell to pay when Alma sees you've taken Birdie."

Doc gave a weary sigh and set his bag on the floor of his carriage. "I'm going to bathe Birdie and buy her a pretty little dress. I'll have her laid out like an angel on a cot in the corner before her mother awakens."

Doc did as he promised and brought the child home in a blue, velvet dress trimmed with lace, but Birdie's death wasn't

161

the end of Alma's sorrows. Silas followed his sister in death the next day. I was nearly overwhelmed with grief, as I'd thought so much of those children. Of course, I also remembered a whore that had given her son to the foul-mouthed wife of a blacksmith, and I remembered a whore that had lost track of her daughter, but I won't speak of those things.

I bought a black dress for Alma, and I bought Silas a suit, white shirt, and a tie to be buried in, and I paid the children's burial expenses. On January 11, 1888, we took them to a burial place Doc Guthrie provided and placed the little coffins side by side, and Rev. F. E. Farrow officiated over their funeral service and offered consolation to Alma.

By this time, Kingston was into a full-blown smallpox epidemic. Doc Guthrie called for the largest tent in town to be used as a hospital for the miners and other men without families in the area who had contracted smallpox. The townspeople supplied cots and linens. Renfield Vicars and Gordon Massy were hired to nurse the sick, but someone foolishly set their pay as a jug of whiskey per day, so I wasn't surprised when I heard that the male nurses were practically worthless. Seven men died under their care while they sat around in a drunken haze.

I called a meeting and asked my girls to help me tend the sick, and every one of them volunteered. The nine of us worked in shifts, so there were always at least three of us to care for the men in that makeshift hospital. Not a single man died after we took over, and not one of us became sick. Rev. Farrow declared that God was protecting us.

I worked the first shift every day, and, when I finished, I'd go to Alma's shack to check on her. She eventually came back to work. I noticed Alma moved through her chores like a woman in a trance. Within a month, Alma drank a whole bottle of laudanum, and we didn't find her in time to save her. Rev. Farrow held her funeral service, and we buried her next to her children.

CHAPTER 23

Business went well for me over the next couple of years. Pretty Face caused no further trouble in those years, and all thoughts of the black wolf faded into distant memory. At the time, many people in the United States were concerned that too many Chinese workers were coming into our land. In 1888, President Grover Cleveland declared the Chinese "impossible of assimilation with our people and dangerous to our peace and welfare." I couldn't help but think of Tom Ying and his partner and their steady determination to make their way in this land with the restaurant business. I still ate at their place every time I went to Lake Valley.

In November of 1888, Benjamin Harrison was elected president of the United States. Cleveland had won the popular vote, but Harrison had won the electoral college vote. I wondered if Harrison felt the same about the Chinese as Cleveland did.

In 1889, I was intrigued by reports of journalist Nellie Bly, who, inspired by Jules Verne, had taken it upon herself to travel around the world in less than eighty days. I envied her, of course. On January 25, 1890, she achieved her goal in seventy-two days, six hours, and eleven minutes, having traveled by steamer, by railway, and even by donkey.

I wondered if Nellie Bly would even survive eighty days as a whore in a whore's world. I thought of the towns I'd been in and wondered about the places she had seen. I considered how every town was a little world in itself, and every home in every town was another little world, everything wrapped up neatly, worlds within worlds, like the little Russian nesting dolls I'd seen in some foreign girls' rooms.

In those days, Kingston's chapter of the Woman's Christian Temperance Union would march down Virtue Avenue and wind through the brothel district from time to time wearing white bows for purity and carrying a banner that read "For God and Home and Native Land." My girls would sit on the porch and watch them as if watching a parade. Reform of prostitutes was one of their aims, and they seemed to enjoy imploring the girls to turn from their wicked ways. The girls, in turn, liked to make catcalls and try to recruit the temperance women to their ranks.

In June of 1890, the temperance marchers were out in the heat, so I went out to the porch and invited them to come in and have some iced tea. One slender brunette with soulful, brown eyes had started walking toward my door when another woman grabbed her hand and jerked her back to the street, shouting, "Helen! Have you lost your mind? Do you want to get a disease?"

The temperance women were a nuisance at times, especially when they staged pray-ins in the saloons and demanded an end to the sale of alcohol, but I had to admit I admired them for their tenacity in standing up for stiffer penalties for crimes against girls and women. In those days, men often got by with raping women and girls by claiming consent on the part of their victims, and, in some areas, the age of consent was very low, so on that issue, I was with them. I knew I'd never join their ranks because one of their requirements was to agree not to drink alcohol in any form. I liked an afternoon whiskey too much to go along with that.

Girls came and went at the Horny Toad, but I remained friends with Joyous Lee, Vashti, Bobtail, and Jiggly. Jiggly soon married a middle-aged miner and left the area, but she sent me a letter a couple of years later to let me know she'd given birth to a daughter. Vashti struck a deal with Joyous to take over part of Emily's responsibilities when Emily decided to move to California. Vashti gave up whoring, started collecting money from guests at the Mother Lode, and did bookkeeping for Joyous, but she still refused to work as anyone's maid.

Bobtail eventually moved to a smaller house called the Do-Gooder. She still looked good, so I would have hired her, but she didn't tell me until the move was made. She moved for the same reason all whores moved: men got tired of seeing the same women. They wanted new, younger flesh. Her move across town worked only because she had a different clientele in the less expensive brothel.

In the wee hours of the morning on Sunday, July 6, 1890, I awakened to pounding on the front door of the Horny Toad, so I grabbed my pistol, pulled on a robe, and went to see who it was. A blond boy of about fourteen stood there huffing and out of breath. "Are you . . . Sadie Creech?" he asked.

"I am, and you'd better have a damn good reason for banging on my door at this hour, you little rotter," I replied, pointing the pistol at him.

It seemed to have no effect on him. "Madam Betsy . . . sent for you . . . Bobtail Betty's hurt real bad . . . and wants to see you. She's at the Do-Gooder."

In my mind, I could see images of Bobtail beaten by some wretched man. I knew it must be bad because Bobtail could take a punch or too and already had, as had most other whores. "Hurt how?" I asked.

"Madam Betsy didn't say."

"Thank you for telling me," I said, and I closed the door and went to get dressed. When I opened the door, the boy was still there. "What are you hanging around for? Did you want money?"

"No, ma'am. I'm going to walk with you to keep you safe."

At that, I laughed aloud. "That's bloody rich, son. Here's a dollar. I can take care of myself. You just go on about your business."

When I reached the Do-Gooder, Betsy Rhodes met me at the door, her blonde wig askew, and said, "Bobtail was calling for you, earlier. Doc Guthrie's upstairs with her now. He was able to stop the bleeding." I walked up the stairway quickly, while Betsy slowly hauled herself up behind me, and I was startled to see the amount of blood on a bundle of sheets in the hallway. Knocking first, I asked if it was okay for us to come in, and Doc said it was.

By the light of an oil lamp, Bobtail looked terribly pale lying on clean linens, but her face hadn't been cut or bruised. I couldn't tell that she was breathing. "Is she . . . sleeping?" I asked, wondering if she were dead.

"She's out cold from the pain I inflicted while trying to clean the wound and stop the bleeding," Doc Guthrie replied. "She'll need laudanum when she comes around."

"What happened?"

Doc's face hardened. "Some sorry, no-good bastard cut off her vestigial tail. As you can see, she's lost a lot of blood."

A flood of sorrow and rage washed over me. I remembered how Bobtail, Jiggly Jane, and Vashti had cared for me after Bill Dunn kicked the hell out of me. "She'll recover, won't she?"

Doc sat there silent for a moment before he said, "It could go either way. There's grave danger of infection. She'll have a lot of pain for a while, and I doubt she'll be able to find a comfortable position for sleeping. Just be aware that any movement will cause the pain to flare up."

Doc left after giving Betsy and me instructions to clean the wound twice a day with carbolic acid. I turned to Betsy and asked, "Who did this?"

"We're not sure. Most of us were sleeping when it happened. I reckon she was down in the parlor well after midnight when some latecomer knocked on the door, and she let him in. Anyway, I heard an awful scream, grabbed my pistol, and came upstairs. By the time I got here, the man was gone. The other girls had come into the hallway, but only Surly Sue had gotten out in time to see his back as he ran out. Her description of a gray-haired man of medium height and dressed like a miner could fit a thousand men."

"Did you ask Bobtail who did it?"

"Yes, but she didn't say. She kept asking me to get Sadie Creech. You must be a good friend."

"I try to be," I said. "Look, there's no need for both of us to sit here. Why don't you get some rest while you can? You can sit with her when I have to leave."

It didn't take much coaxing to get Betsy to go back to bed. As she left, I glanced at her huge bosom. Betsy had been inspired when she saw a photo of another whore with two teacups and saucers balanced on her more than ample breasts, so, for a fee, Betsy served drinks to customers in the same fashion, balancing teacups, highball glasses, or even beer mugs on her tits. I suppose she did that because she didn't get many calls for cups of tea. I'd seen her do it, and I never understood how she managed not to spill the drinks as she waddled across a room.

Bobtail woke up moaning within thirty minutes. I went to her side and told her I was there with her, and she clasped my hand and didn't want to let go. "You need to let me walk across the room to get you some pain medicine," I said. She released her grip until I could give her the laudanum and then reached for my hand again. I sat there until she seemed to be more relaxed. Then I asked, "Who did this to you. Do you know?" She nodded, so I asked, "Why didn't you tell Betsy?"

She whispered, "I'm only going to tell you. I'll tell everyone else I don't know who did it."

Perplexed, I asked, "Why?"

She spoke, barely above a whisper. "Remember what Joyous Lee said about how the law doesn't care what happens to whores? You do care, so I want you to be the law for me. I want you to take care of this man, so he won't hurt anyone else. Promise?"

I squeezed her hand and said, "I promise. Now who was it?"

"Rod Baylor. Him and his wife live out near Pickett Spring Canyon."

I hadn't met him, but I'd seen Baylor's name in the paper a few times after he got in trouble with the law, usually for disorderly conduct. However, I knew his wife, Earlene, who sometimes came into town and sold embroidered pieces to make a little extra cash. She had unloaded her troubles to me regarding her husband, and I knew that she hid her meager earnings from him so she could buy food for herself when he'd go off on a weekend drinking spree. My thoughts were interrupted when Bobtail started speaking again.

"He got mad when I told him my fee . . . said if he had to pay that much, he was taking a souvenir. I thought . . . he was going to take something off my dresser . . . or a piece of my underwear. When he turned me over his knee . . . I thought . . . it would just be a spanking."

I saw her eyelids sinking. I stayed with her until noon the next day, when Betsy came and promised to sit with her or have someone else in the room with her until I could return.

Although I could have used some sleep myself, I headed straight for the Mother Lode to tell Vashti and Joyous Lee what

Rod Baylor had done. I found them both in Joyous Lee's parlor. Upon hearing the news, Joyous shrieked, "Why that cave-crawling son of a syphilitic whore!"

Vashti said, "Somebody need to put a stick of dynamite up his ass and light it."

Her remark gave me the start of a plan on how to deal with Rod Baylor, but I never mentioned my promise to Bobtail. I knew Joyous was probably thinking of taking care of Baylor, too, but, for now, I knew we'd both put him on the back burner and focus on Bobtail.

Vashti and Joyous promised to visit Bobtail, and we made plans to move her and her things into a vacant room at the Mother Lode, just to make sure she received proper care. At last, I went home and got some sleep.

I got up before sunset and found a note Vashti had left for me saying they had already moved Bobtail. They gave her a big dose of laudanum before having a man carry her down to a stretcher on a wagon.

When I went to see Bobtail that evening, she looked worse. I spooned vegetable beef soup into her mouth and tried to distract her from her pain by making her laugh. I told her what Vashti said should be done to Mr. Baylor and what Joyous had called him. Soon, it was time to clean the wound again. When I pulled back the covers, I saw the skin around the base of her spine, which had been white the night before, was now red in an area about the size of a small woman's fist. The reddened skin was quite hot to the touch in comparison to the skin around it. I quickly cleaned the wound and covered her. After I had her settled, I asked Joyous Lee's hired man, John, to fetch the doc.

Within twenty minutes, Doc Guthrie came in to check on Bobtail. He came out shaking his head. "It's infected. Just keep her as comfortable as you can."

Over the course of the next six days, I sat with Bobtail frequently as the infection spread and fever consumed her. I held her hand and soothed her when she became delirious. Sometimes she thrashed about, causing her pain to become unbearable, but she had to bear it until Doc Guthrie came and gave her morphine. Only a deadly dose of laudanum could have relieved it. He told us there was nothing more he could do.

When Bobtail died, Joyous wanted to buy her a dress to be buried in and pay for her funeral, and I didn't argue or offer to help because I was about to do something even more important for my old friend, and my plan was in full bloom. But first, I called Rev. F. E. Farrow, who welcomed whores into his church both in life and in death, to do her funeral.

CHAPTER 24

Three days after we laid Bobtail to rest, I headed out toward Pickett Spring Canyon and paid Earlene Baylor a visit. I took a basket of food, including fried chicken, green beans, boiled potatoes, and apple pie, and we ate together, while she expressed delight over the surprise and told me how happy she was I'd come to see her.

Earlene was a small woman, about forty years old, the nervous type, her eyes always flitting around, as if to make sure she was safe. Her cabin was just one big room with the kitchen, sleeping area, and a sitting area. Examples of her needlework were hanging on the walls, and I was impressed with her elaborate skills at embroidery. She had captured detailed images of birds and flowers in colored thread, but when I complimented her work, she'd look at the floor and say most anyone could do the same.

Finally, I asked, "Is your husband still working the mines?"

"Sure, when he ain't down to the saloons and whorehouses, but that don't trouble me. The more he's gone, the happier I am." She put down her fork and said, "Let me show you what he did to me last week. Look-a here." She pulled up her right sleeve. A wide strip of skin along the inside of her forearm was burned, and I could see where blisters had formed and broken open in the center of the burn. "One night he got mad because a pot boiled over, so he pushed my arm down on the stove and said maybe that would help me remember to tend to my cookin'." She pulled her sleeve down and added, "Ain't the first time he's hurt me, won't be the last."

"Do you have any salve for that?" I asked.

"I been using aloe juice from my plants outside."

I wondered how to get around to my business, which was rather delicate, because my plan to take care of Rod Baylor depended on enlisting Earlene's help. I decided the direct approach was best, so I eyed her and asked, "Have you ever wished you could be rid of him?"

"More than a thousand times," she said, laughing.

I proceeded to tell her about my days at the Mother Lode under Joyous Lee, trying to bring to life scenes from my friendship with Bobtail, Jiggly Jane, and Vashti. Earlene laughed when I told her how Bobtail had lifted her skirt and displayed her little nub of a tail after I expressed disbelief that she had one. Smiling, Earlene said, "You almost make me wish I'd been a whore." Then the smile left her and she said, "But I reckon whores got plenty of bad times, too."

"That's right," I said, finding the perfect opening to tell her of how Bobtail had died because of her husband's brutality. She listened in silence, looking into my eyes as much as she could in her eternal, nervous state. I could tell she believed what I was telling her. Finally, I came to my point. "Bobtail knew the law doesn't care what happens to a whore. If a whore gets hurt, it's the risk of the business. At the same time, Bobtail knew I did care, and she made me promise to be the law for her, and I intend to do that. I'm not going to let your husband get by with this. Now that I've said that, are you going to report me to the law?"

She shook her head, and I said, "Then I'd appreciate your help."

Earlene's eyes moved to the front door, as though she feared her husband were standing there listening to us. Then she gently touched her right forearm. "What kind of help?" she asked, leaning forward with gleaming eyes.

Inwardly, I smiled, knowing she was fully with me. "Let's serve him a nice supper," I said.

"What, are we going to poison him?"

"Oh, no, nothing like that. You leave the dirty work to me. Your hands will stay clean. If things go wrong, you can claim you didn't know what I was going to do, and you'll be telling the truth. Do you trust me?"

She shook her head. "No. I mean, I trust you, but I want to know all about it. If you're the law for Bobtail, then I'll be your deputy. Heck, I'll be the law for me." That sounded perfectly reasonable, so I took a stick of dynamite out of my pocket.

"Where'd you get that?" she asked.

"At the hardware store." I quickly outlined my idea.

Earlene didn't argue, but she asked, "Where will I live after all that, and how will I support myself?"

I hadn't considered that I was suggesting that we destroy her home. "You'll live with me," I said, "at least until the cabin is rebuilt, and I'll pay for that and replace whatever gets broken. You can work for me at the hotels, but I don't expect you'd have to for very long because you could surely remarry." She was satisfied with that, so we decided to have our supper the following Tuesday night, when she felt Rod wasn't likely to go into town before coming home. "What do I need to cook?"

"Not a thing. I'll bring in a delicious meal." At that time, I saw no reason things could go other than exactly as planned, but I should have known better.

I arrived at the Baylor cabin around four o'clock, and we started figuring the best way to attach the stick of dynamite to Rod's chair so that it wouldn't be seen, and then we had to decide about the length of the fuse and how to disguise it. We rearranged a throw rug to hide it and stuffed a good bit of it into a crack that ran alongside a flooring board by the wall. I left about an inch sticking out near the door to make it easy to light. I knew he'd never notice it because he'd be focused on my unexpected presence in his home.

Then we had to figure our timing. I had brought two racks of seasoned beef ribs, a whole one for Rod Baylor and one for me and Earlene to split, and beans, to make it a meal. "Will he eat all of his food?" I asked.

"Every bite," Earlene said.

"Then we can eat until he gets about two-thirds finished with this rack of ribs. At that point, excuse yourself to go to the outhouse, and then I'll tell him I forgot to bring in an apple pie for dessert. I'll light the fuse on my way outside."

"Won't he hear you strike the match?"

"Not if I chatter while I'm doing it."

Around six that evening, Rod Baylor came home. I was truly appalled at how boorish he was. After I'd introduced myself and lied and said that I'd made friends with his wife in a sewing group and had brought their supper, he said, "You say you run the Horny Toad?" I nodded, and he said, "If you gonna eat in my house, it seems you owe me somethin'."

His words shocked me so much I felt my stomach lurch. "Maybe you're right, Mr. Baylor. How about you come by my place and have a romp with one of my girls this week?"

"I like the looks of you. How 'bout you undress and get on that there bed after supper and pay up?"

"Mr. Baylor, surely you aren't suggesting that I entertain you right before your wife's eyes."

He shrugged and grunted. "If she don't wanna see, she can go outside."

I looked over at Earlene, and she winked and said, "Suits me. Let's eat."

The explosion was near deafening from where we were, huddled under my wagon about thirty feet from the house. It blew Rod Baylor right through the roof and rained debris down on the wagon and all around us. We saw Rod's body go up and then fall back onto a stable portion of the roof. Figuring that was the end of him, we took my wagon into town to report the tragic event.

The sheriff, Doc Guthrie, and two other men rode with us back to the cabin. On the way, I claimed we'd heard the explosion after we'd taken a walk down to a little stream while Rod finished his supper. I also claimed that Rod had had a stick of dynamite in his back pocket, which wasn't unreasonable since he was a miner, and that we had no idea how it could have exploded unless Rod committed suicide. Being the nervous type, Earlene was shaking and crying. I kept parroting the same details, not adding or taking away anything, while Earlene cried and confirmed everything I said with nods and whimpers.

At the cabin, two men climbed up onto the roof to retrieve the body for Doc Guthrie to examine. I was thinking I'd take Earlene back to my place and open a bottle of champagne when one of those men yelled, "He ain't dead! He's still a-breathin'." My stomach lurched again. I couldn't believe it, but, sure enough, they brought him off that roof unconscious, but alive. Earlene started crying even harder, which the men took as tears of joy.

"Well, thank God!" I said. "Let's take him to my place. These folks can't stay here with their roof blown off, and I've got a spare room off the back of my kitchen."

Rod Baylor was unconscious for nearly three weeks. His wife

and I tended to him during this time. However, on that very first evening at my place, Earlene picked up a pillow and asked, "Should I smother him?"

"I think not," I said. "He'll probably die without our help." However, as the days passed, I began to regret that decision. Rod Baylor was much more trouble than he was worth. I pondered how best to deal with him.

When he finally woke up, he appeared startled to see me in the room with him. "Do you remember what happened?" I asked. He nodded and groaned. I smiled and said, "It's not half as bad as what will happen if you say one word about it to another soul, and if you aren't up and out of this house within five days, I'll cut your pecker and those swollen bollocks off. Then, if you aren't out of this town, never to return, within a week, I'll cut them off slow."

Four days later, Baylor was gone. Later, Earlene and I learned he'd sold their lot and damaged cabin, leaving Earlene with nothing but the things we'd been able to salvage from the cabin while he was unconscious. I could have kicked myself for not anticipating the sale. "Where would he go?" I asked, feeling the weight of the promise I'd made to Bobtail.

"Probably over to Mogollon," Earlene said. "He used to talk about trying his luck there."

I breathed a sigh of relief, somehow feeling sure that she was right, and I wouldn't have to search the whole West to find him. Earlene then told me she'd decided to go to Texas and take care of her folks, who were getting up in years, so I gave her what it would have cost to repair the cabin and replace her other things and wished her well.

After seeing Earlene off, I sent a telegram to the only man I knew in Mogollon, a former soldier in the Mexican army by name of Tiny Ramirez. It was a miracle I knew he was there, and I only knew because I'd heard a customer talking about him at the bar in the Horny Toad. Tiny was the sort of man who could take care of loose ends, as he'd done for me once before when I hired him to kill Colten Lorne, the man who'd killed my first love. *When Sadie makes a promise, she keeps it,* I told myself.

Weeks later, I rode out to Bobtail Betty's grave and dismounted. The stonecutter had placed the monument Joyous bought for her, which read, "Sarah Lightfoot, 1862–1890, Rest in Peace." I realized I'd never known Bobtail's real name and had never even asked, although, of course, I knew that whores often adopted names for themselves to avoid bringing shame to their families. I took two papers from my pocket and sat on the ground beside the grave. "I've kept my promise," I said. "I tried to do it with dynamite like Vashti suggested, and Rod Baylor suffered a lot, but he lived and moved to Mogollon. In the end, I had to get help, but justice was served."

A canyon wren called *Jeet! Jeet!* from a cottonwood tree as I unfolded the papers in my hand. "I sent a message to Tiny Ramirez, a man I've done business with in the past: Find Rod Baylor. Show him same kindness you showed in Dodge City. My gratitude follows. Little Jill, a.k.a. Sadie, at the Horny Toad, Kingston." Turning to the next paper, I said, "About two weeks later, I received this reply: 'Your friend perished before I could show him any kindness. My condolences.' Then, about a week later, I received confirmation by mail—a news clipping about how Baylor was found in an alley with his throat slit. Immediately, I sent a check to Tiny Ramirez." Tears formed in my eyes, as I thought of Bobtail's fun personality and easy smile. "I hope you can hear me and find peace now," I said. Of a sudden, the canyon wren flew off toward the setting sun.

CHAPTER 25

My status in Kingston and the surrounding area continued to grow. Thinking it would better me, I made the mistake of marrying the ne'er-do-well Casper McKelvey on February 29, 1892, who left me to go to Idaho that same summer after the big mining strike there. He was supposed to send me money, but I never saw it. I'm still angry and have little to say about that. Then came the Panic of 1893, and silver prices fell like rotten fruit. Because of this, I sold the Horny Toad and moved to Hillsboro, a nearby gold mining town. It was a pleasant town with streets shaded by cottonwood trees. Some of the buildings were wooden, but most were stone or adobe. Main Street and Elenora Street, which ran parallel, were the main roads.

The Union Hotel, where the stage always stopped, had a fine bar. This is where I stayed when I first arrived. The Union Church, a red brick structure, was situated a few doors above Muddler's Saloon on Elenora Street. It was pastored by Rev. Roy Honesworth. A few doors down from Muddler's was Fitch's Hardware, which also served as a small lumberyard. On Main Street, there was Doctor Hiram Alston's office, a dressmaker's shop—owned by Hulene Venable—and a bakery, owned by Sylvia Crosswell. There was a post office in George T. Miller's drug store, another drug store, owned by C. C. Miller, a telegraph office, the Black Range Café, an assay office, and other businesses. Tom Murphy's Saloon sat next to the Union Hotel.

Hillsboro was the county seat, so people were always coming

into town to go to court. I realized I could do well there with a hotel. To this end, I bought some property across from the Union Hotel after Howard Muddler, a tall man with reddish-blond hair and a slight paunch, told me it was available for purchase. I liked the property because the stage always stopped in front of the Union Hotel, and I knew that people getting off the stage would look across the street at my place and see another option on where to find lodging. After I bought it, I returned to Muddler's Saloon to tell him the news and celebrate. As a rule, respectable women didn't go into the saloons in those days, but I was the exception. Muddler's soon became my place to go when I wanted to hear the local news and gossip.

Howard Muddler's saloon had a wild feel to it, mostly because of the hunting trophies he had mounted about the place. There were antelope heads, a moose, and a mountain lion. He even had a stuffed grizzly bear standing and showing its teeth in one corner. "Where'd you get all these animals?" I asked.

"Shot every one of 'em myself on one hunting trip or another," Howard said. "What'll it be, Miss Sadie?"

"Whiskey! It's a celebration. Pour one for yourself as well. I bought that land you told me about."

"Damn, that's a good reason to celebrate, and this is on me." When he turned to get a bottle and our glasses, I noticed a strange creature on the counter below the liquor bottles. It looked like a rabbit with antlers.

"What the hell is that?" I asked, pointing to it.

"Ain't you never heard of a jackalope?" he asked. "It's a cross between a jack rabbit and an antelope."

"Bullshit," I said.

Howard smiled and said, "You ain't as gullible as some of the fellers that come in here, particularly them from back East. Otis

Mason put that together for me. You should see his shop down on Lawson Lane. When he has free time, he gets bored and starts mixing up all kinds of critters, and he makes them look real. Why I'll bet he'd be stuffing Apaches if he could get by with it. Ain't nothing he hates worse."

"Why's that?"

"An Apache killed his pa when he was a boy."

"What do you reckon got him started on mixing up animals?" I asked.

"He said he got the idea years ago when he heard about how P. T. Barnum had someone join a monkey's skull to a large fish. Barnum called it the Fiji Mermaid and made a lot of money with it in a circus sideshow."

Howard poured our drinks, and we raised our glasses and clinked them together. "To your new hotel," he said. "When are you going to start construction?"

"As soon as I can get the work hired out."

"If I were you, I'd talk to Aaron Fitch at the hardware store a few doors down. He'll give you the best prices."

As Howard had suggested, I did business with Aaron Fitch. I built the Ocean Grove Hotel and catered to lawyers and businessmen who came into town, reserving a couple of back rooms for the sole use of having women entertain men. From the beginning, I had in mind adding a restaurant to it one day.

I eventually made it to Lawson Lane to visit Otis Mason, the taxidermist. It turned out Otis Mason's shop was just the front room of his house. Otis was a tall, pudgy man with small hands. "Come in, come in!" he called from a workbench. "Come and see this," he said, without rising to greet me.

I walked over and found him meticulously stitching a frog's head to the body of a mouse. "Froggy went a-courtin', and this here's the result of that unholy union," he said, breaking into a laugh. "Tom Murphy commissioned this piece." I introduced myself, told him his friend Howard Muddler had suggested I come and see his work, admitted I probably wouldn't buy anything, but said I'd be delighted to tell others about his work.

"Well, that's just fine, Miss Sadie," he said. "Take a look around."

There were mounted heads of deer, antelopes, mountain lions, other animals, and many had tags with customers' names on them, ready for pickup. There were also a few complete specimens, including a bear, a wolf, and a coyote. Then I came to the corner where he kept his special creations and found a rattlesnake with a duck's head, a young pig with a dog's head, and a crow with the wings and feet of a bat. I marveled at how the bogus creatures were put together so well that they looked real.

Before I left, I told him I kept two rooms at the hotel for the purpose of entertaining gentlemen. "Come see me if you get lonely, and I'll find a lovely girl to keep you company."

"I'll do that," he said, and he held up his frog-mouse triumphantly. "Look-a here. It's finished."

"A true work of art," I said.

Eventually, I came to know most everyone who lived in Hillsboro. I had nearly forgotten about my old nemesis Pretty Face, a.k.a. Lady Claire, until I heard she that she had moved to Hillsboro and set up business. She came to town in March of 1894, probably for the same reason I did. It had been years since I'd had any contact with her. I wasn't pleased to learn she was in the same town, but I thought it didn't matter as long as she kept her distance, and, for a good while, she did. I heard she was still making herself out to be a spiritualist, and, aside from her practice of receiving customers, she was almost a recluse in the house she'd bought.

About a month later, I heard that the Mother Lode had burned to the ground, but everyone inside had been able to get out safely. It seemed odd to me in a house that big that no one would be hurt. I wondered if Joyous had torched it for the insurance money when times got tough. I never got a chance to ask her because she set out for California before I was able to visit with her.

On June 1, 1895, I went to Muddler's Saloon for a whiskey and some friendly banter. As I walked in, Howard Muddler rolled up his sleeves and said, "They say that within half an hour the business portion was in ashes."

"What are you talking about?" I asked.

"A fire broke out in Lake Valley before dawn," Howard said.

"Unbelievable loss for the business owners," Aaron Fitch said. "The poor bastards didn't have a chance, what with that high wind last night. On top of that, there wasn't any water in the town to fight the fire. All they had was what was in the residences."

"What all got burnt up?" I asked.

A bearded man I didn't know said, "The fire started in the Arcade Saloon, but it was empty at the time. Wind took it across the street and carried it two blocks. Keller, Miller, & Co. lost all their buildings and stock. It wiped out the Cotton building, the Chinamen's restaurant, Standish's drug store, the Handel Building, a barbershop, and the post office. Took my house, too. I'm here to stay with relatives."

"I'm sorry to hear that," I muttered, sidling up to the bar.

"Whiskey?" Howard asked, and I nodded.

"I saw them take the man who's charged with starting it into the jail earlier this morning," Aaron said, "a miner by the name of Albert Abernathy. I heard the people of Lake Valley were damned near ready to string him up, but I doubt he did it. He's a one-armed man, for god's sakes. People always want someone to blame."

"If he *is* guilty, I hope they hang him," the bearded man said. I nodded assent, but my mind was still on the news that the Chinamen's restaurant had burned. I wondered what Tom Ying and his partner would do.

The next day I took the stage to Lake Valley to view the ruined buildings. It was a startling sight, but there wasn't much to look at. The fire had totally consumed most of the buildings, and the wind had even taken the ashes away.

CHAPTER 26

In my first year in Hillsboro, I'd had a restaurant built onto the Ocean Grove and hired a middle-aged spinster named Nora to cook. I had money and prestige. Important men, including New Mexico Territory Governor William Thornton, asked for my opinions on issues because they thought I knew everything about everybody after years of keeping my famous black journal. Overall, I was satisfied with what I'd accomplished. I was still attractive, but I had given up any notion of getting married. I divorced the absent Casper McKelvey in April of 1895, and I never expected another romance in my life and didn't think I wanted it. I'd forgotten that people say romance is most likely to come when you aren't looking for it.

As the Fourth of July celebration drew near, I decided to attend all the local festivities. I had seen J. W. Orchard many times because he often drove the stage whenever I rode to Kingston or Lake Valley. He was the owner of the Lake Valley, Hillsboro, and Kingston Stage and Express Line, but I'd never spoken to him at any length until he danced with me at the Fourth of July celebration in Hillsboro in 1895. That day, a group of four miners formed a band and came into town to sing and play music on fiddle, guitar, bass, and mandolin.

When J. W. came over and asked if I'd like to dance, I could tell he'd been drinking, but so had almost everyone else, so I thought nothing of it. I liked the way he put his hands on my waist lightly, as if I were a fragile thing that he might break if he weren't careful. Then the band broke into "Cluck Old Hen," and he was swinging me around as the lead singer wailed the first verse.

The band took its time on the number, adding many verses. As we danced, I noticed that J. W. was an attractive man with his dark eyes, dark hair, and prominent moustache. He smiled and bowed to me when the song ended and said, "Thank you for the dance, ma'am."

"Thank you, Mr. Orchard."

"Please call me Henry," he said. "That's what my friends call me."

We didn't dance any more that day, but we talked a bit, and Henry invited me to sit in the driver's box with him and ride the stage along to Kingston that coming Saturday, and I accepted.

Come Saturday, July 6, the sun was shining that morning as we set out. Two passengers rode inside the Mountain Pride, as the stagecoach was called: T. N. Jobson, a bald-headed miner with white eyebrows, who said he was new to the area, and Jeb Morton, a younger man in a gray suit. The route we took was a winding descent through the Mimbres Mountains, which were part of the Black Range Mountains. Just outside of town, Henry leaned toward me and asked, "Have you ever driven a team of horses?"

I smiled and said, "Once." Then I told him about my experience when the Stanards and their pals tried to rob the stage. Henry let me take the reins, and I started driving that coach through a narrow canyon. At any moment, I expected Henry to take the reins back, but he didn't until it became too hard for me. I thought I simply wasn't strong enough to control the stage.

"I guess I won't make it as a stagecoach driver in these mountains, huh?"

Henry grinned, placed one big hand over both of mine, and said, "I think you'd do all right with more practice. I could teach you how to handle these horses if you'd care to learn."

As we approached town, we heard the most pitiful yelping I've ever heard. There, by the side of the road, was a tiny, white pup with a large, black splotch on its back. The little dog was all alone, no mother or siblings in sight. Henry stopped the coach and climbed down. I heard him croon, "Come here, little feller. It's okay." He picked it up, cradled it in his hands, and brought it to me. As soon as I took it, the little dog started licking my hands with its warm, pink tongue. Then Henry poured water from a canteen into his big palm and offered it to the little dog, which lapped it up quickly. He started to give it more, but I said, "That's probably enough for a little while. Too much too soon isn't good. Do you have anything we could feed it?"

"I have half of a leftover biscuit," he said, reaching for a basket under the driver's box. By this time, Jobson and Morten had climbed out to look at the puppy.

"I'll give you two bits for it," Jobson said.

"Sorry," said Henry, "but the lady wants to keep it." I did, of course. How Henry knew that without my telling him, I don't know. He found an old cleaning cloth under the driver's box and handed it to me. "Put this in your lap in case he pees," he said.

Our finding that little dog together was what cemented my relationship with J. W. "Henry" Orchard. I named the puppy Puddles after he peed in my lap, soaking through the cloth

Henry provided, but Puddles was a smart little dog, very easy to train. I loved him and carried him around in my skirt pocket until he got too big for that.

The next day, Henry and I took a picnic to the mountains and found a shady spot overlooking Lake Valley. Of course, we brought Puddles along. After we had our roast beef sandwiches and a bottle of wine, Henry started singing "Cluck Old Hen," but he stopped in the middle of the first verse to ask, "You remember dancing with me to this song on the Fourth of July?"

"Of course." I smiled, remembering the day, wondering if he was about to ask me to dance with him again right there on the mountain.

"I've always admired you," he said. "You have such a good sense for business."

"Why, thank you. You have a good sense for business, too, operating the stage line."

"Maybe," he said, "but maybe not so much." He picked up his hat and started twiddling with it. I waited to see if he wanted to discuss some particular problem he was having with the stage line, but he surprised me when he looked up and asked, "Have you ever thought about getting married? It seems to me, we'd do real well if we put our stakes in together."

Caught off guard, I was speechless for a moment, but I couldn't find a reason to say no. With Henry's name, I'd have an even higher level of respect in Kingston. In short, I thought he could give me everything I'd ever really wanted. "I think we'd do well together, too, so, yes, I'll marry you." Henry picked me up and started swinging me around, and we laughed until Puddles interrupted us with his pitiful cries after being left out of the celebration. I picked him up, kissed his head, and patted his little pink belly. "You're going to have a daddy now," I said.

★ ★ ★ ★ ★

Henry and I married on Wednesday, July 17, 1895. Elated, I wrote to my sisters to tell them the news. I also wrote to Thurston and Evonia and to Nellie, who was known to the world as Lillian Russell. Soon, gifts arrived—a crocheted tablecloth from my sister, Isabella; money from my other brothers and sisters; an exquisite silver tea service from Nellie; and a hand-sewn quilt from Evonia.

Chapter 27

By mid-August, I told Henry I wanted to learn to drive the stage, so he started working with me, teaching me how to handle a team of horses. We both agreed that it made sense for me to drive the stage because, that way, we'd be covered if one of our hired drivers was unable to work. I soon learned that it took strength and stamina to drive those horses. Although my stamina was far above average, I was a bit low on strength, and Henry sometimes had to take the reins from me to slow the horses. Soon, learning to drive the stage became a point of pride for me. I wanted to do something very few women could do. At that time, I didn't know of any other woman driving a stagecoach.

Instead of despairing, I talked my way to success. As I've said before, I've always known horses, and horses have always known me. Thinking my way through the problem, I decided to discuss it with each of our teams of horses. I'd explain and demonstrate my idea and say, "So, when you feel me give you the special signal, slow down. If you feel it again, stop. Then nobody will be hurting you, jerking on those reins, and, in return, I'll give each of you a little treat at the end of the run." Then I took each team out on an easy run and trained them.

Soon, instead of fighting the teams and pulling with all my strength against the reins, I was able to make them slow down with three light tugs on the reins and stop with three more. Moreover, they'd stop for me sooner than they'd stop for anyone else. They'd also take off for me upon hearing the sound of my cracking whip, which I'd snap at the ground or at rocks. I never used it on their backs. And I never failed to give them their treats at the end of a run—usually lumps of sugar. Once I'd proved to Henry that I could manage the horses on any of the trails we used, I became a fill-in stage driver.

Near the end of October of 1895, it happened that on my first solo run, some Apaches tried to steal my horses, but I was able to get the better of them. I told two ladies outside a mercantile store in Kingston about the experience several days later. The women had seen me drive the stage into town and asked about my unusual occupation.

"Well," I told them, "I didn't realize how dangerous it was when I started training for it. Just last week, a band of six Apache warriors attacked my stage near Hurricane Rock. I'd seen those red devils from a distance and had pushed the team to run as fast as they could. As we got closer, I saw the Apaches were nearly naked, wearing only breechclouts, and they were in full war paint with black, red, and white all over their faces." The women had frightened looks on their faces and appeared to be hanging onto every word.

"What did they do?" one of them asked. She was a chunky woman in a red and yellow dress.

"They caught up with me, came alongside my team, and tried to grab the harnesses to stop the stage. I believed they were set on stealing the horses, and there was no telling what they might do to me."

I paused until the chunky woman's companion, a middle-aged woman in a brown skirt, asked, "How did you stop them? Did you have a gun?"

"No, ma'am. I didn't. All I had was my whip, but I sure know how to use it. I could knock a flea off a dog's rear end with it. Every time one of them reached for the harnesses, I'd crack that whip across his hand, drawing blood, and he'd let go. The biggest Apache kept yelling at the others like a crazy man, so they'd try again, and I'd pop them again. Finally, the biggest one came alongside the team as if he were going to show them how to do it. When he leaned over to grab the harnesses, his breechclout flew up, so I cracked my whip hard across his hind end. Then he made a sound like 'Woo-woo-woo' and took off back toward Hurricane Rock, and the others followed him. That was the last I saw of those warriors."

The two women stood there gaping for a moment, and the chunky one said, "I'm so glad you were able to send them packing."

Her friend nodded and said, "So glad you weren't robbed or worse."

Then I heard a bray of laughter in the background and spotted my old friend Vashti doubled over by a water barrel beside the livery. "Oh, that's rich, Sadie. That's rich," she said, when she could catch her breath.

"Do you find it amusing for a white woman to be accosted by a band of wild Indians?" I asked, and the women beside me gave her a baleful look.

"Naw, I just think that's the funniest story I've heard in a long time." I frowned at her, sighed, and shook my head.

Later, when I found Vashti in a nearby saloon, we had a beer together, and she told me she had married a buffalo soldier by the name of Barret Jones and had two little girls. I congratulated her, and, after we had chatted for a while, she asked, "Why you be telling tales to them silly bitches that don't know a thing about Apaches? You come near making me pee."

"The bloody thing happened," I insisted.

Vashti shook her head. "If six Apache warriors wanted yo' horses, you'd-a never seen 'em 'til they was right up on you,

Indiscretions Along Virtue Avenue

and them horses would be gone, and you'd either be dead or taken as a slave."

"You're wrong. You weren't there, and you don't know cack about what happened."

Vashti snorted, dropped her backwoods English, and said, "What happened is that you were born full of shit, and you still are."

The stage line had other attempted stage robberies, of course. Once I used my whip to run off a group of young hoodlums who were hoping to steal a cash shipment. Another time, our employee, Bill Holt, fooled some outlaws by claiming a cash shipment of $175,000 had gone out the day before, when, in fact, he had hidden the cash in two of the horses' collars. The would-be robbers searched the stage just the same, but they didn't find the money, so we rewarded Bill with a hundred dollars for his cunning. Eventually, I came to like driving the stage so much that I started driving every day for a while.

Being married to Henry seemed like a fairytale in those first years of our marriage. He'd been renting a room from a family in town, so we decided to live at the Ocean Grove Hotel. He wanted me to be happy, so he gave me lovely things. One of my favorite gifts from Henry was a gramophone that played recorded music from flat discs. I'd sit in our parlor in the evenings and listen to symphonies. On our first anniversary, he gave me a beautiful, black stallion I named Onyx. Then he took a notion to build another hotel, and that's how the Orchard Hotel came to be. We moved our residence there.

In the bedroom, he treated me like a fragile thing, and I loved to lie in his arms, where he'd hold me and touch me for hours. I couldn't help but love him. It seemed that even the everyday aggravations of business couldn't mar our happiness.

193

In those days, we were friends with Cecil and Sarah Smith, a couple near our age. Cecil owned an assay office. Sarah was a petite, blonde-haired woman with highly refined manners, who blushed whenever I cursed in her presence. By saying we were friends, I meant that Henry and I would have supper with them or go to dances with them from time to time. I tried to be friends with Sarah, but we never made a connection. She and Cecil were childless, and she'd confided in me that she'd had three miscarriages in the first five years of their marriage.

One day we all rode the stage to Lake Valley to spend the day and attend a dance that night. Sarah and I shopped while Cecil and Henry played billiards in the Arcade Saloon. As we looked at dresses, hats, gloves, and lingerie, I noticed that, if I said I liked something, Sarah would invariably say she didn't like it. Finally, I said, "It's okay, Sarah. I can tell there's something about me you just don't like. What is it?"

Her face colored, and she said, "I've heard about the rooms you reserve so men can romp with whores at the Ocean Grove, and that's your business, but if you like slutty garments, you shouldn't expect me to like them, too. We're here together only because our husbands are friends." From that day forward, we carefully made our way through our so-called friendship while our husbands spent time together.

The Ocean Grove Hotel and the Orchard Hotel were both located across from the Union Hotel. Because of the fire in Lake Valley, I was able to convince Tom Ying, the Chinaman, who was now widely recognized in the area as a fine chef, to come and cook for us at the Ocean Grove. His former partner had moved out of the area. Nora, my spinster cook, was not happy to hear this, but she brightened up when I offered to let her do housekeeping at the hotels until she could find another job as a cook. Within two weeks, she was cooking breakfast and lunch at the Black Range Café.

Since Henry and I also had the stage line and corrals, we employed eight men full time and several other part-time workers with our stage business in addition to several clerks, waitresses, and maids. We owned two eight-hundred-dollar coaches and an express wagon, and we were paid to carry the mail, so our stages ran whether there were any paying passengers or not.

I hadn't had a dog before I met Henry, but now we had Puddles and Henry's hunting dogs, Muddy and Copper. We also had many horses, so we could switch out the teams at certain stops between towns. I loved all the horses, but I especially loved Long Shot and Onyx, and they were never hitched to a stage. I'd take them both for a ride in the afternoons. Every time I left on one of them, Puddles and our other dogs would run alongside me for a ways. Though Onyx was technically a much finer horse, I didn't have the heart to ride Onyx without also taking Long Shot for a ride. This took more time, of course, but it was time I enjoyed.

One day, I came in on Onyx and found a colored boy waiting by the stable. "Ma'am," he said, "I've noticed how you ride both these horses every day and take care of them yourself, but there's no need for you to saddle and curry them horses when you could hire me to do it for you."

"You look a little young to manage all that," I said.

"Oh, I can manage it," he said. "I'm nearly thirteen. I'll do it the first time for free just to prove it."

His eagerness to find work reminded me of Silas, the boy I'd hired to carry my bags when I left the Victorio Hotel and moved into Joyous Lee's place. This boy was wearing waist overalls, a dirty, white shirt, and a straw hat, and he was barefooted. He only appeared to be about eleven years old. "What's your name?"

"My name's Josiah, but everybody just call me Boots."

I dismounted, and Boots took the reins and started removing my sidesaddle from Onyx. "I'll have that brown horse saddled up lickety-split, ma'am. Then I'll rub this'n down."

I was about to remind him that I hadn't agreed to anything yet, but then I noticed how well Onyx was cooperating with him. Onyx didn't usually take well to strangers. "Do it right, and you won't be doing it for free just to prove yourself."

I was quite pleased with his work. From that day forth, Boots was forever hanging about the hotels, ready to run errands or help with chores, and he took pride in his work. Once I saw him struggling to carry two buckets of water at once, and one of our guests called out to him, "Looks like you've bit off more than you can chew, you little runt."

I had to smile when Boots called back, "I ain't no runt. I'm Miz Orchard's stable manager."

Back then, Henry and I kept a small table reserved for us in the restaurant, where we had our meals together as often as possible, and Tom Ying would lay out delicious spreads. I remember one evening we were waiting on our supper when a chubby, blonde waitress named Mary came to our table, red-nosed and teary-eyed, saying, "I'm sorry, Mrs. Orchard. I just can't work here anymore."

Before she could explain, I heard a stream of profanity flowing out of the kitchen, and Tom Ying came into the dining room in his black skullcap yelling, "Sadie Orchard, tell bloody bitches to get back in kitchen! Food pile up! They no serve!" Our guests were looking at me, and I realized they needed their food. Just then, I spotted Nancy, our other waitress, a willowy brunette, who was about to walk out the door.

I called, "Nancy! Mary! Get these customers' food served at once!" It was enough to send them scurrying back to the kitchen.

When the restaurant had cleared, and they were cleaning up, I asked them what that big fiasco was all about. "Tom Ying tried to kill us," Mary said.

"He chased us with a big chopping knife!" Nancy added.

I bit my lip to keep from smiling, knowing that Tom had once chased a man down a street in Lake Valley while brandishing a knife. "Oh, for goodness sakes," I said. "I find that hard to believe."

"He said we were stealing his spices," Mary whimpered, her eyes welling up again.

"Tom Ying is as gentle as a lamb," I said. "You both need work, don't you?"

They nodded, so I said, "Why don't you come back tomorrow and give it one more day?" They agreed, and the next day, Tom Ying apologized to them for frightening them and calling them thieves. I didn't have to ask Tom what had happened because I already knew. Like Henry, Tom drank. Every blue moon, he'd come to work drunk, but I never said a word to him about it, thinking he cooked even better when he was drunk.

CHAPTER 28

On February 1, 1896, a tragic event took place when Colonel Albert Fountain and his eight-year-old son disappeared while traveling near White Sands, New Mexico, about seventy miles from Hillsboro. Fountain, a Republican and an attorney, who had just been to Lincoln and gotten indictments against about thirty men, all Democrats, for cattle rustling, had been headed back to his home in Las Cruces, which is more than seventy miles from Hillsboro. He had many enemies, and he had received death threats. I followed the story in the newspapers and local gossip as many men, including Mescalero Apache trackers, searched for the Fountains.

From what I heard, Fountain's wife had insisted he take the boy with him to Lincoln because she believed no one would attack him along the way if he had a child with him. Men scoured the land looking for the Fountains and gathering evidence, assuming they'd been murdered. Many people believed the rancher Oliver Lee was behind the killings. I knew Lee, who had stayed at the Ocean Grove several times, and I thought he might kill Fountain, but I didn't believe there was any way he'd kill the boy, so I wasn't quick to jump to any conclusions. The bodies of the Fountains were never found. At the time, I had no notion that a trial for the murder of little Henry Fountain would be set in Hillsboro and help Henry and me earn a lot of money about three years later.

★　★　★　★　★

The whores who worked at the Ocean Grove came and went, as all whores did, so I seldom had the same one employed for more than two years. These girls stayed in small cabins across the creek, and, by that, I mean the Percha River. Because it was so small, everyone in town called the Percha a creek. I'd send Boots for the girls when they were needed. Because of this, we had the perfect setup to make a whale of a lot of money later when the so-called "trial of the century" came to Hillsboro, the one in which Oliver Lee and James Gilliland were tried for the murder of little Henry Fountain.

In the U.S. presidential election on November 3, 1896, William McKinley, a Republican, defeated William Jennings Bryan, and, being Democrats, Henry and I were not pleased. This was the same year Henry Ford introduced his first vehicle, the Ford Quadricycle. I felt the world was changing for the better, so it was a grand time to be alive. I'd say the years between 1896 and 1899 were some of the best times of my life. In those days, Henry and I still were tender with one another. He drank, of course, but not so much that it caused any problems between us.

When Oliver Lee's trial came up in June of 1899, my old friend Albert Fall, who'd been my first customer at the Mother Lode, was the leading defense attorney. Judge Franklin Parker, Albert, and his team of attorneys were staying at the Orchard Hotel. By this time, Albert was both an attorney and a politician.

Both our hotels were full, due to all the witnesses, reporters, and spectators from out of town, and the stage line did a lively business as well. I can't decide which worked harder during the trial, the stage-line horses or my girls across the creek. The trial spanned from May 26 through June 12 of 1899. From time to time, I'd go to the courtroom early enough to get a seat, so I heard the testimony of several witnesses, including Pat Garrett and former governor William Thornton, a.k.a. "Poker Bill," witnesses for the prosecution, and Mary Lee and Deputy Tom Tucker, witnesses for the defense.

My heart went out to the Fountain family, but I was very glad when Lee and Gilliland were acquitted because I strongly felt the circumstantial evidence just wasn't strong enough to support a conviction. I knew many of my friends were happy as well, so I decided to throw a supper party to celebrate their victory in court. It was near midnight when the verdict came on June 12—this being because it had been late when all the closing arguments were made, and Judge Parker was about to adjourn until the next morning when Albert Fall requested that the judge allow the jury to begin their deliberations immediately.

After the verdict was given, I rushed to find Tom Ying and tell him my plans for a supper party. Henry had gone out of town that day to look at some horses, and I didn't expect him back until the next day, so I was unable to consult with him on my party plans.

Tom lived in a small house near the Ocean Grove, but he wasn't at home. He wasn't in the kitchen at the Ocean Grove, so I took a lantern and went down into the basement of the Orchard Hotel to check on our provisions. That's where I found Tom, lying on a pile of burlap sacks, smoking opium. Except for my lantern, the only light was from the small flame in the brass opium lamp he used to heat his pipe. "Ah, Sarah Jane," he said. "You look happy tonight." I always liked it when he called me Sarah Jane because it took me back to my childhood every time he spoke it. I had given him my full name when I'd arrived in the area years earlier, and he'd never forgotten it. But he also understood that it was just to be used between the two of us.

Tom used a scraper to remove the dross from his pipe bowl, and then he picked up a long opium needle to stab another opium "pill." This he held over the flame in his lamp for a moment before placing it in the bowl of his long pipe.

"Yes, I'm happy tonight," I said. "Oliver Lee was found not guilty, and I want to make a supper party to celebrate." I knew he heard me, but, instead of discussing the party, he shifted on the burlap bags and patted the space beside him. "If you're happy, it's a good time to try pipe. You'll be even happier and sleep well."

"Tom, you know I couldn't," I said, but I was curious about this drug that promised euphoria.

Tom smiled and said nothing when I settled beside him, took the pipe to my lips, and breathed in the vapor, as he helped me hold the pipe over the lamp. Soon, I felt like I was floating in a river, looking at the stars. I don't know why it seemed that way. Perhaps he suggested it, but I could see the stars just the same. I leaned back against his shoulder, and he told me the Chinese names for many stars as I floated there.

At dawn, I awakened, untouched and fully dressed, on a sofa in the lobby of the Orchard Hotel. I followed the smell of frying steak and bacon to Tom's kitchen, where he was already marinating a side of beef for my party. I knew Tom had carried me up the basement stairs while I was sleeping as if I were a ragdoll, but we never spoke a word of what had happened the night before. I hadn't meant it to be a sensual encounter, but it was, although there was no sex involved. My mind kept returning to the feel of lying beside Tom Ying with my head on his shoulder. I felt I had betrayed Henry and decided it would never happen again.

I tried to put the encounter out of mind and quickly set about inviting guests, including Judge Parker, the Lee and Gilliland families, Cecil and Sarah Smith, Howard Muddle, Aaron Fitch, Hulene Venable, and Sylvia Crosswell.

Oliver Lee and James Gilliland were still in jail, pending their trials for the murders of Albert Fountain and Kent Kearny, a man they'd killed at the Wildy Well shootout when Pat Garrett tried to arrest them. Lee and Gilliland said they refused to surrender to Garrett because they feared he intended to kill them and claim they had tried to escape. They later turned themselves in to Judge Parker in Las Cruces.

That morning, I went to the jail to see Sheriff George Curry, of Otero County, who was there because he was officially in custody of Lee and Gilliland. I invited him and his prisoners, and he agreed to bring Lee and Gilliland to my supper party after they agreed not to try to escape.

Around two o'clock, a boy came with a message from Sarah Smith, asking if it would be all right if she invited a friend to my supper party, so I sent word that it would be fine as we had plenty of food. That evening the Smiths were the first to arrive. "I invited my friend, Lady Claire, but she wasn't able to make it," Sarah said.

"That's too bad," I said, not letting her see my irritation and thankful Lady Claire hadn't spoiled the evening for me by showing up. "I'm sure she would have added some entertainment to the evening. I've seen her do magic tricks, making it appear she pulls flowers and coins out of midair."

"She pulls those things out of the spirit world," Sarah said.

"It's hard to believe she has any special powers because real spiritualists make more impressive displays. I was at a meeting once where Madame Suydam, known as the Fire Queen of Chicago, bathed herself in fire. Now that was impressive. I think Lady Claire is just a two-bit fake. If she has real powers, she should display them more strongly, and you can tell her I said so. Do you think Lady Claire could bathe herself in fire? I truly doubt it."

Sarah was starting to get red in the face. "I'm sure she could if she thought there was a reason for it. She's highly attuned to the spirit world."

"If you say so," I said before turning away to greet other guests. "Tell her she ought to look for something new. People get bored with the same old stuff." Of course, I was trying to irritate Sarah, but I figured she'd repeat what I'd said to Pretty Face, and it would be enough to goad her as well.

That evening, we served plates of tender beef with mashed potatoes, asparagus tips, and sweet corn, with peach pie for dessert. Oliver's mother, Mary Lee, remarked, "I'll declare, that Chinaman has just outdone himself on this meal." After the ladies and children in the Lee and Gilliland families were settled into their hotel rooms, the party became more boisterous, and we made sure the whiskey flowed freely that night. Oliver Lee obviously appreciated the celebration quite a bit because he told me, "Sadie, once all the dust settles and I'm back on my ranch, you come to me if you ever need help with anything. You'll find you have a friend."

CHAPTER 29

The next day, life returned to a normal pace, and Hillsboro seemed a peaceful place without a flood of out-of-towners. As was our custom, Henry and I sat on the porch of the Ocean Grove Hotel after supper, and some of our hotel guests joined us. Puddles, ever loyal, sat right by my chair and had little to do with anyone else. Henry claimed it was because I brought him bits of food from the supper table, so, to prove a point, I had Henry give Puddles his after-supper treats the next night. As I expected, Puddles took them from Henry and came straight to me.

In those days, Henry and I told people the secret to our happiness was mutual respect, but that happiness began to wear thin after the death of Henry's friend and drinking buddy, Harlow Terrell. On March 10, 1900, Harlow was found dead behind the Black Range Café without a mark on his body. There was no sign of foul play or evidence that he'd committed suicide. Henry grieved for months. He began to brood over Harlow's death and became obsessed with finding out how and why it had happened.

I didn't know it at the time, but Henry began seeking help from Lady Claire. I honestly had no idea because Henry and I gave ourselves a weekly allowance that we could spend at our own discretion without any discussion between us, so I didn't say a word to him when I noticed he was spending more than usual. Aside from purchasing clothing he needed, he bought very little, except whiskey. I figured the money was spent on drinking or gambling, but what did it matter? I certainly wouldn't have wanted him looking over my shoulder every time I bought something that struck my fancy. After a few weeks, his spending leveled out, and I thought no more about it.

Soon afterwards, Henry became very critical of me. When I purchased grain for our livestock, he'd bellyache and say I paid too much, sometimes raising his voice at me. Worse, he didn't care who overheard him when he was angry. Many times, he'd start his ranting in the Ocean Grove Restaurant, and I'd see Tom Ying look out from the kitchen for a moment and close the door, or I'd see customers glance in our direction.

Back in our quarters, I'd curse him and insult everything from his appearance to his manhood. When I took Long Shot out in the afternoons, I'd tell him my troubles. Then I'd take Onyx galloping up into the Black Range.

Henry and I argued, even to the point where our differences were written up in the *Sierra County Advocate* on August 10, 1900. That particular argument started on Sunday, August 5, when Henry accused me of paying too much for a load of used shoes I'd purchased for use in repairing the brake blocks on the stagecoach.

"The bloody hell I did, you gormless rotter," I said. "We got a hundred pounds more than in the last load for just a wee bit more." Jackass stubborn, he insisted I was wrong.

"Just let me tend to buying supplies from now on!" he yelled.

"We'd never have things when we needed them if I did, you prat. The only friggin' supplies you're capable of maintaining are bottles of whiskey. I think they've addled your brain."

With that, I left the room and went out into the front yard, and Henry scrambled after me. He pulled his pistol and said, "I'm telling you, you're not to order any more supplies for the stage line."

I pushed my face up to his and said, "I'll order anything I damn well please for the stage line, the hotels, the restaurant, or anything else. Now, give me that gun, you minging bell end!" I reached for the gun and tried to take it from him, and, in the scuffle, he fired a shot into the trees. Then Henry dropped the pistol on the ground and stomped off down Elenora Street.

I could hardly believe it when he returned with Sheriff Max Kahlar and started squalling that I'd tried to kill him. The sheriff asked me if this were so, and I said, "Hell, no! If I'd tried to kill him, he'd be dead! You should know that without even asking, you gormless tosser."

Kahlar asked where the gun was, and I took it out of my pocket. He said, "Ma'am, I'm placing you under arrest for assault with a deadly weapon with intent to kill."

"Why?"

"Well, it's clear you have Henry's gun on your person."

I bristled and said, "Did you expect me to leave the bloody gun laying out on the ground after he ran off?" It took me a while to compose myself enough to explain how the whole thing had started as an argument. "I never even had the revolver in my hand," I said. "I was trying to take it away from that knob head, and he was angry, and he either tried to kill me or squeezed off a shot by accident."

Even though I told the truth, Henry wouldn't back off his story, and Kahlar didn't believe me, so I spent the night in jail, which was enough to make me want to kill Henry.

Then Henry came to the sheriff's office the next day, upset and apologetic, and told the sheriff he wanted to dismiss the charges. I was still of a mind to curse him, but, that morning, I'd cooled off a bit, so, when the sheriff released me, I just asked, "Henry, what the bloody hell got into you? Don't you realize you've dragged our names through the mud?"

"I don't know," he said, as we walked toward home. His

hands were trembling. "A spiritualist, Lady Claire, warned me that you'd be my destruction. When that gun went off, I thought you'd caused it. Now I see it was my fault."

Upon hearing that he'd had dealings with Pretty Face, I laid a cursing on him that left his ears burning. Looking back, I suppose I should have told him about my history with the so-called Lady Claire when we got home. He might have understood and stayed away from her if I had.

The next day, around one, I walked over and stood outside Lady Claire's house on Grayson Street. I wasn't moving my mouth with soundless words as she had outside the Horny Toad years ago but rather just waiting, and I didn't have to wait long. She opened her door and said, "I see a wolf behind you, Mrs. Orchard." She was wearing a black dress, but she didn't have a veil over her face, and she was wearing her eternal smirk.

Her words startled me at first, but then I figured someone had told her the unusual circumstances surrounding Tom Beeson's death. I thought it wouldn't hurt to let her think I believed it was there, so I smiled and asked, "Do you fear evil, Pretty Face? Take a good look at that wolf. It's a part of me."

"Why do you call me Pretty Face?"

"I think you know, you piss-drinking weasel, and if you don't stay away from my husband, I'll make you wish you had."

She took a step forward and said, "He won't be your husband for long. I'll bring you to nothing."

"All right, you pretentious slag. You're a slow learner, but I'll take you back to school." I was trembling, not with fear but with rage.

Pretty Face smiled and said, "Don't threaten me in that phony English accent, Curly Kate. You should go home and check on Long Shot."

A new rage arose in me as I realized that Henry had given

her intimate details, even down to the name of my beloved horse. I shook a fist at her and said, "You should know better than to tangle with me."

When I got back to the Orchard Hotel, I didn't want to go to the stable, but I couldn't help myself. Long Shot was fine, except for a place on his flank that looked like his skin had been torn by a bit of barbed wire. I put salve on the wound and fed him an apple from the palm of my hand.

Several days later, Boots came running into the office at the Orchard Hotel yelling, "Miz Orchard, something the matter with Long Shot! He won't stand up!"

"What are you talking about?" I asked. "He was fine yesterday."

Tears welled in Boots's eyes and spilled over. "I don't know, ma'am. Something bad wrong with him now. He twitchin', and he won't eat, so I put a blanket over him."

I ran with him to the stable and found Long Shot in pitiful condition. He appeared to be having convulsions. "Go quickly, Boots, and get Doc Alston. Tell him somebody may have poisoned Long Shot." Of course, I was ready to kill Pretty Face if she had poisoned my horse.

While Boots ran off, I sat in the straw and clung to my precious horse, trying to comfort him. About fifteen minutes later, Doc Alston arrived and took one look at Long Shot. "Tetanus," he said, "better known as lockjaw." He quickly found the wound on Long Shot's flank. "See this? The puncture wound is what caused it."

"Are you sure?" I asked. "I think someone may have poisoned him. Besides, I put salve on that wound. Can you pump his stomach? Can you—"

He held up one hand and said, "Sadie, all I can do is end his suffering. Suppose you and Boots go over to the hotel office for a minute."

I looked at Long Shot, saw the wild look on his face from where his facial muscles were in spasm, and nodded. I said, "Walk with me, Boots."

We had no sooner gotten into the office than we heard the shot, so I turned and went back outside with Boots following close behind me. I offered to pay Doc Alston, but he shook his head and walked back toward Main Street.

Boots stood in the stable beside me in his waist overalls, and I wanted him to leave, but I wouldn't tell him to go because I knew he loved Long Shot, too. I settled onto the hay beside Long Shot and felt a warm hand on my shoulder, and then Boots was there on the straw with me in that stall, and I put my arm around his waist and pulled him closer so he could touch Long Shot, too, and we cried together.

CHAPTER 30

That evening, I had it out with Henry over his visits to Lady Claire, and he promised he wouldn't see her again. I didn't tell him about my encounter with her earlier that week, but I did ask if she'd ever given him "gifts" from his old friend, Harlow Terrell. He said she hadn't, but she'd been able to conjure Harlow so that he could speak to him. "Do you really believe that? Don't you think she's just faking it?"

Henry shook his head. "It was real. Don't get me wrong: I know everything she does isn't real because she told me so. Sometimes, when the spirits don't show up and she has a paying customer, she'll put on an act, but she says that doesn't happen very often."

I should have wondered why Pretty Face had admitted any fakery to Henry. I should have seen they were getting too close. "Did he tell you how he died?" I asked.

"No," Henry said, smoothing his moustache with his fingers. "Harlow will talk about old times and people we know—anything but that."

Henry's drinking became worse over the next few months, but he wasn't a mean drunk, and it didn't keep him from rolling out of bed every day and going to work, so it didn't trouble me much. Our relationship was still strained at that point, but we were intimate occasionally, and I longed for the days when we'd been happy.

Then Henry took to sleeping in a separate bedroom. I missed having him make love to me, but, for the longest time, I was too proud to admit it to him. I started trying to be particularly nice to Henry in hopes of healing the relationship. I had no idea he was leaving his bed in the middle of the night and tromping down Elenora Street to spend time with Lady Claire. I should have known her whorish charms and the lure of a chance to talk with his old friend Harlow would be too much for him to resist.

On February 25, 1901, I was awakened by pounding on the Orchard Hotel office door, so I put on a robe and took my pistol downstairs to find out what was going on. Sheriff Kahlar informed me that someone had tried to burn the express office between eleven o'clock and midnight, and he asked for Henry. I went upstairs to get dressed and couldn't find Henry, so I went to the scene and learned the fire had first been discovered by W. H. Bucher, cashier for the Sierra County Bank, who was on his way home from a saloon. Witnesses said several men came out of Short's Place, a nearby bar, and put out the fire. We had four horses in the stable at the time, so I would forever be grateful to Will John Reay, who cut them loose. Reay pointed out there was no one in the office when the fire started, but someone had saturated part of the stable with coal oil. Firefighters also found the water pump disconnected. I thanked each of the men who'd helped at the scene and invited them all to come and have a free meal at the Ocean Grove Restaurant. Everyone kept asking me where Henry was, so I told them he was probably in one of the bars or saloons.

In the days that followed, some speculated that Henry tried to burn the place for the insurance money. Of course, I'd considered that possibility, since he was nowhere to be found that evening, but then I didn't really believe Henry would put our horses at risk of death by fire. He was too kind-hearted toward animals for that. Others thought I did it, which was completely ridiculous.

When I asked him about it, Henry said, "If you knew me, you'd know I didn't do it." He stood in the doorway of the Orchard Hotel, holding his hat and twiddling with it.

"Then where were you that night?"

"That's none of your business!"

I tried to get to the bottom of the matter, as I had my sources of information, but I never found out how it happened. Needless to say, I wondered if Pretty Face had anything to do with it.

I was a bit upset when Henry decided to partner with Dr. A. G. Brower on the development of the Dude mine on the Machio in Sierra County around March of 1902. I argued that Henry wasn't a miner, that he didn't know what he was getting into. The tension in our marriage increased even more when Henry lost the mail bid that year. We had a bitter fight when he told me the amount he was planning to bid, and I told him he should bid higher, but he refused. It seemed to me he was purposely losing the bid. Looking back, I feel sure he was listening to Pretty Face instead of me in all the decisions he made. He then sold the stage line to Fred W. Mister in the first week of August that year and soon began doing contract grade work on the Santa Fe Central Railroad, work that kept him out of town much of the time. Though he came home from time to time, it was clear to me that he considered us separated.

In the fall of 1902, coyotes became overabundant in the county, so Sierra County offered a bounty on coyote scalps. Tom Ying was fond of hunting coyotes, and he was very good at it, though it took a lot of skill to track and kill the skittish creatures. Sometime in October, the *Sierra County Advocate* reported the payouts for coyote scalps to eleven different hunters, and Tom

Ying received the highest amount, which was twenty dollars. However, taking time to hunt soon became a problem for Tom in the late fall, leaving him little time for sleep, and it began to interfere with his work as chef at the Ocean Grove. We talked about this and agreed that he should take a break from the kitchen work for a while.

In early December, I hired Amos Booker to take his place with the understanding that it would be a temporary job. On mid-December, I ran an ad in the *Sierra County Advocate* announcing Amos was chef at the Ocean Grove.

When it was time to redeem scalp certificates again, Tom Ying again outdid all the other hunters in the county. In January of 1903, the *Sierra County Advocate* reported that Tom received thirty-four dollars for the scalps he turned in. The next best was G. L. Rosner, who received twenty-two dollars. Twenty-eight hunters were listed. When I read it, I felt proud of Tom. The bounty on coyotes ended when their numbers had dwindled sufficiently.

After that, Tom took some time off to do repairs around his house, and it worked out well. By the time he was ready to return to work at the Ocean Grove, Amos Booker was ready to move on.

At this point, it had been more than two years since I'd threatened Pretty Face, and I hadn't done anything to make good on my threat, mostly because I hadn't heard another word from her. She'd predicted that Henry wouldn't be my husband long, but I saw I didn't have to take her word as the gospel—my marriage didn't have to fall apart.

Around this time, I started to dream of setting things right with Henry and being happy again. On March 1, 1903, I purchased a silky, red nightgown and some new perfume made with roses and jasmine. I had a bath that afternoon and asked Tom Ying to prepare a fine cut of rib-eye, mixed vegetables, and baked potatoes for supper. I dressed in a shimmering pink, satin dress, brushed my hair into a sheen, and went down to eat at the table reserved for us at the Ocean Grove. Henry looked dapper that evening, and, having just visited the barber's shop, he smelled of lime and spearmint aftershave. He was pleasant and suggested we enjoy a glass of whiskey with the meal.

After supper, I went upstairs, changed into my new nightgown, and waited for Henry to come upstairs. Soon, I met him at the top of the stairs and invited him to join me in bed. He looked at me for a moment and said, "I'm sorry. I can't." I thought he meant he was having some trouble common to men and was worried about his performance.

"Henry, it doesn't matter. I just want you to hold me," I said.

Again, he shook his head and said, "I can't."

"Why?" I asked, with tears slipping down my face for the first time in I couldn't remember how long.

He shook his head and said, "Go to sleep, Sadie." With that, he lumbered off toward the small bedroom he'd been using. I stood there staring after him until he closed the door, and then I went to our bed and cried.

Chapter 31

The next morning, my tears had evaporated, leaving nothing but fury in their place. Over our noon meal, I asked, "Why can't you cuddle with your wife every now and then, you good-for-nothing rotter?"

Henry folded his napkin and gave me a sad look. "Consarn it, Sadie! Because it wouldn't be right. Claire would know, and she holds my heart now. I'm powerful sorry, Sadie, but a man can't help who he loves."

I felt as if a thunderbolt had crashed inside my chest. "He can if he doesn't go sniffing around her in the first place." I ran back to our bedroom and got the shotgun with every intention of killing him. He must have sensed it, for he was already outside and running through the yard when I fired at him. I saw some blood fly as a few lead shots pierced his left ear, and the gun recoiled, bruising my shoulder. I was a terrible shot when I was angry. Henry kept running while I fumbled to reload. "You'd better run!" I yelled. "And you'd better not come back again!"

On my way back into the Ocean Grove, I ran into Tom Ying, who was coming out because of the commotion. Tom took the shotgun from me and asked, "You need I should shoot him for you?" His phrasing made me laugh, but then I started crying and collapsed onto the floor. Tom picked me up, placed me in a soft chair, and asked, "What's wrong, Sarah Jane?"

"He's taken up with that lowlife fortune-teller," I moaned.

"He's a fool," Tom said, and he patted me on the shoulder

and returned to the kitchen. A few minutes later, he came back and offered me a cup.

"What's this?"

"Special drink for when husband take up with fortune-teller." The steaming brew tasted like bitter hot cocoa with cinnamon and another spice I couldn't name. I drank it, went to my bed, slept until the next morning, and awakened feeling calm and rested.

Around noon that day, Henry sent Cecil Smith, to ask if he could come back and get his personal belongings. I said, "Yes, but he'd best be quick about it and not say one word to me while he packs his things." A little while later, Henry came in a buckboard. Paying no attention to what I'd told Cecil, he tried to speak to me while he packed his clothes. "Sadie, I never set out to hurt you. It hurts my heart that I hurt you and—" He shut up right quick when he heard me cock my pistol. Henry took his clothing and other personal belongings, including his hunting dogs, Muddy and Copper, and left without another word.

I went to my stable and talked to Onyx that day, but I didn't have the heart to ride him. Not wanting my horse to be kept in on a sunny day because of my mood, I asked Boots to take him for a good ride in my place, knowing they'd both enjoy it. Instead of going back to my room when Boots rode out on Onyx, I settled onto a pile of hay, and Puddles soon joined me. He proved just as good a listener as Onyx. "Your daddy took up with a pretentious, ignorant slut," I said, "so he doesn't live with us anymore." Puddles whimpered, so I rolled him over and rubbed his belly to cheer him up. I leaned over and kissed his ear. "Your daddy can go straight to hell." Puddles gave me a doggy smile, rolled over, and crawled onto my lap.

★ ★ ★ ★ ★

In the days that followed, it seemed to me that Puddles was grieving as well, probably more over the absence of Henry's dogs, Copper and Muddy, than the absence of Henry. Because of this, I decided to give him extra attention. I even asked Boots to take a bit of time to throw sticks for Puddles to retrieve each day.

Tom Ying understood my sorrow as no one else did. One morning, I found a vase of desert wildflowers on the table where I took breakfast, along with a sheet of white paper covered in Chinese writing. I took it into the kitchen later that morning when he was cleaning the stove and smiled at him. "Where did the flowers come from, Tom?"

"Before daylight, I took lantern and gathered them for you before they open."

"Did you leave one of your grocery lists on my table?" I asked, smiling and knowing he hadn't.

"No, I leave note for Sarah Jane. It say you are strong and beautiful woman, and I hope you soon smile again."

All my life, I'd been a proud woman. Not wanting to admit that another woman had taken my husband, I told folks I'd run Henry off because his drinking had gotten out of hand. I made up a story about how he'd hid whiskey in my grandfather clock, causing it to stop, which had been the last straw. Since Henry had been discreet in his affair with Pretty Face, people believed me. They made jokes about how Henry's ears looked like a couple of colanders after I'd finished with him.

After Henry left, I was tormented, thinking of him holding Pretty Face in his arms as he'd once held me. I felt stupid for not realizing what was going on before Henry told me. The hardest part was thinking that Pretty Face had won. Once again, she'd taken away something that mattered most to me. I sorely wished I'd killed her with that shovel years ago.

Feeling beaten and tired, I wished she'd disappear. I was too weak to deal with her. I expected any day to hear news that Henry had moved in with her, but then I learned that he'd taken to staying at Cecil Smith's house when he was in town. I wondered what Henry and Pretty Face were planning.

One day around three o'clock, I took a walk down Main Street, stopping occasionally to window shop. I started to go into T. G. Long's dry goods store just as Sarah Smith was coming out. She said, "Hello, Sadie. It's awkward, isn't it?" She looked beautiful standing there with little wisps of blonde hair about her face that had escaped her upswept hairdo. Her eyes looked clear and strong.

Standing there, I remembered that she'd had miscarriages and had a sudden flash of insight. "It was you, wasn't it?"

"Pardon?"

"You're the one who told Henry about Lady Claire after Harlow Terrell's death, aren't you?"

She pressed her lips together and nodded. "He needed help. I've been seeing her for years, and I can't tell you how much Lady Claire helped me after I lost my babies. She showed me that my babies are little spirits that can talk to their mama plain as day." Sarah looked skyward as her face took on a deeper glow.

I stood there, trembling on the inside with an unspeakable sense of loss. Sarah Smith had brought my whole world into disarray by sending Henry to my enemy, and my brain wasn't allowing me to respond with rage as I wished I could. She'd been deceived by Pretty Face, and her sincere desire to help Henry had torn my life to shreds. Another question made its way to the front of my mind as we were about to step away from one another. "Did you tell her about him before you sent him to her?"

"Of course," she said, "because I knew Henry didn't believe in spiritualism. She told me to offer him a free visit to let him see for himself what she could do."

I backed away from her, my throat beginning to constrict and ache, but there was one more thing. "You'd rather see him with her than with me?"

Sarah studied her fingernails for a moment. "At least she isn't dragging girls into prostitution. She's trying to help people and ease their pain."

I was dumbfounded. I didn't drag anybody into anything. Girls came to me, eagerly seeking employment. To my memory, Sarah and I didn't say another word, and I didn't see anything or anyone else as I walked home that day, not a store, not a hitching post, not so much as a pebble in the street.

CHAPTER 32

Because of my level of fatigue, I might have let the idea of getting even with Pretty Face go if she'd simply stopped after taking Henry. But that just wasn't her way. About a week later, she sent me a bill for five hundred dollars for services rendered to Henry, which included meticulous details of the dates and times, all late evening to early morning hours. It made me so angry I could literally feel the blood coursing through my veins, hot and deep.

After consulting my black book, I remembered Vashti telling me she'd married a buffalo soldier by the name of Barret Jones. As soon as I had my rage under control, I took the stage into Kingston and sought her out, hoping I could get her to curse Pretty Face with one of her spells or at least help me figure out how to handle her. After making inquiries, I found her tidy, little house on the outskirts of town and knocked on the door.

Vashti squealed when she saw me. "Sadie! Let me look at you!" She held me at arm's length for a moment and said, "Come on in. I can see you got something weighing on your mind."

I stepped into her parlor and saw two little girls playing tiddlywinks. "That's Sasha and Ginger, my nine-year-old twins," she said, and the girls waved. "You girls go play in the backyard while I talk to Miss Sadie." Without argument, they abandoned their game and headed toward the back door.

I took a seat in an upholstered chair and admired the way

Vashti had decorated her home. An embroidered piece above the mantle caught my eye and reminded me of something she'd said years earlier. It read, "Her children arise up, and call her blessed; her husband also, and he praiseth her. Proverbs 31:28." I pointed toward it and told her, "I remember when you told me that was going to be yours, and now it is, isn't it?"

"Sure is," she said with sparkling eyes.

Once we heard her daughters laughing and playing outside, Vashti asked, "What's troubling you?"

"You're talking differently."

"Don't you know I have to watch my grammar and speech around my girls? They're going to be cultured women. I don't want them talking like my people back home. What's really troubling you?"

I told her the whole story of my experience with Pretty Face, starting with the day Madame Chantelle threw me out in the street. When I got to the part about Pretty Face telling me she saw a wolf behind me, Vashti frowned and said, "I wonder if she just said that or if she really saw it."

"She just said that," I snapped.

"So you haven't sensed it coming around in all these years?"

"No, I haven't sensed it!" I yelled, dropping my English accent for a moment. "There's no wolf!"

Vashti sighed and said, "If you say so, but I hope you remember it waited thirty years to come for Tom Beeson."

I pressed my lips together, determined not to get into an argument over the wolf. "After I ran Henry off," I said, "she had the audacity to send me a huge bill for services rendered to him."

Vashti frowned and said, "That woman's got it coming." I covered my face with my hands for a moment and asked, "How can I get free of this sooth-saying slut?"

Vashti shook her head and said, "You can't. You aren't in any shape to do that right now. You're a mess. You can't accomplish anything when your heart is all bound up with hatred and bitterness. You've got to put all those bad feelings behind you."

"What?" I asked. "Are you suggesting I start loving that minging charlatan?" I stood as if to go.

"No, I'm telling you to stop being angry and start being smart. Sit down."

I sat and argued, "I am smart. I've always been smart."

"Oh, yeah, you're smart all right," she snorted. "You figured out how to run off a pack of wild Apache warriors with a horsewhip." Then she broke into laughter and doubled over in her chair. "I'm sorry," she said, gasping for breath. "I still laugh every time I think about that tale you told." I sat there frowning at her for a moment, but then I started laughing with her.

When I could catch my breath again, I asked, "Will you work a spell for me?"

She gave me a baleful look and said, "I thought you didn't believe in that."

"Well, now I might. At least I'm willing to give it a try."

Vashti shook her head and said, "I don't work spells anymore. I've been attending Reverend Farrow's church, and I accepted Jesus last year. My husband did the same thing. Now I'm ashamed of all that hoodoo stuff. I stay away from it."

I sighed and said, "Well, I guess I'm in the wrong place."

"No, you're in the right place to get good answers. Let God take that bitterness out of your heart. Give it to him. The Good Book says, 'Vengeance is mine. I will repay, saith the Lord.'"

I'm sure she said more, but I stopped listening. I was thinking about the one thing she'd said that made sense to me—I had to stop being angry and start being smart. I thought I had an inkling of how to do this, and I smiled to myself, remembering how a single offhand remark of Vashti's had given me the seed of a plan for dealing with Rod Baylor after Bobtail's death.

This time, I realized I knew little of Pretty Face's habits. I saw I needed to find out more about her in order to find the right venue to cause her ruin. I also knew where I could enlist some excellent help. When Vashti stopped speaking, she looked at me expectantly and said, "You look better than when you came in. Do you feel better?"

"I feel a lot better and a lot smarter. I'm going to pay that bill Pretty Face sent me."

"Are you crazy?" she asked.

"Oh, I don't mean pay it with money," I said, as I stood to leave.

Vashti sighed, gave me a hug, and mumbled, "You're going to get yourself into a bigger mess than you've ever seen if you're not careful. I hate to see it coming."

CHAPTER 33

I spoke with Edgar Graham, a customer who enjoyed spending time with Sugar, one of my girls across the creek, and worked out an arrangement with him to watch Lady Claire and report her habits to me. Edgar was a clerk at C. C. Miller's drug store, and he was frequently out making deliveries to customers, so he was able to observe much of what went on in town while he was working. Before long, I found out where and when Pretty Face shopped and learned that she always closed her doors to business around eleven o'clock in the evenings. In late May of 1903, Edgar reported that Pretty Face always took a walk along the Percha River around midnight whenever there was a full moon.

"How do you know she always does it on a full moon? You haven't been following her long enough to know that."

Edgar looked at his dust-covered shoes for a moment and said, "You probably ain't gonna like this, but I picked some information out of Henry at the Silver Leaf Saloon. He don't mind to answer questions when he's drunk. He thought I was just interested 'cause she's a fortune-teller."

I was irritated at first, but then I felt pleased. "It's all right, Edgar. God knows he's given her plenty of information about me. As they say, turn-about is fair play. Have you followed her out there yet?"

"Yes, ma'am, on the twenty-second."

"What does she do out there?"

Edgar scratched the salt and pepper whiskers on his chin and tugged at the suspenders over his blue cotton shirt. "Nothing, as far as I can tell, 'cept just stand by that deep pool by that big willow tree and stare into the water. Sometimes she moves her mouth like she's talking, but no words come out. It gives me the willies to watch her out there."

I took some money out of my purse and gave it to him. "I want you to use this to go to one of those meetings she has in her house for people who want to talk to the dead. Watch what she does and tell me about it, especially if you see any trickery."

Edgar scowled and said, "I'd sooner crawl through broken glass than do that. What if she tells me something I'd rather not know?"

"I can see your point, Mr. Graham." I held out another five dollars and said, "Suppose I give you this as well, and, for every hour you spend in that house, you'll get two to spend with Sugar?" Edgar nodded and pocketed the money.

When he was gone, I regretted the deal I'd made with him, thinking he'd probably already told me everything I needed to know. I saw the best solution would be to drown her. To this end, I checked the almanac for the dates of full moons and worked on a plan.

A tiny hope sprang up in my heart that, if I got rid of Pretty Face, maybe Henry and I could work things out and be happy together again. I felt it was still possible to forgive him. Of course, I'd carry the risk of being caught, which could get me hanged. Some folks didn't like Lady Claire's profession, but they didn't think of her as a whore. To the townspeople, she was a respectable woman, and if they thought someone had killed her, they wouldn't let her death go unpunished. Because of this risk, I decided I should kill her myself. That way, it would be kept quiet. I could only trust myself never to speak of it.

I've never understood why, but, the minute I started plotting to drown Pretty Face, I felt a sort of darkness come over me.

I'd killed G. J. Stanard on the way to Dodge City, but that made me a heroine, not a murderer, since he was about to rob the stage. I'd killed Bill Dunn, but, even though I'd wanted to kill him, I'd really had to do it in self-defense, as things worked out, so his case wasn't quite the same. Then I'd tried to kill Rod Baylor, who needed killing, and I'd failed and hired a man to finish him off. Even so, this seemed a deeper sin, one I wasn't sure I'd care to answer for in the end, even with all she'd done to hurt me. I brooded over it, even as I contemplated how best to do the deed.

With Tom Ying's help, I kept the hotel and restaurant business running smoothly, and I never showed weakness to my friends and neighbors. As far as anyone knew, I was glad Henry was gone, and, since Henry had been so stealthy and discreet, as far as anyone knew, he'd only taken an interest in Lady Claire after I ran him off. Though I owned the Ocean Grove, I wasn't sure how the law would see the Orchard Hotel, since he built it during our marriage. I figured that, if I didn't get rid of Pretty Face soon, she'd push him to ask me to buy out his half or force me to sell the place and split the money with him. After all, she had bragged that she'd bring me to nothing.

Still, getting rid of her was problematic. As I thought about it, I couldn't help but wonder if she'd somehow sense my presence on the riverbank while I was waiting to kill her. I also knew I could count on her being armed. I kept thinking of things that could go wrong.

For example, suppose she knew how to swim? Would she get the best of me and shoot or drown me instead? Several times, I walked down to the spot on the river to get the place clear in my mind by daylight and think about what would be visible under a full moon. It became clear to me that I'd have to subdue her before I put her in the water.

Before long, the whole idea of killing Pretty Face and making it look like an accident seemed hopeless and stupid. I wondered if I could hire an Indian to kill her on the riverbank in exchange for a case of cheap whiskey. As it turned out, I didn't need to be thinking along those lines at all. Pretty Face's days were about to end. Without realizing it, I'd already done all I needed to do.

On warm summer evenings, Tom Ying would serve supper to our guests at the Ocean Grove and then sit on the porch, smoke cigarettes, and look at the stars after the restaurant closed. One night, when it was just the two of us out there, he handed me a copy of a political cartoon captioned "The Yellow Terror in All His Glory" that someone had left on one of the tables in the restaurant. It showed a Chinaman in a black skullcap, just like Tom's, holding a smoking gun over his head in one hand, a burning torch in the other hand, and a knife in his teeth, while standing over a fallen white woman.

"You think maybe some people don't like me?" Tom asked, smiling.

I asked who'd left it, and he said, "Hard to say," but I figured he knew.

We both knew there were plenty of people who worried that the Chinese came into the U.S. and lived on starvation wages while secretly plotting to take over everything. This had been a domestic attitude and concern for many years, and, in 1882, Congress had passed the Chinese Exclusion Act, which had prevented the immigration of Chinese laborers for ten years. In 1888, Congress had passed the Scott Act, which kept the Chinese from re-entering the United States after a visit to their homeland, even if they'd been longtime U.S. residents. These were just two examples of many legislative acts that put the Chinese at a disadvantage. I found it ironic that white people were so worried about the Chinese after having taken the land away from the Indians.

When I crumpled the lurid picture, Tom said, "What? You don't want to frame it?"

"I want to set it afire and shove it up somebody's arse while it's burning, and I would if I knew who left it."

Tom crushed his cigarette and said, "Ah, Sarah Jane. You want to shelter everyone. Someone need shelter you." In the moonlight, I noticed his eyes were beautiful, glittering like black diamonds.

On June 19, I was finishing breakfast at the Ocean Grove Restaurant when Edgar Graham came in and practically dragged me to the porch of the Ocean Grove Hotel. "I've got news for you, Sadie," he said, "and I 'spect you'll want to hear it. I'm sure glad to be finished with our business, and I'm ready to collect my pay—that's two hours with Sugar for the one I spent in that conjure woman's house last night."

Edgar plucked at his suspenders. "What news?" I asked, wishing he'd make it quick. However, I knew Edgar loved to tell a story and insisted on meting it out bit by bit.

"Lady Claire threw one of them parties last night—called it a séance. Me and four other people went, including a fine-looking, blonde-haired woman—Mrs. Boughton Wilson—and her two teenage daughters, and a feller by name of Morgan Claus. It was the damnedest thing I ever seen." Edgar took my arm and guided me to a chair. "I reckon we ought to sit down for this."

I took a seat and watched him settle his lanky frame into one of my straight-backed chairs. "Did she pull any stunts?" I asked.

"Oh, yes, ma'am. Before she even let us in the house, she asked each of us who we hoped to contact that evening. Seemed to me, if she had special powers, she ought to know without being told. I told her no one special, I was just there for the show. Well, she didn't like that. She said, 'This isn't a show, Mr.

Graham.' The widow said she and her girls wanted to ask a question of her departed husband, and Morgan Claus said he wanted to hear from his fiancée, Priscilla Johnson, who died back in 1872. I felt sorry for him, still pining over that girl."

Edgar scratched his beard and stared across at the Orchard Hotel. "She took us into her parlor, lit a tall, black candle in the center of a table covered with a black tablecloth, and had us sit around it. After a few minutes, she said there were spirits in the room that wanted to speak. Soon as the words were out of her mouth, her body started twitching, and her eyes rolled back in her head. I thought she was having some kind of a fit."

I snorted and said, "Yeah, I understand. I've seen her do that a time or two."

Edgar shook his head and said, "Then a young woman's voice came out of her mouth, speaking tender words to Morgan Claus. The gist of it was that she'd always loved him, loved him still, and was forever lingering near him, watching over him. Lady Claire went on for several minutes, asking him to remember things any sweetheart might remember, like how it felt when they held hands and walked along together. Then she held her empty hand palm up and said, "A gift from Priscilla Johnson." When she turned her hand over, a fresh daisy dropped into Claus's hands. By the time she was done, that old feller was bawling so much that she asked him to leave, saying Priscilla had left, and he'd heard what she needed to tell him. He went away thanking her and pressing more money into her hands, while them Wilson women sat there with tears streaming down their faces. Then I heard the rumble of an approaching thunderstorm."

I sighed and said, "She just tells people what they want to hear."

Edgar nodded and said, "Looks like it. I figured she'd go through the same rigmarole with the Wilson women and send us all packing."

I sat there waiting for Edgar to continue while he rolled a cigarette and lit it. A look passed over his face that I couldn't read, perhaps fear or doubt. He took a long draw on his cigarette and blew the smoke toward the sky. "Lady Claire said her trance had left her, so she needed to cleanse herself so she could hear the spirits clearly again. 'To do this,' she said, 'I'm going to bathe myself in fire. Don't come near me until the flames are gone, as I've never done this in the presence of others until this night.' She went over to a washbasin in a far corner, swished her left hand around in the water, and drew it out, covered with foam that was running down her arm and dripping off her elbow. During a flash of lightning, I saw some of that foam fall onto her dress right over her belly. Next, she passed her right hand over the foamy hand, and her left hand ignited, sending a flame nearly to the ceiling."

Of course, as he spoke, I remembered telling Sarah Smith about the old news story I'd seen many years ago in Kansas City. I supposed Sarah had passed the idea of bathing in fire along to Pretty Face, who may have taken it as a challenge or simply realized more people would come to her if her tricks were more sophisticated. "How long did it burn?" I asked.

"Far too long. Just as her hand started blazing, a clap of thunder crashed right beside the house, and there came a sudden downpour. I guess the thunderbolt startled her because she jerked her flaming hand down to her side, and her dress caught fire, shooting flame out in front of her where that foam had dripped on her clothes. She started screaming, and I nearly knocked the table over trying to get over and help her. I tripped over a small footstool, fell, and busted my knees on the floor. As I got up, I wavered a moment, trying to figure out how best to put the fire out, and then I grabbed up a throw rug and beat it out.

"All them women in the room were screaming along with Lady Claire, and, God help me, Sadie, that rug took the skin off that woman's belly. Her chest, thighs, and hands were burned, too, but not as bad. I got the Smith women out of that house onto somebody's porch across the street and ran for Doc Alston in the pouring rain."

I felt my pulse pounding in my temples as he spoke. "Is she dead?" I asked.

"Naw, but I 'spect Lady Claire will die 'fore long. When I came back with the doc, a crowd had formed on the porch across the street, and people were trying to comfort the Wilson women, who were hysterical. I reckon Henry and his friend Cecil Smith heard all the commotion because they come running up, so I hung back and let Cecil and Henry go in with the doc. Then Cecil had Lady Claire taken to his house where him and Mrs. Smith and Henry could look after her. Sorry to have to tell you that part."

I sat there stunned for a moment. "Thank you for telling me," I said. "You've been through a lot. You take four hours with Sugar instead of two, and divide it up any way you want."

Three days later, around one thirty in the afternoon, Hulene Venable, the dressmaker, came to visit. "Have you heard the news?" she asked. "That woman your husband took up with is dead."

"No," I said. "Sit with me."

Hulene settled her nearly two hundred and fifty pounds into one of the straight-back chairs on the porch of the Ocean Grove and pushed a swatch of gray hair from her forehead. She was sweating, as she'd walked the whole way from her shop on Main Street, a distance of about half a mile. "Boots!" I called, and he came around from the back yard. "Get some iced tea from Tom Ying for Mrs. Venable and me."

"Yes, ma'am," he said.

Boots returned quickly with a tray that held a pitcher of tea, two glasses with ice, napkins, forks, and dessert plates laden with lemon pound cake. He placed it on a table between us and walked back around the building. "Thank you, dear," Hulene murmured as I poured the tea.

After she'd taken a sip, Hulene said, "She died around two o'clock this morning. I wasn't there, of course, but Doctor Alston's daughter, Nina, who helps her father at times, said the burns on her belly were infected, and the stench was horrendous."

I pressed my lips together and shook my head. "I've always heard it's best to speak well of the dead, but I can't help feeling she got what she deserved."

"That's what I think."

"When did you talk to Nina?" I asked, as Hulene took a bite of pound cake.

She chewed and swallowed. "I saw her this morning when she came to be fitted for a dress for her sister's wedding in November."

After Hulene left, I wondered what I should do, if anything. For a moment, I even wondered if I should offer Henry a word of condolence. Then I caught myself. I'd do no such thing. I knew that thought had come from the part of me that still loved Henry. I decided, as the old saying goes, that he'd made his bed, and he could lie in it.

After the dinner rush was over around two, Tom Ying came over to the Orchard Hotel and headed to the basement. I was sitting in the lobby in my favorite blue chair. Tom nodded to me and said, "Low-life fortune-teller tells fortunes no more."

CHAPTER 34

On Tuesday June 23, 1903, there was a lot of movement on Elenora Street, as Henry and his friends made ready for the funeral at the Union Church. Around eleven, I walked over to Muddler's Saloon, a few doors down from the church, to get a better look. Howard Muddler was washing glasses when I went in. Aaron Fitch, who owned the hardware store and had a half-finished beer before him, was saying, "I heard that widow woman and her daughters weren't no help to Edgar, just sat there screamin' and watching that conjure woman burn."

Howard nodded solemnly then asked, "Beer, Sadie?"

"Yes, beer's fine. Are the Wilson women still in town?"

Aaron belched. "Naw, they already on a train to El Paso. Edgar told me that 'fore they left, the widow asked Doc Alston who she should see about getting a refund since she didn't get to talk to her departed husband, and the doc told her far as he knew her money got burnt up when Lady Claire Johnson's clothes caught fire. Said he figured she was out of luck."

"I'd never heard Claire's last name before," I said.

"Well, that's how she used to sign for goods on credit at the hardware store, at least until Henry started taking care of that sort of stuff for her. She sent Henry in for some butane and Fels-Naptha soap a few weeks ago. I don't carry butane and had to special order it. I wonder how many times she practiced with it before she tried that stunt."

"How did she learn to do that trick?" I asked.

"I heard C. C. Miller worked it out for her. As a pharmacist, he knows a lot about chemistry." Aaron ordered another beer. Then he frowned and said, "I'll bet she put too much butane in that soapy water when she tried the trick that night."

"Must have." Pretending ignorance, I asked, "What's going on across the street? I saw people taking flowers into the church."

"That's where they're having Lady Claire's funeral," Howard said.

"Seems odd to have a fortune-teller's funeral in a church."

Howard handed me a mug of cold beer. "People tell me Rev. Honesworth had some big reservations until Henry gave him fifty dollars and promised to buy a silver communion set for the church in exchange for doing her service there. Money opens doors, Sadie, but I doubt it will open the pearly gates. That woman was dealing in devilish stuff."

I grinned and said, "I guess it's a matter of perspective. The temperance women claim you're dealing in devilish stuff."

Howard ran his hands across the white apron that covered his large paunch. "Now that Temperance League's the real devilish bunch. A few years ago, a woman by the name of Carrie Nation went into a saloon in Kansas and broke all the liquor bottles with rocks." He spread his hands, palms up, before me. "Ain't there some commandment about thou shalt not destroy thy neighbor's property? But what did she care?"

Something scratched at my mind while he was talking. Fitch had called Pretty Face Claire Johnson. I recalled the night at Joyous Lee's brothel when Pretty Face had dropped a river rock onto my table, saying it was a gift from Lewis Johnson. I wondered if she might be related to the man who'd killed my grandfather years ago. That could explain how she'd known about him. I supposed anything was possible. "You going to the funeral?" I asked.

Howard said he was going to stay put and keep his saloon open, but Aaron said, "You damn right I'm going. I want to see how they laid her out. It's a public event. Anyone can go."

At that, Howard broke into a large smile. "I know you better than that, Fitch. You're going 'cause people are saying her spirit might show up. You know she was tryin' to fool people with that fire trick, and you still think she was able to conjure spirits."

Aaron scowled at him and said, "Go screw your mother."

Howard turned to me and said, "Sadie, why don't you go? That'd give people somethin' to talk about."

"I just might," I said. "What time does it start?"

"One o'clock, but go early or you might not get a seat."

I could hardly believe what I saw when I arrived at the Union Church at twelve thirty. First, as I approached the doorway, there was a tiny explosion and a flash of light. Henry and C. C. Miller were standing up front with Omar Turner, the undertaker, and his assistants, B. G. Vanhorn and Reuben Wade, and I saw they had the coffin in an upright position to the right of the pulpit. Pretty Face was wearing a beautiful gown, covered with lace and embellished with seed pearls. Her face was uncovered, and her eyes were wide open, but a veil covered the dent I'd put in her head years ago and the ribbon they'd tied in place to keep her mouth closed. Four large baskets of creamy yucca flowers stood at the front and filled the air with a fresh fragrance that almost overpowered the smell of death in the sanctuary.

Several rows of pews had been moved to accommodate a photographer who was about to put his camera away. "Wait!" Henry called. "Do one more of me and Claire. I want to make sure you get a good image." I stepped back from the doorway and stood in the churchyard shaking my head. I wondered if it had been Henry's idea to dress that hellish bitch in white. *In a wedding gown!* I figured Henry must have been planning to marry her. I'd expected to see her laid out in black with a veil of black netting over her face, the way she'd been so fond of dressing.

Soon, the photographer came out of the church with Cecil Smith in tow, and I heard the men inside pushing the pews back into place. I walked back down to Muddler's Saloon to wait until more people arrived. "You ought to go take a peek," I told Howard.

He took his apron off, smoothed his moustache, and said, "I believe I will."

About ten minutes later, he returned, muttering, "That's almost a sacrilege, but I gave Henry my condolences anyway."

"Give me a whiskey," I said.

Howard served my drink, and I paid him and lingered over it until he said, "Hey, you better go. It's almost one."

I slipped into the church, which was nearly full, and took a seat near the back beside Aaron Fitch just as the organist started playing a shortened version of Chopin's Funeral March. Pretty Face's coffin was now lying across a table up front. Henry and the Smiths, who had gone outside, filed into the church, paused for another look at Pretty Face, and took the seats reserved for them. Then B. G. Vanhorn and Reuben Wade lifted the lid and placed it over the coffin.

"I hope the Millers covered the mirrors in their house when she died and took her out feet first, so she won't come back to haunt them," Aaron whispered. I nodded and looked over the crowd, hoping they hadn't. It was very hot, and most of the women were wearing black and working the paper fans provided by the undertaker. I thought they were crazy because working a fan always made me feel even hotter. The men were in dark suits of various shades.

Just as Rev. Honesworth took his place behind the pulpit, a

shadow fell over the whole church, although it had been sunny all day. I heard a couple of women gasp, as if they thought Lady Claire had caused it. After giving the women a stern look, the reverend began reading, "*The Lord is my shepherd; I shall not want. He maketh me to lie down in green pastures: he leadeth me beside the still waters. He restoreth my soul: he leadeth me in the paths of righteousness for his name's sake. Yea, though I walk through the valley of the shadow of death, I will fear no evil: for thou art with me; thy rod and thy staff they comfort me. Thou preparest a table before me in the presence of mine enemies: thou annointest my head with oil; my cup runneth over. Surely goodness and mercy shall follow me all the days of my life.*" He then looked out over the congregation.

I knew the Twenty-Third Psalm and was aware that he'd omitted the last phrase, *and I shall dwell in the house of the Lord forever.* I figured it had something to do with his full expectation that Lady Claire was already in hell. The preacher continued, "This is a tragic time. Some in this room will experience sadness of heart for years to come." I smirked, thinking it would be more accurate if he'd said *one* instead of *some.*

Honesworth continued, "Indeed, we must all tremble before our vulnerability to death." As he spoke, I felt a minor vibration in the room. The reverend paused, clutching the pulpit, as the light tremors grew, and I realized we were having a minor earthquake. The church's brass collection plates clattered to the floor from a small table near the back as the tremors shook the whole church. Then Pretty Face's coffin toppled off the table up front, and she rolled out of it onto its lid and lay there on her side, her eyes seeming to look straight into mine.

Several women, including Hulene Venable, fainted. Others screamed and clamored to get out of the church. A plump redhead with bulging, blue eyes pointed to the corpse and cried, "She's the cause of this!" Then B. G. Vanhorn nearly tripped over his own feet in his haste to usher the redhead out of the church. Conversation in the pews rose like the hum in a hive of bees.

When the tremors ended, Rev. Honesworth said, "Even the earth trembles for us in our vulnerability unto death." He nodded to the undertaker's men, who quickly settled Pretty Face back into her coffin and onto the table. Then he said, "Now, let us take comfort in some words from Psalm 145. *The Lord is righteous in all his ways, and kind in all his works. The Lord is nigh unto all them that call upon him, to all that call upon him in truth. He will fulfill the desire of them that fear him: he also will hear their cry and will save them. The Lord preserveth all them that love him: but all the wicked will he destroy. My mouth shall speak the praise of the Lord; and let all flesh bless his holy name forever and ever.* Amen."

Again, the Rev. Honesworth nodded to the undertaker's men, and they nailed the coffin lid in place. "We will now proceed to the burial site." I figured he was glad for an excuse to cut the funeral short.

Six pallbearers lifted the coffin and placed it in a hired carriage outside the church. I realized the sun had returned and was shining brightly, but I hadn't noticed when it came back out. There were several hired carriages outside to take the guests to the graveside, but I thought I'd seen enough and turned to go home. Then Henry was beside me. "Thank you for coming," he said. I sighed, thinking what a mess he'd made of the happy life we'd had, and I felt like cursing him, but I couldn't bring myself to do it. I nodded and climbed into a carriage, having decided to go to the graveside after all.

Henry had his beloved Claire taken to a cemetery outside of town. It was in a lonely place, I thought. Everyone waited as the undertaker's men carefully lowered the coffin into the ground. Then Aaron Fitch's cousin, Emma Jean Fitch, a scrawny woman with light-brown hair, stepped forward to sing "Amazing Grace." Just as she started, a light wind pushed the black netting of her hat into her mouth, and she thrust it back, leaving the hat askew on her head.

When she finished, the Rev. Honesworth read from Psalm 46:1–2, *"God is our refuge and our strength, a very present help in trouble. Therefore will we not fear, thought the earth be removed, and though the mountains be carried into the midst of the sea."* He paused a moment and said, "Let us now lay Mrs. Orchard to rest." He nodded to Henry, who picked up a handful of dirt and threw it into the grave. I was stunned, thinking Rev. Honesworth had made a mistake, and I wasn't going to let it pass.

"That's not Mrs. Orchard," I said. "Her name is Claire Johnson."

Rev. Honesworth said, "She's Mrs. Orchard now. I married her last Sunday afternoon."

My mouth went dry. "But you couldn't have. Henry's married to me."

Rev. Honesworth smiled and said, "Let's discuss this after the service, my dear. Kindly step over and wait for me by one of the carriages."

"No, I'm not moving an inch." I felt everyone's eyes on me, but I didn't care.

Then Henry came to me and said, "Sadie, I divorced you on Claire's birthday."

I felt my stomach lurch. "You utter minging rotter!" I yelled. "How could you divorce me and not even tell me? You're the lowest beggarly, prick-eared feck I've ever seen! You make me puke!" And, just to prove it, I threw up on his shoes. I glanced over at Emma Jean, and her mouth was agape.

Henry looked around and said, "My former wife is sick. Will someone please take her home?"

Then Omar Turner led me to a carriage, and I walked with

him willingly while cursing and shouting at Henry, "Arsehole! You put that bloody, hell-bound, plug ugly slag in a wedding dress! I hope she gave you a disease! I hope your cock and bollocks rot and fall off!" I paused long enough to take a deep breath and yelled, "I hope you die a worse death than she did, you good-for-nothing bell end!"

Omar Turner was smiling to himself when he helped me into the carriage, but I knew he wouldn't be smiling when he turned back to face that crowd. B. G. Vanhorn, who was following us, climbed into the driver's seat. At that point, Henry and the other graveside attendees had their backs to me, apparently trying to pretend they couldn't hear me. I saw Cecil Smith had placed a hand on Henry's shoulder. As the carriage started moving, I shouted, "Buggers!" Cecil withdrew his hand, and I heard B. G. chuckle.

CHAPTER 35

On the ride home, I was physically sick. The thought of Henry divorcing me on Pretty Face's birthday, as if part of a gift, was too much for me. I had to get B. G. to stop the carriage so I could throw up again. It didn't seem right that I could be divorced and not even know it. I remembered the poker game hosted at Emmett Fowler's ranch, where my first love, Garland Spade, was killed, and the story of how Fowler had divorced his wife when she was visiting family in the East. I knew that in the territories men made the law work in their favor. Something needed to be done about that, but women didn't even have the right to vote.

Upon arriving back at the Orchard Hotel, I was emotionally exhausted, so I went to my quarters, had a glass of wine, and tried to take a nap, but sleep wouldn't come for a long time, and, when it did, it brought strange dreams. I was wandering through long hallways searching for a wedding dress, one I'd never owned, since Henry and I had simply gone to the courthouse and stood before Judge Parker to take our vows. Then Pretty Face entered the dream, sat up in her coffin, and told me she'd bring me to nothing. Next, I was swimming in a lake surrounded by mountains when a mermaid with a monkey's face swam up beside me, startling me. I must have lost my mind for a little while that night. I awakened and had an evil thought, one I knew I shouldn't act on, yet I hurried to set it in motion.

It was nearly six o'clock. My thoughts were swirling like a dust devil in the desert. I hadn't won. I'd planted a seed that led to Pretty Face's death when I told Sarah Miller about the fire queen's trick, but I hadn't killed Pretty Face or frightened her into leaving town. She'd died because she made a stupid mistake. That wasn't vengeance, but I'd have revenge.

I hadn't eaten since breakfast, and I didn't care. I knew exactly what I wanted, and it wasn't food. I opened my strongbox, took out two hundred dollars, and called for Boots to saddle Onyx for me. Then I headed down to Lawson Lane in search of Otis Mason, the taxidermist.

I'm sure I was out of my mind that evening because, along the way, I muttered to Pretty Face, "I'll teach you to stay out of my dreams. You won't trouble me again, you mangy gobshite."

As I peered at him from the olive-green sofa in his parlor, Otis ran his hands through his thinning, black hair. "I don't know, Sadie," he said. "That could land me in jail if I got caught, and, if anyone saw me working on her later—"

"You won't get caught. No one's going to pass by that god-forsaken graveyard in the middle of the night. It's a fresh grave. It won't take you long to dig her up. And you can work on her in a back room." I took a hundred dollars out of my purse and put it on the table between us.

He sighed and wiped the sweat from his face, but he didn't touch the money. "That ain't enough considering the risks involved, and, even if I wanted to do it, I got a horse, but I ain't got a wagon to transport the corpse, and I cain't just ride back to town with a dead woman sharing my saddle with me."

Without blinking, I placed another hundred dollars on his coffee table. "I'll have Boots bring a wagon over in a little while. You can bring it back in the morning."

Still, Otis didn't touch the money. "She's a human being," he argued.

"She's half Apache, though she kept that a closely guarded secret," I lied, remembering that Howard had told me Otis hated Apaches. "She lived with the Lipan Apaches for years, and I happen to know that she learned her connections to the spirit world from her grandfather, who was a medicine man. She got that dent in her skull when another Apache woman accused her of being a witch and whopped her on the head with a stick." I paused and said, "That half-breed whore has done me many wrongs over my life, not the least of which was stealing my husband. Won't you help me?"

Otis raised an eyebrow. "Half Apache? An Apache killed my father when I was twelve years old."

"Really? I'm so sorry to hear that."

Otis recounted the story of his father's death. He told about how he and his mother and siblings had seen times when they just barely avoided starvation afterwards.

"It sounds like I'm offering you a chance for a small measure of vengeance as well."

He nodded, and his eyes glittered as he asked, "What you want me to make of her? One of them mermaid creatures?"

"Certainly not. I want you to shame her! Give her a mule's face and a donkey's ass."

I expected him to pick up the money at that point, but he said, "Sadie, I can't make just anything. The animals I mix have to be of similar size. This is more complicated than cutting down antlers and putting them on a jackrabbit. What you gonna to do with her when I finish, anyway?"

"I'll hide her in a crate in my quarters and look at her now and again for my own satisfaction."

Otis nodded and said, "I'll have to think on this a bit, but

I'm sure I can come up with something you'll like. Is that all right?"

"That's fine," I said. "How long will it take?"

"Give me three or four weeks, and if I have to go to some expense to purchase animals, I'll expect you to pay for them. I'll have to keep the thing hidden, too, so I'm also going to charge you whatever I have to pay for a crate to fit it in. I'll let you know when it's ready."

"Agreed," I said and shook hands with him.

CHAPTER 36

On Thursday, June 25, 1903, Otis Mason brought my wagon back around noon, so I invited him to eat with me at the Ocean Grove, where we had roasted chicken with rice and green beans at a table in a far corner, removed from other guests. "I'm assuming you had no trouble last night," I said.

"Not a bit, but it was spooky out there. I heard a wolf howl, and it sounded right close, though I never saw it. I had my pistol and a rifle with me, so I weren't too worried about it. I dug up the corpse and put it in the wagon. Then I put the lid back on the coffin and covered it up again as quick as I could. I hope you aren't set on having her dressed in that wedding gown, 'cause there was no way I could move her without getting dirt on that dress. Worse than that, her bowels let go when I lifted her, and she added some dirt of her own."

"That's okay. She needs a cruder outfit. You can burn that slag's dress for all I care."

Around one o'clock that afternoon, I wandered over to Hulene Venable's shop. She was pinning emerald-green lace to the bodice of a dress. She put the work aside and spoke with me for a few minutes. After fainting in the church, she hadn't gone to Lady Claire's graveside service, but she'd heard all about it and learned that Henry had divorced me and married the fortune-teller. She said, "He sure deserved the tongue lashing you laid on him."

I agreed; however, instead of cursing Henry further, as Hulene and I discussed my situation, I cried and spilled the secret thought I'd been holding in the back of my mind. "We might have gotten back together and eventually been happy again," I said, "but I don't see how I could ever forgive him now." I dabbed my eyes with a handkerchief and asked, "Why would he marry that slut when she was on her deathbed?"

Hulene patted my arm with her pudgy hand and said, "At the bakery yesterday, Sylvia Crosswell told me she'd heard that Henry had been planning to take Claire to California to get married this fall. Maybe he wanted to let her have her wedding before it was too late, or maybe he just wanted to secure the inheritance. She had money from what I hear, and she owned her house."

I felt like a poleaxed ox when she said that. In all my anger and aggravation, I'd forgotten about that, though I should have seen it right away. I looked at Hulene sharply. "Did you make her wedding dress?"

"No, and I wouldn't have if she'd asked, since you and I are friends. They must have gotten it somewhere out of town."

"Did you know he'd married her before the funeral?"

She shook her head. "I don't think anyone did besides Rev. Honesworth and the Smiths."

At about two thirty, I found Tom Ying shivering under an old shawl while chopping vegetables for the evening supper rush, although the kitchen was still hot from where he'd had the stove going for dinner. Touching his forehead, I found he was burning hot, so I sent him home to rest and put a CLOSED sign on the restaurant door. Then, for the first time in years, I cut up a chicken and made soup, using some of the celery and onions Tom had already chopped. Around five o'clock, I took a pot of soup over to his house, which was built shotgun style, the rooms aligned one after another so you could stand in the front doorway and fire shotgun pellets through every room and out the back door. I found Tom a bit worse, his breathing labored, so I walked to his front porch and hollered for Boots to bring me a pail of cold water.

"Do you want me to get Doctor Alston?" Boots asked as he set the pail by Tom's bed.

"No," I said, as I bathed Tom's face. "Tom has his own medicines here, and he'll tell me what to use. I want you to go over to the Ocean Grove and tell Nancy to give you some clean sheets and another blanket for his bed."

Once Boots had brought the linens and left, I removed Tom's shirt, bathed his chest and back, and changed his sheets. Tom endured the cold washcloth without complaint while shivering like an old woman in a cold wind. He ate a portion of the soup I'd brought and asked me to make him some ginger tea, so I did. Before I left, I served him a cup and left a pot of it beside his bed. I was tempted to sit with him through the night, but I knew it would get out and set tongues wagging all over town if I did. Tom nodded his thanks to me, and I promised to return the next day.

The following morning, I sent Boots over to check on Tom and help him as needed. Around noon, I took a pot over to the Black Range Café, paid them to fill it with vegetable beef stew, and took it to Tom. I could tell Tom was better, though still weak, and he said he'd come to work the next morning. "No you won't," I said. "I have a sign on the restaurant door that says it's closed until June 28. I want you to take another day to get your strength back."

Tom smiled and said, "Maybe I chop wood tomorrow instead."

I had Boots take breakfast and dinner to Tom on Friday, June

26. Then, around two that afternoon, I walked over and knocked on Tom's door, but there was no answer, which seemed odd, so I let myself in. Passing through the front room, I found Tom lying on his bed, holding his long opium pipe over a little brass lamp he'd set on a table beside the bed. He breathed the vapors, and said, "Smoke with me." Then he moved over and patted a spot on the bed where he'd made room for me.

"Tom, you know I can't. People will talk. Someone probably saw me come over here and started timing how long I stay." Tom patted the bed again, so I went to his front room and locked the door. When I came back, he was heating another pill of opium over the lamp.

I got on the bed beside him, and he held the pipe for me as I breathed in its vapors several times. I was about to take more, but he said, "Enough! You want to become opium fiend?"

I realized he was right and giggled. He asked, "You want I should name the stars for you again?" Then the pipe was gone, and those stars were shining on the ceiling for me, even when I closed my eyes. A few minutes later, Tom apparently forgot the stars and started making requests of me. "I want your hands," he said as I lay dreaming, so I gave him my hands, and he applied soft, feather-like strokes to my fingers, my palms, and the top of my hands.

He kept moving from part to part. "I want your forearms." "I want your feet." "I want your back." His touch was exhilarating. Soon, all my clothes were in a heap on the floor, and he was fully dressed and had yet to touch my breasts or sexual parts. He must have spent nearly an hour touching me before I became aware that he was doing much to pleasure me while I was doing nothing for him.

I slid my hand across his chest and down his belly, but he caught it and said, "Sarah Jane, relax. Learn to receive."

Then I looked up, and, instead of stars on the ceiling, I saw a cerulean sky in which a crescent moon was visible. I lay there panting as Tom Ying slowly explored every part of me and eventually made it impossible to relax. As the afternoon shadows grew long, I cried out in ecstasy under his ministration.

The next morning Tom cooked breakfast for customers at the Ocean Grove Restaurant. I'd spent a largely sleepless night trying to figure out what was happening between us. Tom was my friend, but he was strange in some ways, and I wondered if what he'd done was simply his way of repaying me for taking care of him when he was sick. Regardless of how he saw it, I had a huge problem. I wanted Tom Ying, though I wasn't clear on how he felt about me. If he felt the same, we'd have to hide our feelings from our neighbors if we didn't want to get ourselves killed. I was sure no one in town would tolerate a white woman taking up with a Chinaman.

CHAPTER 37

As the days passed, my desire for Tom Ying quickly became a tight coil of passion in my chest. I felt like a woman out of her mind wanting him that way and fully understanding the impossibility of the situation. To make things worse, Tom grew more reserved around me, offering very little encouragement. He started heading home after work at night rather than joining me on the porch of the Ocean Grove Hotel. More often, I'd hear "Mrs. Orchard" from his lips instead of "Sarah Jane," even when no one else was around. But then I'd catch him looking at me from across a room, imagine I saw longing in his eyes, and wish I could live forever under his gaze. I tried to forget my attraction to Tom, but it came back every time I saw him or heard his voice.

Three weeks passed, and, true to his word, Otis Mason rode up on July 16 to tell me he'd finished the work I'd commissioned. It was near suppertime, so I invited him to eat with me at the Ocean Grove. Over beef ribs and roasted potatoes, I smiled and said, "Tell me about what you've done."

"Oh, no, ma'am," he said. "You'll just have to wait and see it with your own eyes." He took a long draught of beer and added, "I 'spect you'll be mighty pleased." Over a dessert of apple cobbler, Otis took an envelope out of his pocket and handed it to me. He said, "I burnt that dress, but I cut off them seed pearls and put them in here in case you want 'em."

"Thank you, Otis. I might put them on the bodice of one of my dresses." After supper, I had Boots saddle Onyx, so I could ride with Otis back to his place.

An empty wooden crate stood against one wall in Otis Mason's back room, near his unmade bed, and I could make out the figure of a woman at the foot of the bed. He had the curtains drawn, so it was hard to see anything until he lit a lantern and trimmed it. Then I was speechless for a moment when I saw his creation. Otis had Pretty Face draped in burlap from her neck down to her knees. He'd attached a pig's nose to her face, removed her ears, and attached pig's ears to the top of her head. These hung down over her forehead. Her stringy, brown hair fell slightly below her shoulders, and it appeared that Otis had given her a rough haircut. Her close-set eyes, once blue, were now beady, black, glass eyes that seemed to regard me with sadness, and Otis had found a way to make them look smaller. She stood there in the white, lace-up shoes she was buried in.

"Since she was burnt, I had to use two pigs to get it right, a young one for the snout and some pinkish-white skin and a good-sized sow for those big ears and other parts. What do you think?"

"It's perfect. You've done remarkable work."

"Just wait 'til you see the rest," Otis said. "That woman didn't have no skin on her belly, so I had to do more work than I expected." He pulled back the burlap, and I saw that he'd removed her breasts. Pretty Face had hairy pink and black speckled skin across her torso and two long rows of brownish sow's tits. He'd stitched the outer lips of her cunny closed in the front and extended the sow's skin down over it to make it smooth and give her a chaste look. "Now, let me show you her back." We walked around, and he removed the burlap completely. Her back and arse were covered with stiff boar's bristles, and the skin underneath the bristles was black. To round out the presentation, he'd attached a curly, black pig's tail to the base of her spine.

"I didn't have to replace the skin on her back, but I thought it would look better if I did. You want me to make her a rough dress out of that burlap?" Otis asked.

"No, she's an animal now. She doesn't need a dress."

Otis smiled broadly. "She does look like a natural born pig woman, if I do say so myself."

"Bravo, Mr. Mason. What more do I owe you?"

"I had to buy the crate and them two pigs, but fifty will cover it."

"That crate is rather wide," I said.

"Well, I didn't think you'd want me to deliver something that looks like a coffin."

"You have a point, Otis. I'll give you fifty in cash, or you can have twice the amount of time with my girls that fifty would buy. Which do you prefer?"

"Time with the girls is fine. Have Boots bring your wagon to me tomorrow, and I'll deliver it tomorrow after the supper crowd has cleared out of your restaurant."

"You bring two things in that crate," I said, "and I'll say I'm not happy with the delivery and send one of them back to you. That way, no one will know I bought anything from you."

I walked around Pretty Face again and said, "There's just one more thing I'd like to do, if we can. This woman used to wear red lipstick and circles of rouge on her cheeks when she was young. Do you have some kind of permanent stain that would give the same effect?"

"I've got some red ink, but you'd best apply it since you know exactly how you want it to look."

He produced the ink, and using a small brush, I carefully

painted her lips and cheeks and stood there admiring my work. "Do you want to take a bit of that off before it dries?" Otis asked.

"No, it's perfect. She always overdid it." On impulse, I added, "Mr. Mason, you deserve a bonus. Take four times what fifty dollars would buy with my girls."

Boots was whittling a piece of cottonwood when Otis Mason pulled into the side yard of the Orchard Hotel after supper the next day. I was reading in the lobby when he arrived, and I went outside just in time to hear Otis ask Boots to give him a hand taking the crate inside. "For now, just put it in here," I said, pointing to the little bedroom Henry had used when he stopped sleeping with me. Then I sent Boots out to put the horse and wagon away. Otis quickly used a small crowbar to open the crate, where he'd stuffed a couple of old blankets between Pretty Face and a stuffed wild boar. I went to the window and yelled, "Boots, don't put the wagon up yet. This is going back where it came from."

Otis quickly took the wild boar outside, put it in the wagon, and covered it with his blankets as Boots looked on. When he drove off, Boots asked, "Why he not put it back in the crate?"

"I bought the crate off him to store some things in."

"You done the right thing," Boots said. "That old boar was ugly. It wouldn't add a thing to this here place. I wish you'd get him to bring a bear or mountain lion."

Revenge was sweet. In the days that followed, I felt a lot of satisfaction when I'd pull back the lid on that crate and look at Pretty Face. I'd take her by the waist and pull her out into the middle of the room and smile. She'd said she'd bring me to nothing, but I'd won in the end. She stood there naked before me in her white wedding shoes, showing off her pig's tits and hairy black arse. I dearly wished I could have her picture taken and send it to Henry.

CHAPTER 38

By October, Pretty Face was haunting my dreams, repeating words she'd said in her lifetime. She'd say she saw a wolf behind me or tell me she'd bring me to nothing. It came to a point where I wouldn't even enter the room where I kept her.

Soon, I began finding wolf prints around the hotel and became convinced the unholy bitch was drawing evil to my place. The prints were huge, and I was certain I wasn't mistaking Puddles's paw prints for those prints. They looked much like the ones I'd seen at Tom Beeson's place and the ones I'd found near the place where Tom and his horse had plunged to their deaths in a ravine years ago. When I mentioned them to Tom Ying, he said he doubted a wolf would come into town. I tried to show them to him, but when we went outside, they were always trodden over, never as clear as what I'd seen. Tom said he thought it was probably just a big dog.

Then one evening, Boots found Puddles dead in the side yard of the Ocean Grove, mauled. I had just come in from a ride on Onyx when Boots told me, so I went to see my dog, collapsed on the ground, and cried. Puddles's neck had been snapped, and his belly had been laid open, leaving a bloody mess of intestines spilled onto ground. In that moment, it seemed very possible to me that I hadn't won at all, that Pretty Face was reaching from beyond the grave to take away the things I loved. When I could speak, I asked, "Did you see this happen?"

"No ma'am. I went down to the hardware store to buy some nails for Tom Ying and found him when I come back."

"Will you bury him for me?" I asked.

He nodded and offered me his hand. "Let me help you up, Miz Orchard. You should go inside while I bury your dog."

When I refused, he got Tom Ying to come outside. Tom didn't ask me to get up. He just picked me up and started walking toward the Orchard Hotel. I started pounding his back with my fists, yelling for him to put me down, and trying to kick him. Once inside, he asked, "Why so angry, Sarah Jane?"

"Don't ever touch me again! You can't make love to me, then act indifferent to me, and then pick me up as if I'm a little child. You made me want you, and then you acted like nothing had happened between us."

Tom said, "I want you more than you know."

"Then why don't you show it?"

He shook his head. "You have no future with me, Sarah Jane. I can save money, have more money than any man in town, but I can't have white woman and live in fine house with her. Chinaman and Sarah Jane have no future in this place."

He turned to go, but I said, "Hold me," and he put his arms around me. Nestled in his arms, I started crying again. I told him, "I don't care if we can't have much of a life together. I just want whatever minutes we can steal."

After that, Tom started coming to me at odd hours in the middle of the night after I gave him a key to my quarters. Having Tom with me caused my nightmares to go away for a while. Making love to him was unlike anything I'd experienced with other men. He'd enter me, vary his thrusts in depth and intensity, and then withdraw as if he'd lost interest and start caressing me again. "Tom, please, I want you to finish," I'd say.

Sometimes, he'd comply, and sometimes he'd say, "Relax,

Sarah Jane. I choose when." He always made me cry out from the pleasure he gave, but he didn't realize he left me feeling inadequate when he refused to finish. I tried to explain it to him once, but he said, "This isn't a whorehouse, Sarah Jane. I'm not your customer." Eventually, I came to understand that it had something to do with some Chinese ways and beliefs I didn't understand. I had to learn to let Tom Ying be Tom Ying.

By January, Otis Mason had become extremely fond of a new girl named Saffron, a lovely girl with strawberry-blonde hair and narrow hips. Like Nancy, she also worked as a maid at the Ocean Grove when needed. I told her she was welcome to stay the night in the back room at the hotel after entertaining men if it was late and she didn't feel like walking back across the bridge over the Percha to her cabin. Once Otis discovered Saffron, he never paid for time with Nancy again. Saffron was a strange girl, and she seemed to think a lot of Otis Mason and took an interest in his work. One day, she padded into the Ocean Grove Restaurant to show me that he'd made her a mouse with a frog's head because she'd seen the one he'd made for Tom Murphy's Saloon and admired it. I figured he'd soon get tired of paying to be with her and simply ask her to marry him.

That summer, I began having nightmares about Pretty Face again. She'd taunt me, telling me vulgar details of her evenings with Henry. She'd always end her monologues with a threat that she'd bring me to nothing. Sometimes she'd tell me the black wolf was coming for me soon. When I awoke, I'd call her a liar or sling threats back at her. It was all I knew to do.

Soon, things started getting out of hand. One day, I was fully awake and simply walked by the room where I kept Pretty Face when I heard her say, "I'll destroy the Chinaman." It sounded like she was standing right beside me. I didn't see how I could have imagined anything so vivid.

When Tom came to sit with me on the porch of the Ocean Grove that evening, I told him the whole sorry mess of my experience with Pretty Face, starting with the day she'd lied and gotten me thrown out of Madame Chantelle's brothel to the day Otis had delivered her to the Orchard Hotel. Tom listened patiently without interrupting. Then he said, "I want to see this pig woman."

I told him to go and see it, that I wasn't going near it again. When he came back, I said, "I guess you despise me for what I've done."

Tom shook his head and said, "You have temper. You do such thing. I have temper. I chase people with knife."

When I told him Pretty Face had threatened to kill him, he smiled and said, "Fortune-teller can't destroy me. Even your own holy book say a curse causeless shall not come."

"Where does it say that?"

"Somewhere in Proverbs."

"How would you know that?"

Tom sighed and said, "In China, missionary come to our village when I was fourteen. I help him speak Chinese. He help me speak English. Sometimes I helped him read Bible in Chinese."

That same evening, I started reading Proverbs and found the saying in the second chapter, but the scriptures were of no comfort to me. After what I'd had done to her corpse, I supposed any curse Pretty Face wished on me might come, having plenty of cause.

When I shared this conclusion with Tom Ying, he said, "No, Sarah Jane. Fortune-teller bring this fate on herself with her actions. Fate use you as instrument, same way fate use lightning as instrument when she set herself on fire. You torment self, giving this dead woman power." His words helped, and the dreams stopped for a while.

In November, Otis Mason saw me at Muddler's Saloon and asked if he could speak with me for a moment, so we moved from the bar to a table near the back and ordered another round of beer. "Have you ever dreamed about her?" he asked.

"Who? Saffron?" I asked, teasing. "Sorry, I only dream of men. But she seems quite taken with you, luv."

Then I saw the fear in his eyes, and all silliness left me. "The fortune-teller," he said.

"A time or two, and it's never good."

Howard brought our beers to the table, and I took a sip as Otis ran his hands through his hair. "She's going to kill me," he said. "I have nightmares of her standing by my bed, and she torments me. She says she'll send someone to kill me."

I sighed and said, "I think our minds are playing tricks on us. A friend of mine helped me put the bad dreams in perspective. He said she put her own self in the shape she's in through her actions. We were just instruments of fate. Don't imagine she has any power over you."

Otis sighed and downed half his beer. "I hope you're right."

CHAPTER 39

Tom Ying and I heard Saffron's screams around five in the morning on February 15, 1904. Tom jumped out of my bed, put on his trousers and his coat, and went outside through a back door, while I grabbed my pistol and threw on some clothes. By the time I got outside, Tom had gotten Saffron to go back inside. She was keening softly, sitting on her bed in the back room. I peeked in at her and said, "I'll be right in," before turning back to Tom. "What happened?" I asked.

Tom nodded to a vague form on the ground near the back fence. "Is Otis Mason," he whispered. "Is bad. Take her to Orchard Hotel now. Don't let her see him when sun comes up. I get sheriff."

I walked Saffron back to the Orchard Hotel and gave her a large draught of laudanum. Soon, Nancy arrived for her morning shift at the restaurant and came over to see me, after finding it dark and empty. I had her sit with Saffron and went back outside.

Sheriff Max Kahler was with Tom Ying behind the Ocean Grove, and a small crowd had formed in the gray light of dawn, including the undertaker, Omar Turner. Someone had thrown a sheet over the corpse.

"It's got to be the work of a renegade Apache," Kahler said, "maybe Massai or the Apache Kid." I heard murmurs of assent.

"Why in the hell would you think that?" I asked.

Max Kahler gave me a pained look, as if he were getting

ready to explain a difficult concept to an idiot. "Ma'am, his throat is slit. His horse, rifle, pistol, and bullets are gone. His body has been mutilated Apache style with his privates removed and stuffed in his mouth."

The hair on the back of my neck stood on end when I heard this. I couldn't help but think of what Otis had told me a few months earlier at Muddler's Saloon. When the body was removed and the other men left, Tom said he'd found Saffron on the ground beside the body. She'd dropped her lantern, and it had gone out. He'd gotten her settled in her room, taken her lantern, lit it, and examined the corpse.

"Do you think the sheriff is right?" I asked.

He shrugged. "Probably right."

I told him about my conversation with Otis at Muddler's Saloon, and he asked, "What now you want me to say, Sarah Jane?" I could see his point. It was crazy to think Pretty Face had anything to do with this. *Otis was just in the right place at the wrong time,* I thought. Even so, I wondered why an Apache on my property wouldn't have taken Onyx and the hotel guests' horses as well. *He must have been in a powerful hurry.*

Needless to say, Otis Mason's death convinced me that I needed to get Pretty Face out of my house. I just wasn't sure how to go about it. I considered burning it, but I knew some rotter would come along by the fire. I couldn't let someone find human body parts in a fire I'd started.

On March 3, 1904, I thought of the story of how P. T. Barnum had commissioned someone to create the Fuji Mermaid, and I saw what I needed to do. That same day, I sat down and wrote a letter to Otto Ringling, of the Ringling Brothers Circus, billed as "World's Greatest Shows." At the time, Otto Ringling was considered the king of the circus business.

Dear Mr. Ringling,

For many years, I've owned a great curiosity of nature that will surely be of interest to you and contribute greatly to the sideshows you offer. In the 1880s, when I lived in Telluride, Colorado, a hunter by the name of Homer Martin was hunting wild boars in the mountains when he shot and killed a creature that appears half woman and half wild boar. He had this creature stuffed, and I eventually convinced him to sell it to me. This specimen is remarkable. I invite you to visit my Orchard Hotel in Hillsboro, New Mexico Territory, at your convenience to view this rare freak of nature and consider purchasing it for your collection. I assure you, you won't be disappointed.

Kind regards,
Mrs. J. W. Orchard

Months passed, and my nightmares continued. I'd rail back at Pretty Face and declare she had no power over me, that I was the one who had power. Whenever I thought I heard her voice, I'd threaten to set her pig's ass on fire.

Otto Ringling did not respond to my letter. I wondered if he'd even received it. Finally, on July 22, I was in Muddler's before suppertime when Boots stuck his head inside the saloon and said, "Miz Orchard, there's a midget in a top hat wants to see you up at the Orchard Hotel."

I scowled at him. "A midget, you say. How tall is he?"

"Almost as tall as you," he said, drawing laughter from several men in the room.

"Then he's simply a short man. A midget would be much shorter."

"Maybe so, but he looks like a midget to me."

"Go tell him I'll be there in a few minutes." Boots took off, and I finished my whiskey and headed back to the hotel at a leisurely pace, so as not to be winded when I arrived.

The stranger was a remarkable sight in his black suit. He wore a monocle, and his coat had tails. It seemed the largest thing about him was his dark-brown moustache. "Hello, madam. I'm Mr. Ambrose Bizzec. I'm here to see you on business."

He stood less than five feet tall, and, when he removed his hat and bowed to me, I saw that he was bald on top.

"A pleasure to meet you, sir." I offered my hand, and he shook it. "Will you need lodging here tonight?" I asked, seeing he had a large valise beside him.

"That would be helpful."

"Have you had supper yet?"

"No, ma'am."

I called for Boots and said, "Put Mr. Bizzec's bag in room seven, and have one of the maids get him some water for his wash basin and some towels, and then tell Tom Ying to prepare a fine supper for Mr. Bizzec and me." I turned back to Mr. Bizzec and said, "Go and refresh yourself, sir. We can discuss business over supper. I'll send Boots for you when it's ready." Heading back to my quarters, I wondered what the little tosser wanted to sell me. I got dressed and went to have a chat with Nancy, thinking I could sell him her services.

Thirty minutes later, we were sitting in the Ocean Grove Restaurant, and Nancy brought out our food. Nancy was wearing a light-blue dress that made her eyes look even bluer and showed off her slender figure to her best advantage. Her dark hair hung free, but she'd curled it and brushed it until it shone. Following instructions I'd given her during our chat, she allowed her body to touch Mr. Bizzec as she served our food and drink. "Oh, excuse me, sir," she murmured, as if it were an accident.

After we'd cut into some fine rib-eye steaks, Mr. Bizzec

handed me his business card from the Ringling Brothers Circus. "Mr. Otto Ringling sent me as his agent to assess and possibly procure a curiosity you have for sale. Are you prepared to show it this evening?"

"I am. I'm just surprised. I thought you'd send word before you came here."

"Ordinarily, I would have, but other business brought me near this area, so I decided to stop and see if I could meet with you."

I took a sip of cold beer and asked, "How did you come to work for Mr. Ringling?"

Mr. Bizzec sniffed and said, "I wanted to be in the circus, so I went to him when I was a boy of fifteen, but, alas, I didn't have any skills of note or any physical deformities that would merit bringing me on as part of the show. I couldn't sing, dance, or juggle. I couldn't walk a tight rope. I wanted him to have someone train me in some skill, and he tried, but I failed at every turn. I nearly killed myself on a trapeze one day. Mr. Ringling took mercy on me and hired me to clean up after his animals. Soon, he had me buying their feed. Within a few years, he noticed my skills at business negotiation, and he started sending me to make all types of purchases on his behalf." Mr. Bizzec sniffed again and said, "Sometimes I still dream of being a trapeze artist."

I smiled and said, "From what you're telling me, I'm sure you'll understand the value of the item I have for sale."

Later that evening, I heard Mr. Bizzec gasp when I opened the crate and let him gaze upon Pretty Face. He tried to cover his gasp with a cough, but I knew I had him. "Hmm," he said. "I'll have to admit it's fine work. Which taxidermist did the former owner use?"

"I have no idea, and it's too late to ask because he's dead

now," I said.

"Ah, well, that doesn't matter. I can offer you two hundred dollars for the piece."

"Don't waste my time, Mr. Bizzec. Surely you understand I have more than that invested in her."

We continued to dicker until he offered five hundred. I was tempted to accept since all I really wanted was to get Pretty Face out of my house, but something in my nature wouldn't allow it. "Seven fifty," I said.

We sat there in silence for a few minutes, staring at Pretty Face. I was trying to think ahead of him. I figured I was close to his limit, but since he'd told me his boss thought he was a fine negotiator, I knew he didn't want to pay what he considered top dollar. It seemed the best way to deal with him was to try to inflict some fear. "I've written to all of Ringling's competitors," I lied, "and I included photographs with those letters, so I feel sure I can get my price."

I paused and looked at him intently for a moment. Then, I asked, "Mr. Bizzec, do you think Mr. Ringling will be pleased with you if you let this piece get away? And how will you feel when you see it on someone else's show bill? Think of the hundreds of people lined up in every town to see her, every one of them with the price of admission in hand—hundreds of people lined up in towns all over the United States for many years to come."

He sighed and sat there thinking.

"I know it's a big decision. I hope you'll make the right choice. I really want Mr. Ringling to have it because this piece doesn't belong in an inferior circus. Good night, sir." I got up and started to leave the room.

"All right," he said.

"Excuse me?"

"I can do seven fifty," he said, "but only if you'll include this fine crate, my lodging, my supper and tomorrow's breakfast, and some blankets to cushion the piece."

"Done," I said, and I shook his hand.

"I thought I was good," he said, "but you're quite the negotiator, Mrs. Orchard."

"You'll soon feel very good about this deal," I promised. "You know what? I want you to feel good about it right away, so I'll sweeten the pot and provide you with some fine entertainment. Did you notice the waitress who served our supper?"

"Of course. She's a beauty."

"Yes, and she's good at waitressing, but her real talent is in making men very, very happy. I'll have her knock on your door shortly." Mr. Bizzcc's moustache started twitching. He was literally trembling in anticipation as he headed down the hallway to room seven.

On Thursday, August 25, 1904, I received the following letter from Mr. Otto Ringling:

Dear Mrs. Orchard,

I am absolutely delighted with my purchase of your pig woman specimen. We're billing her as "The Pig Woman of Borneo," and customers are lining up to see her in many towns. I've never seen finer work by a taxidermist. We have covered her white shoes with deerskin boots to give her a greater air of authenticity. Thank you for thinking of me, and please let me know if you come across any other oddities of interest.

Respectfully yours,
Mr. Otto Ringling

I found that getting Pretty Face out of my house took all things supernatural out of my mind for a while. Too soon, I forgot her threats to bring me to nothing. Too soon, I let go of all thoughts of the black wolf I'd fought at Tom Beeson's cabin. I didn't realize that my mind would play games with me later, calling forth both Pretty Face and the black wolf, but I eventually discovered some threats and apparitions do not die.

At the time, I didn't understand that it's impossible to desecrate another human being and come out unscathed. I had a euphoric sense that I was about to blossom into what I was always meant to be. I had no notions of the battles left to fight. At the time, I was not much over forty, and I vainly believed I could still pass for twenty-nine. I thought I finally had life by the tail.

AUTHOR'S NOTE

There are many conflicting reports regarding Sadie Orchard's life, and Sadie frequently added to the confusion by giving false information. In this book, I've made every effort to use the most reliable information. However, the date of her divorce from J. W. Orchard remains in question. One source states that Sadie was divorced in 1901 without giving an exact date. Dr. Garland Bills, author of the forthcoming *Sadie Orchard: Madam of the Black Range,* wrote to me, "We haven't been able to confirm, much less date, the divorce. Perhaps the best guess is 1901 or 1902." In this book, I've shown the divorce taking place early in 1903 to serve my storyline best.

ABOUT THE AUTHOR

Harper Courtland, a native of Eden, North Carolina, holds an M.A. in English from Old Dominion University. A former news reporter and a cancer survivor, Courtland works as a writer/editor from her home in Virginia. She has published short stories and poetry in literary magazines and anthologies. *Indiscretions Along Virtue Avenue* is her first novel.

The employees of Five Star Publishing hope you have enjoyed this book.

Our Five Star novels explore little-known chapters from America's history, stories told from unique perspectives that will entertain a broad range of readers.

Other Five Star books are available at your local library, bookstore, all major book distributors, and directly from Five Star/Gale.

Connect with Five Star Publishing

Visit us on Facebook:
  https://www.facebook.com/FiveStarCengage

Email:
  FiveStar@cengage.com

For information about titles and placing orders:
  (800) 223-1244
  gale.orders@cengage.com

To share your comments, write to us:
  Five Star Publishing
  Attn: Publisher
  10 Water St., Suite 310
  Waterville, ME 04901